Best yu

Salt and Pepper

Into the Cruet

Jackie Huck

2QT Limited (Publishing)

Best Wishes
Pauline Henderson

First Edition published 2014 by
2QT Limited (Publishing)
Tatham Fell Lancaster LA2 8RE, United Kingdom

Author/Publisher disclaimer:
This novel is a work of fiction, although the working conditions and
discipline of that time are, according to the authors recollection, factual.
However the names and events and place names are the work of the
authors imagination and any resemblance to actual persons, living or
dead, is entriely coincidental.

Cover Design and Illustrations by Pauline Henderson

Printed in Great Britain by
Lightning Source UK

A CIP catalogue record for this book is available
from the British Library
ISBN 978-1-910077-23-8

For Eddie in remembrance, and love

Other publications by the author:

Cats Like Me

A collection of poems and writings about Cats
Available as Hardback ISBN 9781908098290 and
Paperback ISBN 9781908098122

Chapter 1

It's an overall not a uniform

As I fell through the sewing room door of Benjamin Hale General Hospital that July morning in 1964, I had a head full of expectations and little else. Too eager and poor to await my eighteenth birthday, I had been accepted as a nursing cadet, although my father had been at pains to point out that 'you'd earn a sight more up at t'mill.'

I was greeted by a squat, frog-faced woman in pink, who gave me a look normally reserved for a snotty child without a hanky. Her badge announced she was Mrs Frost, Assistant Sewing Room Attendant, a title that accounted for her attitude.

'You're late!' she snarled, as the clock hit ten past nine. 'These are yours.' She thrust a heap of garments into my outstretched palms. 'Put one on, that leaves you with five. Here's your cloak and laundry bag, everything has your name on. This is your locker key. Don't lose it! You're number 146, in the basement.'

Five other girls were already pulling on yellow outfits which would not have looked out of place in the workhouse. 'I look like a skivvy with yellow jaundice!' said a girl whose golden locks resembled a laburnum in a storm.

'It's a good fit. You must remember it's an overall, not a uniform,' said Mrs Frost.

The blonde gave another twirl. 'It doesn't fit anywhere, it's like a mail sack.' She was half a head taller than my five foot five, a corncob of a girl, nibbled in all the right places, with sky-dyed eyes which shot out of a pale complexion. Her made-up eyebrows swept up as she spoke, her voice drawled a lazy Lancashire accent, red-glossed lips scowled as she looked with disgust at her reflection in the wall mirror. From her discarded clothing it was clear she was more used to leather and denim.

Another girl with a bony chin and heavy brows was busy buttoning a similar yellow overall. 'It's very serviceable, and yellow and jaundice mean the same.'

The blonde gave her a look that would have wilted a prize petunia, as I searched for a spare table. 'Just drop them on the floor,' she said. 'Have you ever seen anything more ghastly? It's like baby's poo.'

The overall was an odious colour resembling the yellow colour-wash on many post-war walls. It was a button-through dress with no waist, hanging in a straight line from the armpits. Short sleeves reached the elbow but were so wide that two plump arms could fit up each opening. Rules demanded the length be six inches below the knee, but they tended to sweep the ankle like grandma's nightshirt, with a cushion-sized pocket on each side of the skirt. Ghastly just about summed them up.

'No one wears black-seamed stockings these days,' said bony chin, her eyes on my snaking seams. 'That went out years ago.'

'First I've heard about it,' Blondie put in. 'The only reason my stockings haven't got seams is that I couldn't find any.'

The door crashed open. 'Are you lot not ready yet?'

asked the new arrival, obviously a senior cadet with an air of exaggerated importance. Her glance wafted across my seams, and I felt like the new girl at school who'd turned up with the wrong-coloured gym knickers. 'Right, come on!' The order given, she spun on her heel and was off.

The others, heaped with possessions, followed and I tried, rapidly scooping up overalls, laundry bag, cloak, coat and holdall. Loaded like a camel I stumbled for the door, only to hear a tinkle as the vital locker key slid through my fingers.

I peered over and around my stack but the locker key, reluctant to leave the sewing room, had vanished. Blondie was wedged in the doorway. 'Get a move on,' she said. 'The Yellow Commander has gone and we'll lose her if we're not careful.'

'I've dropped the key.'

'What?'

I gave up, dumping my gear like the rag and bone man's wares. 'I've dropped the locker key. You go on, I'll catch up.'

'Us idiots should stick together, we're an endangered species,' she said, kicking the door closed and chucking her pile down besides mine. 'Where do you think it went?'

'It must have bounced.'

We went down on hands and knees, two yellow pigs snuffling around the floor. We could have been invisible: cadets were often invisible.

The sewing room lay over the laundry on the northern outer reaches of Benjamin Hale and was accessed by a rickety wooden staircase, its rubbed, creaking banister ready for collapse. The heat from the laundry hit like a tropical jungle and followed up the stairs, causing sweat to ooze. The sewing room lived up to its designation and was crammed with material and machines. Strip-lighting from an off-white, long-since painted ceiling glared down on the workers, an assortment of young and middle-aged women bent intently over their machining.

Every uniform and overall for all levels of staff was produced in this claustrophobic workplace. Theatre gowns and cotton masks were made and repaired, as were sheets, pillowcases, curtains and tablecloths. The windows brought in little light as most of them were obscured behind piles of cloth. Bales of varying shades of blue, white, pink and yellow filled every available space, and cotton bobbins with the attendant pins, binding, buttons and lace were crammed onto shelves and tables. The machines were crowded together and the clamour was constant.

'Is that it?' Blondie asked, pointing under a nearby machine table where something shiny was lodged in a crack in a floorboard. I put my head down so my nose brushed the floor and spied a small key peeping out between piles of fluff and bits of cotton.

'However did it get there?' I gasped. I tried to get my hand under the bottom shelf but my knuckles wouldn't fit.

'Let me try.' Blondie grovelled about. 'No good, we'll have to prod it out with something.' She dragged out a cane from a dusty corner. 'This might do. I wonder what they use it for.'

'For beating cadets who lose their locker keys?'

'I think we're going to get on.' With a smile, she extended a hand around a table leg. 'Vale Pepper.'

I started laughing as our hands met. 'Susan Salt.'

'A match made in the cruet. I'd already decided I didn't like any of that other lot, so you and me will be friends.'

It was a delicate manoeuvre, with an inch and a half working room. The cane reached the key easily but there was a tiny gap in the floorboards, which lovingly waited for the key to vanish down forever. We considered moving the table but the combined weight of table, industrial sewing machine plus overloaded drawers put us off, and we were clearly not going to get any help from 'the workers'.

'I expect table-moving and helping cadets in distress is not in their job description,' Vale observed.

'Do you think she'll give me another if this one disappears?'

'No chance,' said Vale. 'You'll have to spend your nursing career humping uniforms, oh excuse me, overalls from place to place. A bit like one of the labours of Hercules.'

'Who?' I was trying to wriggle the key out and not getting very far.

'Oh, some big feller from mythology. I had a cat called Hercules but a bit like your key, he went down the nick. Let me have a go.'

She was more successful and the key started to move, jumping out of the groove into the fluff. 'They don't clean under here very often,' said Vale as she swept the cane from side to side, pushing an assortment of cotton, cloth, toffee papers and pins out from under the table. I delved in and with a sigh of relief pulled the key out.

'Whatever are you two doing?' said a voice above a pair of sling-back shoes. I travelled upwards past the stockings and noticed the beginnings of a ladder. The Assistant Sewing Room Attendant bent down.

'I lost the locker key.'

Her expression would have curdled cream. 'Well, that's a good start! I hope you've found it. These keys can't be replaced, they stopped making those lockers thirty years ago. If a key goes missing the locker has to be scrapped. Have you any idea how much a new locker costs?'

I shook my head. 'Do you know where the rest of the cadets went?'

'So, you've lost them as well,' she smirked. She was about to turn away when she suddenly relented. 'If you remember, I told you that the lockers were in the basement.

I expect they've gone to put their things away.'

We left, heading back into the laundry heat. Steam rose from the presses and, feeling like an overdone sponge cake, I stumbled after Vale with relief into the morning air. 'Any idea where we'll find the basement?'

'Not a clue but it must be under one of these buildings.'

'Benny's' was really three hospitals in one. The 'new hospital' where we stood had been tagged onto the old workhouse and infirmary back in the thirties. It was built of red brick interspaced with white seams and designed in a large E. It sat apart, an aloof relative condemned to look down on its poor relations.

An oval roadway with green swathes of lawn divided the new hospital from the original workhouse block. The infirmary had been endowed in the nineteenth century by Old Benjamin, who'd made his money in the Lancashire cotton industry.

Like a couple of castaways holding their worldly possessions, Vale and I stood outside the laundry. The large block of wards stood to our left and we could see bed-backs and flowers through the windows and figures moving about. Since it was nearest, that's where we headed.

'I hope no one I know sees me dressed like this,' said Vale. 'I feel a right frump.'

'They might grow on us,' I answered, struggling not to drop my load.

'Like warts. My only consolation is that Miss Clever-Pants looked even worse than me.'

'It's very serviceable,' I mimicked.

'For working in a custard factory. I dread to think what she wears normally if she thinks this is acceptable.'

A sign read WARDS 14–19 outside the red-brick, but there was nothing about a basement. I went to push the door open as an elderly woman with greying hair, and an expression like a trout out of water, pulled it from the other side. Her look put me off but Vale was not so easily daunted.

'Excuse me, you wouldn't know where the basement is? We're new cadets and we're supposed to put this lot in our lockers, but we've lost our guide and if I don't put them down soon me flipping arms are going to fall off.' As she spoke a yellow overall toppled from the pile and draped itself across the woman's shoes.

I would have picked it up but I was in danger of dropping everything. The woman bent, picking up the overall with two fingers as if it were a tramp's bed-rug. I decided she was one of the elderly cleaners who mopped somewhere important like the operating theatre. She did look vaguely familiar but grannies have a habit of doing that.

'If you turn left and follow the corridor to the end, you'll find a flight of steps going down into the basement,' she said in well-educated tones. The door slammed on her departing back. 'Poor old soul,' I thought. 'She must have fallen on hard times. Fancy expecting someone that age to scrub floors.'

'Thank God for that,' said Vale, as we reached the bottom of the staircase, Granny's directions having proved correct. A depressing corridor lay before us. The gloom was emphasised by a few ill-lit bulbs that hung from a ceiling lost in dirt. It rattled and banged from the miles of heating pipes that ran its length. We started along and soon saw rows of battered, dull-green, tin cabinets, which were about a foot wide and nearly six feet tall. 'Geronimo! We have lockers!' said Vale.

'For lamp-post sized giants. What's your number?'

'278,' said Vale, looking at her palm.

'Mine's 146. I wonder why they're so far apart?'

'Perhaps the ones between fell to bits.'

'Where have you two been?' I started at the stern voice behind me. 'I've been looking everywhere for you.' It was the 'Yellow Commander'. On closer inspection I saw she wore a name badge which announced that she was Nursing Cadet Roberts.

'I dropped my locker key in the sewing room and by the time...'

'Well, you've no time now to put things tidy. You'll just have to dump your stuff. We're due at Miss Patton's office, and there'll be hell on if we're late.'

'We can't find our lockers,' offered Vale.

'All the cadet lockers are in our changing room,' said Roberts, indicating a door. 'Get a move on,' she ordered.

The cadets' changing room, which I was to discover was the only place in Benjamin Hale specifically for the use of cadets, resembled a dungeon. The walls were circled by rusty heating pipes which shuddered and vibrated as if they were about to explode. Many generations of cadets must have passed through its dingy portals since it was last decorated, and thin slices of old plaster drifted to the dirt-engrained floor. The only illumination came from two dim light bulbs which swung on cobweb-coated cords from a dusty ceiling.

We scuttled into the room where the other four waited, their lockers neatly stacked with overalls and outdoor clothing, bags hung up and hair spruced. Roberts tapped her foot as Vale and I rushed round the lockers looking for the right numbers. I found Vale's but couldn't discover mine.

Roberts looked at her fob watch. 'We'll have to go,' she said, one hand already on the door handle, 'but you must get that hair up!'

'Is there a mirror?'

Roberts indicated a foot-square object over in a corner. Its edges were chipped and browned, leaving a bare six inches for essential grooming.

Vale muttered something about anything being good

enough for the peasants, scooped up her mass of hair, twisting it round, and with a slick movement drew an elastic band over it. A tail-comb appeared from her pocket and with a few dexterous tucks the hair was swirled into a large bun. The laburnum was transformed into an attractive doughnut.

I stood, still lockerless, clutching my pile as Roberts opened the door and prepared to march. 'We've five minutes and we'll just make it if we rush. You'll have to catch up.'

'Oh no!' shouted Vale. 'We're not being left behind again. Come on, Sue, squash your things in with mine.' As the others vanished through the door, we somehow managed to shove five overalls, linen bag, coat and bag into Vale's locker, which was now so overloaded it refused to shut. We pushed, Vale getting her knee up against the lock, swearing. She grabbed her cloak, and we belted after the Commander.

We caught up with her on the stairs with the others close on her heels. Roberts walked as if she were training for the Olympics; her gait never flagged and I wondered how many miles an hour she was covering as we left the red-brick building and crossed a long stretch of hospital tarmac.

Benny's was not a beautiful place. It had developed in hiccups from the original workhouse, spilling out like garments escaping from an over-stuffed case. Southern-facing windows looked onto the urban sprawl of Thorpe, a small industrial town tagged onto the outskirts of Manchester. Those lucky enough to have a northerly view gazed across green farmland to a distant thin ridge of hills. The 'Swinging Sixties' were leaving Benjamin Hale behind; it neither swung nor changed, but bumbled along like an elderly rheumatic gentleman who just hopes to keep going.

We were heading for the oldest part, which had been the original workhouse block. Red brick turned to black stone, deeply engrained with Lancashire coal dust. We entered through a rear door with ADMINISTRATION written on a plaque.

'Cloaks off,' ordered the Commander, as she swung the cloak off her shoulders, folding it neatly over her arm, red side in, straps tucked away and navy side out, all in one action. Apart from a brief pause as she opened the door, her pace never slowed until we reached a series of puce doors on a brightly-lit corridor. There were two straight-backed chairs against the wall but they were clearly not for cadet bottoms.

Roberts gave us an appraising look before knocking on a door labelled DEPUTY MATRON.

'Enter!'

Vale was fighting cloak-tags and showing more red than navy blue as we shuffled through the door. We lined up before a desk which held two telephones, three neat piles of files and a general assortment of papers and pens, and found ourselves under the scrutiny of Miss Patton, second only to Matron at Benjamin Hale.

She was edging fifty, round, with thick glasses. Her eyes were like big dots behind the lenses and her prominent cheekbones bulged, as did her lips and bulbous nose. A frilled cap perched in regimented order, allowing only a small show of silver hair to peep out. Her ample bosom swelled within a purple, long-sleeved uniform with lace collar and cuffs. She reminded me of an overcooked suet pudding with no soft centre.

Vale, last through the door, managed to get a cloak strap stuck. We waited in silence as Miss Patton watched. Vale tugged, splitting strap from cloak, leaving a woolly length of red material hanging in the door like a marker flag. Gathering her composure, she reopened the door and swept the offending strap into one of her voluminous yellow pockets. I caught her eye as she slid into line, realising with horror that we were on the brink of the giggles.

Miss Patton sat very straight in her chair, her backbone standing clear of any support. I wondered if she always practised perfect posture or was putting on her iron maiden act especially for us. When she spoke, her voice was clipped like a radio announcer. There was no welcome; she looked at her watch, frowning. 'You have an appointment to see Matron at ten, which gives you a quarter of an hour to tidy yourselves.' It had to be me she was referring to; everyone else looked immaculate.

'When you go in to see Matron, she will ask for your names. You will say Nursing Cadet, your surname, then Matron,' she instructed. I was amazed we weren't ordered to curtsey or kiss the carpet.

'This being your first year as cadets, you will work on various departments across the hospital. After your seventeenth birthday, you may be allowed to work on the wards. During term-time you will attend the college of further education two days a week, then work three days, plus Saturday mornings, in the hospital. Outside term time, you will be at the hospital for the whole five and a half days.'

She picked up one of the files from her desk. 'Nursing Cadets Browning and Pierce, you will be together in the outpatients department. Nursing Cadet Hudson, you will be in the laundry.'

Poor sod, I thought, all that heat.

'Nursing Cadet Nightingale,' she continued, eyeing 'Smarty'. Vale gave a spluttery cough while I concentrated on two paper clips which had dared to venture down by a table leg. 'You will be working in the main X-ray department.'

The Nightingale beamed. 'Thank you, Miss Patton.'

'Nursing Cadet Pepper, you will be working in the accident and emergency department and…' she paused; where was left? kitchen cleaner; please God, not the sewing room! '…Nursing Cadet Salt, you will be in orthopaedic outpatients.' I hadn't a clue what orthopaedics meant, but at least it sounded like it might have a remote connection with nursing.

Miss Patton had apparently endured us for long enough. 'The Assistant Matron, Miss Pettigrew, is responsible for the nursing cadets at Benjamin Hale. Cadet Roberts will take you to your departments after you have seen Matron.' She dismissed us with a nod. Vale opened the door and, like a batch of novice nuns sent away to do good works, we trooped out.

Matron's office lay at the opposite end of the corridor. Roberts led the way but at a demure pace. 'When she said her name was Nightingale, I thought I was going to explode,' Vale whispered in my ear. The relief burst out of us and we filled the hallowed corridor with laughter. It was as if we'd set off the fire alarm; only Hudson (she of the laundry), who most likely felt if she didn't laugh she'd weep, dared to join in. Roberts stopped in her tracks, the Nightingale and companions nearly colliding with her. The Yellow Commander blazed; she was just about to give us a mouthful, when a door opened and a duck of a woman waddled out.

'Who's making that noise?' she demanded. The laughter died. 'Can't you read?' She indicated a SILENCE sign. 'There's a meeting going on. If I hear you again, I'll take your names and report you to Matron.' She slammed the door behind her.

'Daft bat,' said Vale.

Roberts looked mortified. 'It's me that will get into trouble. I'm responsible until I drop you off. So for goodness' sake keep quiet.' I felt like a troublesome parcel that she was having difficulty delivering.

The waiting room outside Matron's office contained an unmatched assortment of chairs, smelled of beeswax polish and had a table with a terracotta vase of fresh roses. The cleaner must have taken pride in keeping the area spotless: the burgundy carpet didn't show a speck of dirt and the net curtains were pristine. An oil painting of an imposing man set against a background of factories gleamed in its replica golden frame. 'I suppose that's his nibs, Old Ben,' whispered Vale. Roberts frowned and I was sure the Nightingale tutted.

In a whispery voice, Roberts told us to straighten our hair. She handed round our name badges, which had to be placed on the right side of the overall, seven inches down from the shoulder and two inches in from the centre of the breastbone. 'And make sure they're straight.'

The clock showed 9.55am. Her eyes flicked round her charges, making sure we were turned out right. 'Since you've worn those seams, make sure they're straight.' Vale and I spent the remaining time 'seam aligning'. I wriggled, she directed, in sign language of course. As the clock touched ten, I suddenly felt a desperate need for the toilet. Roberts went to the door, knocked and a red light flashed. 'That means she's not ready for you or engaged,' she informed us. 'When the green light comes on, you can go in.'

So we waited.

Miss Cooper-Ffinch, Matron of Benjamin Hale, held one of the few positions of true power that were available to a woman in the male-dominated world of the 1960s. She was a supreme being, answerable to no one except the hospital board. To every nurse in all ranks, the majority of the doctors, all departmental workers, receptionists, porters, cleaners, cooks, to all within the boundaries of the hospital, her word was law. She did a personal inspection of every ward and department at least once a week. She was revered and feared by almost everyone, and at that moment I would have sooner faced a black widow spider.

My bladder distress grew worse with the passing minutes. I prowled around like a stray dog looking for a convenient lamp-post. I passed a nervous hand through my well-combed locks and fiddled with my new name tag, hoping it was straight and the designated inches down and across. Vale whispered, 'It's like waiting outside the dentist's when you're due ten fillings.'

I stared at old Ben; his grizzled looks vaguely reminded me of an old photo of my maternal great-grandfather who, I'd been told, was something big in sewers. I spent some time debating if they'd ever met. 'How's the mill doing, Benjamin?' 'Oh, not so bad, getting fourteen hours a day labour out of the gals, and only lost two squashed under the machines last week. How's the sewers?' 'Sloshing along nicely. Lots of rats, of course, but the lads are used to that. We must get together for a good claret some time…'

I jumped as a buzzer sounded, scattering rats and fallen machinery. The green light winked and the Nightingale opened the door. We followed in single file.

It was a large, imposing room with rosebud wallpaper. A few red leather, straight-backed chairs were assembled against one wall. An old fireplace, long unused, had a white china vase of dried flowers in the hearth, and an old-fashioned wooden clock stood on the mantelpiece alongside a framed photograph. The curtains were pale lavender draped back in evenly-matched hangings, allowing the July morning sun to stream in through the bow window.

These were unimportant impressions as my eyes travelled from the carpet, up the legs of the antique mahogany table to the woman who sat observing us as we lined up before her. Her uniform was similar to Miss Patton's, but in smart navy-blue, her only adornment a shiny badge pinned below her top button. My eyes worked their way up the dress, over the collar and jumped to her stiff frilled cap, sitting like a crown. I settled on her face as sweat pricked under my new yellow overall, and I met 'Granny the Cleaner' for the second time that day.

'Good morning.'

Meek courtiers before the queen, we chanted, 'Good morning, Matron.'

The way she studied us reminded me of my elderly aunt Alice, the most miserable woman I'd met in my sixteen years. Her meek little husband had died when I was ten; I always believed it was the only way he could get peace from her constant nagging. Their terraced house was perpetually gloomy as aunty dictated that the lights must stay off until it was almost dark. A weak fire glowed with a few coals but gave out little heat, and her new carpet was rolled against the wall in case, heaven forbid, it might get walked on. Her thin, pale face sported a hooked nose, and if her lips ever raised in a smile, I never saw it.

'If you would tell me your names,' Matron said.

We went along the line starting with, 'Nursing Cadet Nightingale, Matron,' who naturally got her script right. The others didn't do too badly until she came to Vale, who must have been rethinking every word they had exchanged a short while before. After a moment's pause she managed to croak like a toad with laryngitis, 'Nursing Cadet Pepper, Matron.'

I was on! Lights! Curtain! Action! My mouth was dry, my bladder full. My mind and tongue tried to coordinate my short speech, and failed. 'Matron, Cadet Nurse – Sat – Alt – Salt,' I managed.

She gave me a glance reserved for an imbecile. 'I hope you benefit from your time as nursing cadets. It will give you an insight into many areas of the hospital. You have been selected for cadetships out of the many applications that I receive. Should you find the work or the discipline too much, there is a waiting list of girls quite willing to fill your places.'

I didn't know whether to feel flattered to be one of the chosen or threatened as I pictured the queue of hopefuls lining up to fill my yellow overall.

'Nursing Cadet Roberts will take you to your places of duty. You have a lot to learn, but you will quickly fit in to the hospital routine.' 'Or else…' I felt she should have added.

With a dip of her chin she indicated the interview was at an end and, trying not to run, I led the way out. I'm sure Ben winked from his portrait as we silently left the waiting area, sucking in large lungfuls of sunshine as we emerged outside.

'I'll take you down to the main infirmary foyer, where you must sign the book every morning before you go on duty at 9am,' said Roberts, already into her stride. 'You're not allowed to wear your overalls outside hospital property, so you must arrive in the morning with enough time to sign in, go to your lockers and change, then be ready to report on duty at nine. I always sign in about 8.30, that saves rushing, especially when we have to go up to the new hospital to the changing room, then back down to the infirmary for work.'

'Of all the little old ladies to drop overalls on, I had to choose Matron,' whispered Vale.

'At least you managed your name. I was that nervy, I made a right mess of things.'

'Are you two listening?' Roberts was running through a complicated list of rules and procedures as we hurried along. 'And whatever you do, don't be late,' she finished. 'We won't have time for morning break. I'll take you to where to sign in tomorrow morning, then drop you off at your departments.'

'Any chance of using the toilet?' I asked in a small voice.

'You won't be able to keep running off to the toilet when you're on duty,' Roberts scolded. God, I thought, I'm not even allowed to pee! 'If you really can't wait, we pass the nurses' home and you can pop in, but you'll have to be quick.'

Two minutes was all I was allowed, then we were off again through a small wooded area with flowerbeds, between two low buildings, across a yard and in through another door. Down two corridors, right turn, left turn, more doors; by now I was completely lost. I'd have done better in Hampton Court maze. As we went through a final swing door we came into the main ante-room of the infirmary buildings, with a half-moon table standing against one wall.

'That's where you'll find the book,' said Roberts. I eyed the table as if it were a sacrificial altar. 'You come in here, sign in, then get a move on up to your locker.'

'But that's a heck of a trek,' Vale observed.

'That's why I always get here for 8.30. Come on, no time to waste. You're first Salt,' she said. I jumped when she said my name. 'The orthopaedic department is just across the yard.'

I hated to show my ignorance but I was sure the others wouldn't know either, with the possible exception of the Nightingale. 'What's ortho-podic?'

'Orthopaedic,' she corrected. 'Bones, joints, people with fractures; it's a very busy department, a good place to start.'

I decided I hadn't done too badly; it was certainly an improvement on the laundry. With high hopes, I headed up the concrete ramp.

Chapter 2

Orthopaedic

Sister Mandrake regarded me with a look one reserves for a bin full of maggots. 'This is Nursing Cadet Salt, Sister,' said Roberts.

'Thank you, Roberts,' Sister answered, as the senior cadet made a hasty retreat. 'Straighten your hair before you come on duty in my department,' she snarled. 'You'll find the other cadets in the day ward.'

Like a stray kitten, not knowing where to go or what to do, I stood looking up and down the unfamiliar corridor. A young man on crutches came limping towards me, a paper in his hand. 'Where do I take this, nurse?' he asked. He pressed the white form into my hand. I gave him a bewildered look but I couldn't help feeling a thrill; it was the first time I was ever addressed as 'Nurse'.

I was saved by a man who popped out through a door marked PLASTER ROOM. Hoping he wasn't some terribly important doctor, I latched onto him with relief. 'This gentleman's looking for X-ray.'

'Down't ramp, 'cross yard, through Cas and follow't sign,' he answered in broad Lancashire. The chap on crutches limped away with a nod of thanks. 'Hallo,' the other man said. 'Are you't new cadet?'

'Sister said I had to go to the day ward, but I don't know where to find it.'

He smiled, showing a row of teeth in dire need of a dentist. 'Down't corridor an' ward's at th' end. What's your name, lass?'

'Susan, Sue.'

He fingered my name badge. 'Nursing Cadet Salt. Sister Mandrake would 'ave me guts if she 'eard me callin' you by yer first name.'

'Oh,' I stammered, 'I'm sorry.'

'Don't worry about it, pet.' He was a head taller than me and looked like he was drifting towards retirement. His face was crinkly, like crepe paper, and his short spiky moustache seemed stuck on like small bits of grey brush-head. He wore a white coat overlaid with stiff splashes of plaster, some of which speckled his cheeks. 'You'll get use to all t'rules. My name's Digby, I work in't plaster room. If you need help you just come an' find me. Now you nip along to t'ward an t'tother cadets'll be there.'

'Thank you.' I could have hugged him.

I made my way up a highly polished corridor which ended in a set of blue swing doors with, WARD written over the top. Gingerly, I popped my nose inside. It was a small unit with eight beds, four up each side. I couldn't see all the beds, as some were surrounded by heavy green curtains. It smelt of disinfectant and reminded me of newly cleaned toilets. A cadet nurse with an air of quiet competence bustled through a gap in the curtains and spied me peeping through the door. She frowned and beckoned me in.

'Are you Salt? First day? Some good you'll be.' I nodded, whether to confirm my name or in agreement of my uselessness, I wasn't entirely sure. 'Hang your cloak on one of the hooks behind the door and don't use one that's got a name over it. You better comb your hair while you're at it; Sister has a thing about hair. Then you'll have to test the wees.' I must have looked more vague than usual. She shook her head. 'We're short staffed; the other junior cadet, Mellor, is off sick. Barnes and I can cope in here but the wee hasn't been tested. I'll show you how to do the first one then you'll have to cope with the rest. When you've finished the wees, there'll be Sister's tray to clear and the cleaning to start.'

I hadn't a clue what she was talking about. 'I know it's difficult but it's Monday morning and we're up to our eyebrows. The clinic is hectic, Sister Phipps is in there, Sister Mandrake is working between the plaster room and the ward. She's not in the best of moods, so stay out of her way.' With this last instruction at least, I was quite happy to comply.

I deposited my cloak as instructed and, using a tiny mirror the size of a cigarette packet, tried to put my unruly hair in order. My nose filled the reflection and I weaved about trying to bring my brown locks into focus. I had an ordinary face with nothing special to distinguish it. Brown eyes lay above high pale cheeks and a rounded chin. I wasn't skinny but no one could call me fat, and I'd always prided myself on having good legs with shapely ankles. I took after my mother, being on the odd side of five foot four, and I'd been told I walked with a natural sway to the hips. I suppose, being so nondescript, I might have made a good spy. I wasn't the person to stand out in a crowd. The senior cadet, who said her name was Thompson, interrupted my grooming and rushed me out of the ward and into a tiny room just outside. It was narrow, dingy and cluttered. One wall contained a sink and a draining board which held a collection of bottles, all containing yellowy or orange fluids. There was a four-ringed gas hob with a shabby kettle and pan sitting on the top. The remainder of the room was filled with cupboards rubbed with age, the blue paint flaking off.

'This is the sluice,' said Thompson. 'They bring their wee in anything from scent to lemonade bottles. I'm always amazed how they get it in.' As Thompson produced a tray, I had a vision of trying to pee into the tiny opening of a perfume container. There were glass tubes, pipettes, bowls of varying sizes, various coloured chemicals and even a cracked cup on the tray; this I hoped was for a well-deserved cup of tea when the task was complete, and not as the last resort for the suicidal.

'We test reaction, specific gravity and for sugar.' I tried to look intelligent and failed, wondering how Vale was coping. 'This is litmus paper,' Thompson continued as another cadet appeared at the door. I presumed she was Barnes.

'That late admission's just arrived,' she said, ignoring me. 'Will you be long?'

'I'm just showing – what was your name? – how to test wee.'

'Sue – Susan – Salt,' I stuttered.

'Hell! Don't let Sister Mandrake hear anyone call you by your first name.'

Barnes looked at me with little hope, like a new set of false teeth that would take a lot of settling in. She spoke to Thompson. 'She'll never pick it up that fast.' For once I agreed. 'Shall I test them quick, while you sort out the admission? Sister will be along any minute and she'll play pop if she sees us standing around here.'

Thompson nodded. 'Right, go through to reception, you'll find that in the waiting room, and see if the receptionist has any urgent errands. After you've done that, go to Sister's office and collect her tray and wash up the pots. Then get busy on the cleaning. Have you got all that?' I felt like a parent suddenly presented with triplets, not sure which one to feed first. Reception, clinic, errands, trays, cleaning, sluice revolved in my mind, and I wished I'd been left alone with the wees.

I headed back up the corridor, feeling vulnerable. A collection of the wounded had arrived in my absence and was sitting in wheelchairs lined up against the wall. They were either the newly plastered waiting to set, or waiting to be plastered. Most were legs or ankles, with the occasional arm. The 'legs' had the foot-rest of the wheelchair raised, so that their broken limbs jutted out like parking barriers. They should have had red flags tied onto their protruding toes in warning as the corridor was narrowed by half, with the steady passage of people pushing up and down the reduced space.

Many of the injured being young men, it was akin to the aftermath of a battle. I gave them what I hoped was a professional smile and made my way carefully along the obstacle course, heading for a double door at the end. I was half way along the line when the waiting room door opened and a young girl on crutches appeared, pursued by her mother.

'Well, you're not going near that lad's motorbike again, our Norma, or me and your father will have something to say. I always said that boyfriend of yours drives like a maniac, didn't I say?'

'Yes, Mum,' she said, giving me a look her mother couldn't see.

To allow Norma and Mum passage, I had to back out, bumping an unplastered foot. The poor lad let out a yell as if he'd been shot. Norma lost her balance, put a hand out to save herself and clutched another leg. There were more yells and Mum, who was having difficulty getting through the small gap, bumped a third leg. I was busy apologising to everyone when Sister Mandrake swept out of the plaster room with Digby.

'Come on, mate, you're next,' said Digby, expertly manoeuvring one of the wheelchairs back through the plaster room door.

Sister Mandrake addressed the waiting line. 'We'll take you in turn, just be patient. We're very busy this morning.'

There was a lot of muttering. 'I've nowhere else to go, been waiting all day. Another week or so won't matter,' one spotty youth put in. Sister's face silenced further levity.

Having dealt with the patients, she turned on me. 'Where are you going?' I shrank under her frown. She reminded me of a goose I once met on my uncle's farm. It acted as a guard dog, flattening its neck and heading, bullet-like, for the ankles of any intruder.

'To – wait – wait – room,' I managed.

'You've no time to waste wandering round on a Monday morning. The plaster room is a mess, go and start the cleaning. And straighten your hair!' Thompson's instructions had just about settled in my head; now they'd been over-ruled by Sister, who I was sure must have priority.

Digby was busy plastering an ankle. He gave me a wink. 'Start over there on t'sinks,' he advised.

The plaster room was square and busy. A large table filled the centre, with a circular light overhead. Three white sinks, interspaced by draining areas, filled one wall of the room; there were cupboards everywhere, most hanging open, their contents spewing out. A shelf at head height held tins and bottles. Under and at the side of the sinks were rubbish containers and more cupboards. The place looked like a grenade had exploded, chucking chunks and flakes of plaster of Paris everywhere.

As Digby plastered, I cleaned. It was not a matter of what to do but where to start. The sinks were heaped with brown waterproofs thick with plaster. The drainage areas were lost under boxes, bits of wet and dried plaster, old bandages and an assortment of metal dishes. If the sink was a disaster area, the floor was even worse: there was plaster everywhere. Digby wore white Wellington boots but my new black lace-ups were soon flecked in bits of white.

I plunged into one of the sinks. 'Use a bit of gumption,' advised Digby. He stopped plastering for a second, laughed and pointed to a pint-sized tin on the shelf in front of me: GUMPTION it proclaimed in large black letters. This was my introduction to this renowned cleaning product which was to become my constant companion. I levered off the lid and saw a pale stone-coloured mixture with the consistency of heavy dough. Its distinctive aroma was a combination of drains, cabbage and unwashed socks, but I was to discover that a small amount applied to any surface, combined with water and a good helping of elbow-grease, would remove most muck and stains.

For the next half hour I was lost in the mess. I chucked all the lumps, both wet and dry, into the bins, scrubbed the sinks and draining areas, and washed and polished bowls. When I'd finished, the sinks sparkled. The room was still awash with plaster; Digby, having completed the plastering of an ankle, was now onto an arm. I was just about to start on the rest when a side door from the plaster room opened, and Thompson rushed in.

'Good grief, here you are. She's screaming out for a cadet in reception. Sister's tray still hasn't been washed up and it's 11.15. She'll play hell if it's not done before noon!'

'But—'

Thompson cut me off. 'You'll have to start listening to what you're told.'

I tried again, thinking I should at least get some recognition for my beautiful clean sinks. 'Sister sent—'

'Reception! Now!'

Thankfully the corridor was emptying, with only a

bony teenager with acne and a sneezing pensioner who was filling an enormous white hanky still waiting for plasters. I followed my ears and found myself in the orthopaedic waiting room. These were the days before timed appointments. Anyone who'd had a fracture on either Saturday or Sunday attended the Monday morning orthopaedic fracture clinic; these were added to the re-plastering brigade, with the plaster removal and check X-ray gang thrown in for good measure. The whole lot bundled in at 9am and it was first come, first served. The heaving crowd struggled for space; the lucky ones were seen in order, the unfortunate ones submerged beneath lost notes or X-rays.

I squeezed in through the door, apologising to two girls leaning against it who I'd nearly toppled. The place had thinned out slightly, the fortunate having gone. Every remaining head turned to me in expectation.

'I've got to go to the lavatory for a blood test, which way is it, nurse?'

'Do you know if they've found my X-ray's yet?'

'If Gran doesn't get seen soon, she'll have to have the toilet.'

'Our Jean's feeling bilious. 'Ave you got a bowl she can use?'

Our Jean wasn't the only one. I gave them what I hoped was a comforting smile. 'I'll find out.'

Every seat in the room was taken, laden wheelchairs were parked in the aisles and a collection of crutches and sticks poked out between chairs. I could see the reception desk in the far corner with an anxious bunch of patients grouped around it. It reminded me of the queue around the ice-cream girl during the cinema interval when the ices are running out.

A young woman in her late twenties, with red hair and glasses, was trying to explain to an old man that he'd be seen soon. Resting on a crutch he hobbled back to his chair, muttering, 'We got better treatment in the desert!'

'Thank Goodness, you must be the new cadet. I'm Fran, Mrs Hughes when Sister's around,' and she stuck out a hand. 'I've got a pile of jobs for you.'

'They're asking about toilets and someone's feeling sick,' I said, indicating the waiting hoard.

'Oh don't worry about that lot, Sister Phipps will be out of clinic in a few minutes. Now, here's what I want you to do: these X-rays are missing, you'll have to chase them up.' She pressed a list of names into my damp palm. 'Then go to medical records and find these notes.' More names. 'Try not to be long, they've been waiting since nine. Oh, and before you go, pop into the clinic. Sister Phipps has some bloods to drop in at the lab.'

I felt like asking if she'd got a map. I was rapidly developing a door-opening phobia as I poked my head through the battered swing entrance to the clinic, wondering what unpleasant reception might be waiting for me there. It was a large oblong room with two beds, an assortment of chairs, cupboards and an important-looking desk holding a good scattering of medical notes, X-rays, forms and letters. Two doctors in white coats were busy examining a patient, and a sister I hadn't yet encountered slid towards me. I presumed she was Sister Phipps. She pressed three white forms accompanied by small plastic bottles containing blood into my hands, mouthed 'Laboratory', and went back to the doctors.

It was nice to be out in the sunlight but, in my state of mind, it could have been thick with fog. I had a list of important tasks, a strict timetable and not a clue where to go.

The orthopaedic department was a bungalow-type annexe adjacent to the main entrance of the hospital. Set on an incline, a tarmac ramp with a red handrail ran from the main door. After six yards it swept down to the right between two flower beds, forming a fairly steep gradient. I followed the track and found myself behind a parked ambulance. Paths went off in all directions, into the main block of the hospital, left to a large outcrop with OP emblazoned above the door, and through a small labyrinth of scattered buildings.

Time was ticking away and panic was setting in when I spotted a yellow overall, going at top speed, heading north. Like a greyhound out of the trap I sprang into action; surely another overall would take pity on me, she must have been new once. She rounded a corner, I broke into a gallop; this overall knew her way around. I was starting to put on a sweat in the hot sun as I reached the corner, only to see a flash of yellow disappearing but I wasn't going to let her escape. I went after her like a lemming heading for a cliff. Suddenly she emerged and we met head on; it was Vale.

'It'd be easier to find your way around a bloody rabbit warren, than this damn place,' were her first words. 'I don't suppose you know where "Lapor-atory" is?'

She clutched a bundle of blood samples, like mine. 'Snap!'

'How're you getting on?' she asked. 'I can't decide if I've joined the army or been sent to Borstal.'

'I know the feeling.'

'I've cleaned every sink in the place three times and they don't supply rubber gloves. I'll need a jar of hand cream a night at this rate. Everybody shouts and no one tells you anything.'

I wanted to linger and share pain stories but the clock was ticking. 'I know what it's like. I've got Gumption and Sister Mandrake.'

'Oh, I've met Gumption, I've nearly gone through a tin already.'

'Do you know where X-ray is?'

'I'll swap you for "Lapor–atory"?'

'I think they mean laboratory.' I held up my bottles.

'Right, we'll combine efforts, two lost heads are better than one. I've been to X-ray already, I'll show you afterwards. Sue, look!' She pointed to an insignificant building signed LABORATORY. I had a feeling we'd walked past it twice and I'd now lost my way back to orthopaedic. We dumped our bloods at the hatch and beat a speedy retreat.

Vale pounced on a passing male in a light-brown uniform coat, with PORTER written in red over the pocket. 'Be a love, we're new, lost and in danger of screaming.' She fluttered her golden eyelashes, 'Could you point us back to casualty?' He succumbed in a flash. 'You're a real darling,' she purred.

If I thought orthopaedic was busy, it was calm against the turmoil of the accident and emergency department, which resembled a mainline railway station. There was a constant flow of traffic as it was the main admission centre for anything from road accidents to heart attacks, as well as a thoroughfare used by many of the staff. Ambulance men wheeled in the newly injured, others propelled out those able to go home. Porters whizzed around with chairs and trolleys, armfuls of notes or bottles. Patients were being diverted up to wards and back and forwards from X-ray and assorted clinics. Doctors and nurses hurried around the crowd assembled in the main waiting hall, and the WVS wheeled a trolley dispensing tea and sympathy.

'I'll have to be off back into Bedlam,' said Vale. 'Gumption, here I come. I might see you at lunch if they ever let us eat. Oh X-ray's that way.' She pointed to a swing door as she rushed off.

I joined the stream of people heading into the infirmary building and the unique hospital smell hit me. It was a confusing mixture of strong disinfectant and cleaning fluids, with an underlying hint of body smells which were impossible to eliminate, especially in A&E where sweat, blood, vomit and wee all merged.

A set of polished, worn doors led to into a wide hallway which resembled a high street. A constant surge of people passed in both directions, everyone sure about their course except me. I noticed another brown-coated porter and thought I'd try Vale's approach. I'm not into fluttery eyelashes but I can look helpless. I was to find that porters, mainly middle-aged to pre-retirement men, were a bunch of gents. They were the saviour of many a perplexed cadet and treated us like daughters. They were always ready with a hanky, cup of tea and fatherly advice. The one I found gave me a big smile, walked me down the hallway and pointed to a glass-covered passage that ran alongside the kitchen.

The X-ray department had been designed either by a fool on a tight budget or somebody with a grudge against the NHS. It was one of the added-on bits which joined the main infirmary building by a short walkway. Most patients and staff went in this way, which was really the back door. Two trolleys and a few wheelchairs were choked up in the doorway; they really needed a policeman on point duty. I waited with the clock ticking, while they backed and pushed. I was to discover that there were two ways to find missing X-rays, experience or luck, and at that point I had neither.

Similar to orthopaedic, the patients were lined up along the corridor but on both sides. It resembled a jammed conveyor belt with a sprawl of wounded and attendants. These were the days of 'wet plates' (I was to discover later); after the X-ray was taken, it had to be allowed to dry and then checked before the patient was sent back. If the doctor was in a hurry, the wet plates could be carried, still dripping, to be examined. Drying took about half an hour and casualties, plus booked appointments, repeat and check X-rays were arriving all the time; it was like a battery farm with the chickens all pecking for space.

I eased my way up the narrow passage and looked round for the Nightingale, who must be an expert by now having spent at least two hours in the department. There was no sign of her. I noticed an unknown cadet who'd been caught in the traffic jam, obviously a senior from a ward as she wore an apron and was looking after a crinkled old woman on a trolley. Her patient, propped with pillows, had the colour of a navy cardigan I'd worn at school and looked as if she might expire at any second.

'Excuse me, do you know where I find missing X-rays?'

She gave me a look similar to Sister Mandrake. I expect she'd been working at Benny's long enough to have got in plenty of practice. 'We shouldn't be long, Mrs Briggs,' she said sweetly to the patient, before dismissing me with, 'You'll have to ask at reception.'

I didn't bother asking where reception was, but continued on through the wounded. A young woman holding a curly-headed, crying child stopped me. 'Do you know if the plates are dry yet, Nurse?'

I must have given her a mystified stare. Whatever was she worrying about the pots for? Perhaps they'd promised her a cup of tea and a biscuit when they were done – and that reminded me, Sister Mandrake's tea-tray was still waiting. 'I'll go and see if they've been washed up,' I reassured her.

Opposite the top entrance was an unmarked door; my door phobia was now reaching frightening proportions. I tapped and was tapping again when a voice behind me said, 'There's no one there. Vera's off sick. I'm filling in. What d'you you want?' She pushed past me into the office.

'I've been sent from orthopaedic, they want these three

X-rays.' I pushed my list towards her.

'When were they taken?'

'I've no idea.'

She pushed the list back at me, and rattled off a set speech. 'If you haven't got a date, you'll have to search the index. If they're not in the index, they're new and waiting to be reported on. If they're in the index but had new films, they'll be in Mr Johnson's office. If they're in the index and old, you'll find them in the filing room. If they've been removed from the filing room, someone must have them for another clinic. That's the index.' She pointed to a wardrobe-sized metal cabinet that filled a quarter of the room.

I stood before the index, which seemed to have about a hundred drawers. It was 11.35 and I'd been gone fifteen minutes. I took each name in turn: Ellis, Sylvia, thankfully a bit unusual, so there was just the one. I fished her out in triumph. 'That can't be her,' said my helpful new companion over my shoulder. 'That's the file where they're all dead but interesting. Is she dead and interesting?' she asked,

'She might be interesting but she was sat in orthopaedic when I left so, unless she's died of frustration waiting for me to find her X-rays, she's very much alive.'

'There's no need to be sarcastic. Cadets that are sarcastic, get nowhere. I'm usually in eyes on a Monday, I only fill in when Vera's off. Then I do teeth on a Tuesday and nerves on a Wednesday. And on a Thursday evening,' she confided in a whisper, 'I do the special clinic. Try the left hand side, I think them's the last five-year index.' As expected, I got nowhere. 'Must be waiting to be reported on,' she advised.

'Where?'

'They're most likely to be on Mr Johnson's secretary's desk. Third door down, across from the X-ray rooms.

But she won't let you have them,' she added, as I sprinted through the door.

Another door. Behind this one I found a lady in her early thirties with pink cheeks and brightly painted lips, who I presumed to be Mr Johnson's secretary. For once I received a smile. 'Can I help?' She spoke in a superior manner, enunciating her vowels, like someone who'd taken elocution lessons.

'I've been sent from orthopaedic, there's three X-rays wanted for the clinic.'

'Have you the names?' I handed over my list once more. 'Were they taken over the weekend?'

'I think so.'

'Then they'll be somewhere on the shelf, in alphabetical order, but I can't let you take them.'

'But they're needed.'

'They can't be removed from here until Mr Johnson has done his written report. He'll be starting on them after lunch and you will be able to pick them up at four.'

I was glad someone around here got something to eat. 'But the orthopaedic receptionist said she must have them now.'

'That will be Mrs Hughes?' she said, her smile fading. Her lip gave a little twist, as if she had an uncomfortable piece of meat stuck in a front tooth. 'Please tell Mrs Hughes that she knows very well that X-rays can't be removed when they're in for report.'

My goal was so near. Trapped between Fang, and the prospect of returning empty handed to orthopaedic, I decided to appeal to her motherly side. 'I'm sorry to be a pest but it's my first day and everything's going wrong. Would it be possible to borrow the X-rays, just while the clinic's on, and I promise I'll bring them back right afterwards.'

She gave me a toothy smile and I noticed a smudge of

lip-gloss. 'Oh, it's awful being new, isn't it? My youngest sister's a student nurse at Guy's, in her third year.' She swelled with pride. 'You'll soon get used to it. After all, a cadet's not a nurse, more a domestic, but you'll pick up a few things. Mrs Hughes knows she can't have access to the weekend X-rays if they're in my office. We've had this little argument before. She really should know better. It's not your fault dear, you weren't to know.'

Defeat; my first morning as a 'domestic' disintegrating. Now I was undecided: should I abandon the X-rays and try and find medical records, or return to orthopaedic empty handed, and sort out Sister's tray? I thought of the patients anticipating my return, eagerly watching the door, reassured that 'the cadet won't be long'.

'Can I help?' The voice came from a pretty girl in a white coat.

I was not far from tears as I blurted out my troubles, ending with a sniffled, 'And she's got my X-rays and she won't let me have them.'

'Oh dear, you are having a bad morning. Have you got your list?' It was getting a bit crumpled as I handed it over. 'Wait there, I'll just be a sec.'

She returned a few minutes later clutching three large brown X-ray folders. How she'd managed to extract them from Fang, I had no idea. 'They've not been reported on so they'll have to be returned when you've finished with them. Oh, and a tip for the future: if you want X-rays from Mrs Waring, get into her office between ten and half past, that's when she goes for her morning coffee. And whatever you do, don't mention Fran Hughes.'

'Why,' I asked clutching the folders as if they were the lost treasure of the Sahara.

'Fran pinched her husband!' she whispered with a giggle. 'Good luck.'

I found my way back into the sunshine, having learnt

my first lesson in hospital gossip and stopped a passing porter to ask the way to medical records, which turned out to be above outpatients. Another dilemma: should I head straight there and start another hunt? I only had half my list and it was 11.45. I'd been gone nearly thirty minutes. At that moment the hospital gates and the way out looked very inviting. Had I really looked forward to this day? I'd been a nursing cadet for two and three-quarter hours, and it was still only Monday morning, but if things didn't improve, I'd be going to the Wednesday nerves clinic. Filled with apprehension, I made a decision and headed back to orthopaedic.

Chapter 3

Rice and Ice

Thompson was heading out of the department and met me by the handrail. 'Wherever have you been? Have you got those notes and X-rays?'

'I've got the X-rays, and delivered the blood.'

'Is that all? Where's the notes? Don't you realise there's patients been waiting since nine? The clinic's coming to an end and they still haven't been seen. The doctors and Sister Phipps are playing war.' And 'of-course it's all your fault' she should have added. 'Take the X-rays through to reception and I'll dash to medical records and get the notes. Hopefully I'll be back before Sister Mandrake notices, or I'll be in trouble next!' ('And that will be your fault as well.' I could read her thoughts.) She snatched the list out of my hand and belted off with the final instructions, 'Go and clear Sister's tray, you can manage that surely?'

Fran was rather nice about it as I pushed my hard-won treasure at her. 'Did you have a tough time getting them?' I nodded. 'I should have warned you about Mrs Waring, she's a real cow!' I kept my information to myself. 'Take them into the clinic. What's happening about the notes?'

'Thompson's gone for them.'

'Oh well, they should be here soon. Don't worry,' she added, 'you're doing fine. First days are horrendous, you'll laugh about it one day.' I was sure that day was a long way in the future as I crept into the inner clinic. Sister Phipps was on me in a second. She held out her hand and mouthed, 'Notes?'

I was beginning to wonder if she had laryngitis or if nurses weren't allowed to talk in the clinic. 'They're on their way,' I whispered, confident that the highly-efficient Thompson would discover their hiding place, even if Matron was sitting on them.

Sister bounded back to the doctors and I withdrew. The waiting area had thinned out leaving just a handful, most likely the 'missing vital information brigade'. I gave them a smile and escaped back up the corridor, which thankfully was now empty. I glanced at the clock; it was ten to twelve and Sister Mandrake would play hell if her tea tray hadn't been done before noon. That gave me ten minutes. Digby!

I popped into the plaster room. Digby was busy mopping the floor. He looked up. 'How you gettin' on pet?'

'Terrible! Where do I find Sister's tray?'

'Her office, just across,' he pointed. 'If the door's closed, knock.'

'Thanks.'

The door lay open. A wooden tray, covered by a neatly embroidered cloth, sat on her desk. It held two delicate cups and saucers, sugar bowl, milk jug, teapot and plate with biscuit crumbs. Sisters Mandrake and Phipps took tea in style. I was just about to carry the tray away when the phone rang. I looked around for someone important to answer it, but there was just me.

'Hallo.'

A female voice answered, predictably fractious. 'Is that orthopaedic?'

'Yes.'

'Who's speaking?'

'Su-Susan – Salt, Cadet.'

'Who!'

'Cadet – Nursing – Salt.'

'Is Sister Mandrake there?'

'No. Well—'

'I want to speak to Sister Mandrake.'

By now my palms were getting sweaty. 'I'll get her.' As far as I knew she was in the ward so, laying down the receiver, I went up the passageway and in through the ward doors.

Barnes was helping a young girl on with her coat and two ladies who had returned from their minor ops, were having a cup of tea. I saw a flash of navy blue as Sister slipped between a set of green curtains. I popped in my nose; she was attending to an elderly lady with her arm in plaster. 'Excuse me, Sister.'

It was my second encounter with the Dragon and the look she gave me, if possible, was even worse than the first. 'Well?'

'You're wanted on the telephone.'

'Who is it?'

I swallowed. 'She didn't say.'

'Go and take a message.'

My brow was becoming damp as I hurried back to the phone. 'I'm sorry, Sister's busy. Can I take a message?'

'It's important I speak to her.' The speaker was getting crosser. 'Tell her it's...' Of course I didn't catch the name. Dare I ask her to repeat it? No!

'I'll tell her.' Back to the ward I went, heart pounding and the perspiration getting worse.

Sister was still behind the curtains. 'She wouldn't give me a message, she says she needs to speak to you.'

'Who is it?'

'I didn't catch her name.' Sister gave a snort of disgust,

apologised to the patient and, nearly knocking me over, stormed out of the ward. Knowing I still had to collect the tray, and seeing that it was two minutes before twelve, I followed.

I saw the office door close as I rounded the corner and stood outside, bewildered. Dare I knock and get the tray? Would it be wrong to disturb her while she was on the phone? Should I go and do something else? But what? I was still pondering when she came back out, angry. 'Don't you know how to answer a telephone?'

It should have been possible to tell her that I'd hardly ever touched a phone. Few working-class households had a telephone in the 1960s. It seemed an expensive luxury when no one we knew had a phone, so who would we ring up? There were numerous telephone boxes around for emergencies, though fortunately I'd never had to dial 999. Mum went to the call box occasionally to ask the GP to visit if I was poorly, and I had learnt the rudiments of putting in money and pressing buttons A or B when I was in the Guides. But I felt that none of this information would have impressed Sister, who was convinced that fate had lumbered her with a half-wit in a yellow overall. She proceeded to give me a sharp lesson.

'You say: "Orthopaedic department, Nursing Cadet Salt speaking." Then, if the person on the phone does not inform you of their name and what they want, you ask them!' She shook her head; I was going to need a lot of work. I suppose she was wondering what she had done to deserve the likes of me.

She glanced at the tray and then at her watch. 'One of the other cadets can do the tray, you'd better go to first lunch.' With a flash of starched apron, she hurried away on her black lace-ups, like a highly bred greyhound fresh out of the trap.

The relief of being dismissed for three-quarters of an

hour was tempered by the fact that I didn't know where to go and the unnerving prospect of returning for the afternoon. If my morning had been a disaster, whatever would my afternoon be like?

I remembered passing the kitchens on my way to X-ray. Kitchens, food: could the dining room be somewhere near? The only way I knew was through casualty. It was a little quieter than my first visit and I soon found myself on the far side. I headed towards the smell of food, feeling hungry, although my first morning as a cadet had not been the best preparation for a hearty appetite. I met Vale coming in the opposite direction; she looked like I felt. 'Where are you off?' she asked.

'First lunch, but I don't know where the dining room is, and you?'

'First lunch, but I don't know where the dining room is.' We stood outside the kitchen as a strange, sickly smell wafted out through an open window. It reminded me of pig swill and I dreaded to think what was being served up for our delicate stomachs. Vale was examining her hands. 'They're raw and my feet are killing me. I don't think I'll go back after lunch, I feel like going home.'

I wasn't sure if she was joking. 'Let's find a porter,' I said.

'I could do with keeping one with me. How did you get on at X-ray?'

'It was like pulling teeth.'

She nodded. 'Did you try and get some X-rays from that damn secretary? I came very near to wrapping the things round her head. You'd think she owned them.'

We met a porter pushing a metal meal trolley. 'Which way's the dining room?' I asked.

He pointed to a door round the back of the kitchen. 'Go through there, love, then up the stairs. Dining room's at top.' I thanked him, and we headed up.

We discovered that the nursing staff dining room

slotted neatly over part of the kitchen area. In the sixties, various levels of staff dined apart. I never really thought about the doctors eating arrangements but I assumed it was somewhere select with white tablecloths. The porters and other hospital 'under-staff', who were the unappreciated essentials of the hospital, most likely ate in some cobwebby basement smelling of stale cigarettes and onions.

It was a bizarre arrangement but the more responsibility and training you received, the less financial reward you received. On the other hand, though vital to the hospital but untrained, the ancillary staff were less appreciated but much better paid than the nurses. I suppose it was really all Florence Nightingale's fault. Nursing was a vocation; nurses would find their reward in heaven. Earthly riches were not to be expected and definitely not received. What was received was a strange reverence. From the day I put on my yellow overall, and had the word nurse (though a very fluid term for a cadet) attached to my name, I was given a special status by the public at large.

The dining room creaked with age. The ceiling plaster ran in cracks like a road map. The faded lime-wash walls were bright only because the room had windows on three walls. Antiquated cream-painted radiators were spaced beneath the windows and an odd selection of easy chairs, many with bits of stuffing escaping, ringed each radiator like circling wagons. The tables, each capable of seating around twenty people, were laid out like a convent refectory, with a long top table and a number of others running end-on, each covered by a green-and-white checked tablecloth. Hard wooden chairs, designed for posture not comfort, were assembled at the tables. The top table had a cream cloth, a few bowls of fresh flowers and a couple of glass ash-trays.

The room was fairly quiet as Vale and I walked in. A

scattering of student nurses in their distinctive pale blue uniforms sat at some of the tables. The table furthest from the door accommodated a group of yellow overalls, all busily tucking into the stew which we were to discover was a mainstay of the menu. The top table stood empty. 'Let's sit here,' said Vale. 'I've had a belly full of bossy senior cadets this morning. I'm not having them for lunch as well.'

I agreed and we settled ourselves facing a glass bowl of roses. 'Do you think they serve us, or do we have to go and get it?'

'We'd better find out. No one tells you anything round here and I'm starving.'

A serving hatch filled part of the wall behind us and a woman in a well-stained white overall and a mop cap stood at the other side. 'Large or small?' she asked as we approached. We exchanged puzzled looks as she stood poised with a ladle. 'Large or small?' she repeated.

'Large or small what?' asked Vale.

'Stew.' She had a slight lisp, and it came out as 'spew'.

'I'll have a small,' I said, my appetite shrinking.

'Me too,' said Vale.

'Small' when it was dished out was ample for a hefty navvy. It looked awful but smelt good. 'Do you want bread?' asked the ladle holder. We declined and headed back to our table which was still empty.

'We're getting a few funny looks,' I said to Vale, as we started on the stew. It was quite tasty, loaded with potatoes and carrots but light on the meat.

'New faces, I suppose. Everyone's been looking at me all morning as if I had two heads. Mind you, this rather delicious doctor did give me a wink.'

'You're not really going home after lunch, are you?'

Vale played with her spoon, twirling it around in the thick gravy. 'I'm very tempted. The only thing that would make me stay is not wanting to prove my mother right.' She made a face. '"You won't last a week, perhaps not even a day, my girl. The first time you break a fingernail or get told off, you'll give them a mouthful, and be away home." She'd love to get her "I told you so", in.'

I was going to ask about her mum, when I saw a couple of sisters coming into the dining room and heading right for our table. 'Oh, good grief,' muttered Vale, 'that's all we need.'

They approached the table and gave Vale and me scowls which would have frozen a lava flow. They pulled out two chairs and sat at the far end of the table. A few seconds later a member of the kitchen staff bustled over, gave them a card each, which I presumed was the menu, and stood patiently as they decided what they wanted. 'They even get a choice,' Vale whispered.

The kitchen maid wrote something down and bent nearer to one of them who said something and pointed in our direction. 'Now what?' said Vale, as the maid headed towards us. The low murmur of voices in the dining room fell quiet and I heard a few giggles. A red flush started up my neck as I realised that all the diners were looking at us.

'Excuse me, cadets,' said the maid, quiet nicely, 'but this table is reserved for the senior nursing staff. Would you please move to the nursing cadets' table?'

Vale cursed quietly and looked ready to argue. I wanted the polished floor to open up and swallow me. Feeling like a pair of tramps who'd wandered into the Ritz, we scooped up our plates and headed for the cadets' table, our progress followed by many pairs of eyes. By the time we were seated in our correct, lowly position, I had lost any will to eat and just wanted to bolt for the door. Vale glared at the other cadets and said, 'Why didn't one of you tell us?'

Most of the yellows ignored us now that the entertainment we'd provided was over. 'Welcome to

Benjamin Hale,' said Vale. 'Such a friendly spot.'

A cadet called Evans turned towards us. 'Where are you working?' she asked.

'Accident and emergency,' said Vale.

'Oh Cas is great fun – as long as you get on the right side of Tizzy,' said Evans.

'Tizzy?' I asked.

Vale answered. 'Sister Tissleton, everyone calls her Tizzy. That's something else nobody told me.'

'What?'

'I was scrubbing away, queen of the Gumption. I'd heard the cadets and the nurses talking about Sister Tizzy, so of course I thought that was what she was called.'

'Good grief,' said Evans, 'you didn't call her that?'

'I was mid scrub,' said Vale, 'when suddenly this navy blue uniform towered over me. She's a giant. I knew sisters had frills round their caps, so I supposed this must be her. "You'll be Pepper, the new cadet?" she said. "It's obvious you don't know how to clean a sink, do it again girl." "Yes, Sister Tizzy," I said.'

The rest of the cadets at the table had broken off their conversations to listen and as Vale spoke, they all cracked out laughing. Their hilarity grew louder as Vale went on: 'She gave me the strangest look and I wondered whatever I'd done. Then she bent down so her nose almost touched mine and bellowed "TISSLETON, girl! TISSLETON!"'

As we all joined in the fun, I decided that the other cadets might not be too bad when I got to know them. We were all in the same boat, it was just they knew how to handle the oars.

'Is there afters?' I asked Evans.

'There's an interesting selection. Rice pudding or ice cream or, if you smile sweetly at the kitchen lady you can have rice and ice, rice pudding with a splodge of ice cream in the middle. Recommended.'

'Sounds lovely.'

We followed the cadets and took our stew plates back to the hatch. 'You cadets all want rice and ice?' the lady with the ladle asked.

'Yes please,' we chorused. For the first time since my arrival I started to feel at one with the others. 'You cadets,' she'd said, and that included me. This was the first day on the pathway to my dream of being a nurse. No one said it was going to be easy but surely if I tried hard and learnt as quickly as I could, in time I'd settle down. Everyone feels strange when they're new but newness wears off, the unfamiliar becomes commonplace.

I watched Evans as she dropped a large blob of ice cream into the centre of her steaming bowl of rice. 'They have their own paddy fields behind the laundry,' she confided with a grin. 'That's where you get sent to work when you sit at the sisters' table and call Tissleton Tizzy.'

I made sure I arrived back on orthopaedic promptly and hurried into the ward. Thompson was busy changing bed sheets. 'Have you reported on duty?' I shook my head, something else no one had bothered to tell me.

'Go and find Sister Mandrake, then you say, "Reporting back on duty, Sister".'

Terrified she might think I'd been late back, I scuttled up the corridor. The plaster room was deserted, as was her office. The waiting room was empty and Fran had vanished from behind the reception desk. This 'hunt-sister-to-report-on-duty' was to become a daily expedition. I was sure that she vanished purposely just when I needed to say my prepared speech. This first return-from-lunch-report found her in the clinic, deep in conversation with an important looking 'white coat'. I hovered in the background, wondering if I should wait, interrupt or return in a few minutes. These protocol problems were to haunt my first few months and were a continual dilemma. This time I hung around, pretending to tidy an examination couch, wrapping the blanket first one way then the other. I tucked in already neat corners and set the soap in beautiful alignment on the sink. After being ignored for five minutes, and having relocated the blanket six times, I tried a discreet cough.

'Did you want something Cadet Salt?' She spat.

My new-gained composure evaporated and for a terrible moment I thought I might deposit my 'spew' and rice and ice over her shiny shoes. I opened my mouth to say my lines, which I'd been mentally practising over the blanket, but 'Sister-duty-reporting-on-back' came out. She gave me that look as I confirmed her earlier opinion that she had been saddled with a fool. 'Have the other cadets gone to second lunch?'

They could have gone to Timbuktu or the paddy fields behind the laundry for all I knew. 'I don't know, Sister.'

'Go and tell them to go. You'll be on your own while they're away. Clean the sluice. If you want me, I'll be in my office.'

With an almost inaudible, 'Yes, Sister,' I hurried off. I passed on her instructions to Thompson and Barnes, who were off with practised haste, leaving me for three-quarters of an hour, as the only visible person on duty in the department.

This was to become a strange time of the day for me. Only the 'dispensable' went to first lunch; the others went to second lunch when the clinics and morning work was done. Sister Phipps only worked mornings and was off at twelve thirty. Fran and Digby had an hour for lunch, which they also took as soon as morning clinics were finished. The senior cadets nearly always went to second lunch, and Sister Mandrake usually had her lunch in her office, with the door securely closed, and only the brave would dare disturb her. For forty-five minutes I entered a surreal world. Apart from a few patients who were waiting for ambulances, all was quiet. The morning minor operation people had either gone or were ready to go, and I was left in limbo.

That first day I wandered around like a stray dog. The sluice was fairly tidy. I gave the sinks a wash and brush up, hung the towels neatly on their pegs and polished the draining board. I went into the ward. Just one lady was sitting in her coat, her left foot sporting a bandage.

'Are you alright?' I asked.

'Just waiting for the ambulance, dear. Sister said it wouldn't be long.' She'd no sooner spoken than an ambulance man came up the corridor pushing a wheelchair.

'One for the Blue Light Express,' he cried, giving me a wink. The lady was moved competently into the wheelchair and away they went. As his voice faded, silence descended.

Half the beds were either stripped or in the middle of being remade. I had a feeling I was expected to clean them all up and have the work done by the time Thompson and Barnes returned. This was one challenge too far. I was presented with so many questions, with no one to supply answers. Did I change every item on the bed, or just the sheets and pillowcases? Where did the used linen go? Where was the clean bedding? If I solved those problems, was there some special way of making the beds. I was bound to do it all wrong.

I left them and headed for the plaster room, which was in disarray again. My carefully washed sinks were a mess, the floor was pitted with old plaster and discarded casts and boxes were strewn around. Did I plunge in and clean this lot up? A voice in my head echoed, 'That Digby is always getting the cadets to do his work.' Would the senior cadets be angry if I cleaned up? Would Sister think I was lazy if I left it? Not for the first time anxiety was rapidly becoming my middle name.

I tiptoed passed Sister's office, dreading that she might pop out and ask what I was up to. The last patients had left the waiting room and, after the chaos of the morning, an eerie calm had settled. I spent a few minutes straightening chairs, before drifting around the desolate clinic plumping up pillows. I went from place to place, terrified to stop and be caught slacking but perplexed about what I was supposed to be doing. Outside I could hear vehicles moving about and distant voices. Then a phone started to ring, its demanding tone reverberating through the department. Like a hound on a scent, I followed the sound to reception where the black phone on the desk rang into the empty room. After my first attempt at phone answering, I was not overly keen to pick up the receiver but felt I had to. A man's voice answered.

'Is that orthopaedic?'

'Yes.' I remembered my previous instructions. 'Nursing Cadet Salt speaking.' I glowed with pride at having got my speech out correctly.

'Mother can't make it today.' The voice reduced to a cough as the elderly gentleman on the other end cleared his catarrh.

I searched for a pen. 'What's her name, please?'

'She can come tomorrow.'

'What's her name?'

'She'll need the ambulance. I'll tell the surgery to book it.'

'I didn't get her name,' I shouted, he was obviously hard of hearing.

'I haven't got any more change, we'll be there tomorrow,' and the line went dead. Certain that my first important telephone message had not gone according to plan, I made a cryptic note and left it for Fran.

Life started to return to the department with the

delivery of a large metal box of laundry, followed in rapid succession by Digby, the senior cadets and the first afternoon patients. Thompson shook her head in despair as she surveyed the ward. 'Whatever have you been doing?' she asked.

'Well, I didn't really know what to do after I'd cleaned the sluice. There was no one around.'

'You'll have to learn how to use your initiative, Salt,' she said. 'There won't always be someone around to tell you.' I was tempted to inform her that even when there was someone around, no one told you a damn thing. 'Anyway,' she continued, 'you can put the linen away then go through to reception and see what Mrs Hughes needs.' She directed me to the linen cupboard, a small walk-in storeroom decked from floor to ceiling in wooden shelves. A square metal box the size of a captain's trunk waited outside. As I unlatched the top, I discovered it was crammed with bed linen and towels.

So I found the linen cupboard, which became a place of refuge. The other two cadets were to tell their friends that, 'Salt spends all her time hiding in the linen cupboard.' Which in part was true. It was safe, yet visible. The cupboard was two doors up from the plaster room, not far from the main entrance. It had the advantage of not being out of the way, so I could easily be found if I was required, but private enough to provide a sanctuary. Also, if I was there I could always look busy; it was amazing how carefully linen could be removed from that tin and how slowly it could be placed on the shelves. Then items needed refolding, rearranging, lining up in precise order. Never had that cupboard been so tidy or loved. I discovered countless ways to arrange the pillow slips, sheets and blankets. At least once a week I took everything off the shelves, scrubbed the wooden slats then put everything back in order. I had all the towels sorted into hand and bath, with teacloths separate. I even discovered the secrets hidden on the remote recesses of the top shelf, which I had to use a small stepladder to reach. I found a few sets of ancient lace curtains, a box of Christmas tree decorations, an assortment of embroidered tray-cloths and an elderly pair of navy-blue knickers!

Reluctantly I tore myself away from the linen cupboard back into the minefield which was the rest of the orthopaedic department. It was starting to fill up for the afternoon clinic and a trail of humanity was making its slow, painful way into the waiting room. As with the morning clinic, everyone was told to turn up for 2pm but where the morning clinic was full of wounded accident victims, the afternoon's injured were the persistent backs, achy hips and all those recalcitrant joints.

Fran was busy with a stack of X-rays and notes. She gave me a smile as I slipped behind the desk. 'How's it going?'

'A bit better.'

'Did you leave that note on my desk?'

'Yes. I think he was deaf and all he would say was that Mother would come tomorrow, not today.'

Fran laughed. 'We'll have to see who turns up.' She was busy writing a list. Over the next few months I collected enough lists to paper a house. 'These are the lists for tomorrow's clinics.' I looked puzzled, as usual. 'Each morning we have the fracture clinic. The notes and X-rays should automatically be sent here after they've been seen in casualty, so we shouldn't have to worry about them. Some that come in the morning are check-ups or for repeat X-rays. They're booked in at the first appointment, so their names are in the book.' She showed me the appointment book with a register of names. 'Every afternoon we have the orthopaedic clinics, where patients referred by their GPs by letter come to see one of our two surgeons. These are the letters for tomorrow's clinic.' This time she showed me a pile of letters.

'Now,' she explained. 'We have to make sure that notes and X-rays are available for every patient. The fracture clinic notes and X-rays are pretty straightforward,' (after my morning adventure in the X-ray department, I didn't quite agree) 'but the afternoon clinics are more difficult. If a new patient has been seen anywhere in the hospital over the past twenty years their notes and X-rays have to be found. That's where you come in, as chief hunter.'

It made a change from being chief cleaner. She passed over the list; it was very long. 'These are the afternoon appointments. The ones with the cross have been seen before, so they'll have old notes and X-rays. Start in medical records. Find Mr Ray, he's the main filing clerk. He'll show you where to look and how the system works. If you run into problems, bring back what you've got. One of the other cadets will help when they've got all their work for Sister finished. Try not to be too long, I don't want you to get in trouble with Sister Mandrake. She might have some other jobs she wants you to do. Good luck,' she added, as I set off on my mission.

It should have been easy to find the medical records department on the top storey over the general outpatients. That frenzied seat of activity lay a short walk from orthopaedic and I was fairly confident as I went in through the main doors. It was 2.15 and a number of clinics were in full swing. The waiting room was crammed and there was a steady movement of nurses, cadets and the general public. All I needed were the stairs.

There was a large reception area where four middle-aged women were constantly busy. The telephone rang continuously, and those patients who were not sitting down waiting were queuing before the desk clutching various bits of paper. I decided I'd better not ask at reception; an enquiry for the staircase was bound to get my head chewed off.

Across from the waiting area was a series of doors with a corridor going off both right and left, but no sign of a staircase. I turned left, hoping to come across it, and found myself in the ladies' toilet queue. An enormously fat woman in a brown coat, gripping a small chrome kidney-shaped dish, was directly in front of me. She turned a puffed, crimson face in my direction as she saw the yellow overall.

'I don't know how I'm going to manage, nurse,' she said, indicating the bowl. 'I've been told to pee in this but I don't think I can hover and hold it all at the same time. What do you think?' I tried to picture the mechanics of the operation and I couldn't help thinking she was going to have difficulty. 'I don't really want to go. I mean you can't always perform to order, can you, nurse?'

I gave her an encouraging smile and bounced away up the other corridor. I met a cadet coming at speed. 'How do I find medical records?' I asked.

'Up the stairs,' she said as she ran off. I'd clearly asked the wrong question but it was too late, she'd gone.

I decided to explore and ventured further down the corridor. I was rapidly coming to the conclusion that hospitals were designed by people who had been rabbits in a past life. I passed a number of doors before finding another corridor going right which led to a side exit from the department. Yet another corridor headed off left, with more doors but still no stairs. Perhaps there was a lift, or maybe the medical records' workers were brought in by helicopter each morning and struggled in through a skylight.

I was debating what to do next when a door opened and a doctor popped out. 'Thank goodness,' he said seeing me. 'Take these to the lab and tell them to phone me with the results.' He thrust two plastic specimen bottles into my hands before ducking back inside. I had acquired some revolting looking stuff like frog-spawn with lumps which floated around in an obnoxious yellow fluid. I tried not to heave and set off to try to hand them over to the correct person.

It is a fact of life that when you want someone you can never find them; if you have no need they spill out of every door. I knew that the specimen bottles must have been intended for either Browning or Pierce, the outpatient cadets. If I could find one of them, I could deliver my unwanted produce and discover where the stairs were. I set off on an up-and-down-the-corridors hunt. I travelled back the way I'd come, politely side-stepping various patients who all wanted to ask me directions, and eventually landed back at the waiting room and reception desk. The fat lady was just returning from her lavatorial task and, as she saw me, she waddled over. She held the kidney dish at arm's length, as one might an unexploded bomb. It was full to the brim; she'd evidently managed to 'go' quite well.

'Here you are, nurse,' she said proudly. 'I hope there's enough.' It slopped around and, as she pushed it towards me, I was in danger of a drenching. In one hand I held the bottles, their repulsive contents swimming about; the last thing I wanted was a kidney dish filled with wee in the other. I looked around desperately for a nurse or cadet but only the sour-faced receptionists could be seen. I had a feeling they would not welcome the fat lady's gift.

'I think you have to take it to the nurse who asked you to do it,' I said, still dodging.

'I can't find her,' she said as her hand started to tremble. 'I'll have to give this to someone soon or I'm going to drop it,' she bleated, wobbling towards an empty seat. With an effort she sank down on her large bottom. 'This heat is making me feel a bit faint,' she said, trying to drag out a hanky with her free hand. The wee slopped in the dish and a small amount dripped onto the floor. She patted her brow, where the sweat was trickling into her eyes. 'I've not been well for ages, love,' she confided. 'I've waited months for this appointment and I wasn't really well enough to come but I wasn't going to miss it. Our Joan was going to come with me but she's got bad feet and they swell in this warm weather.' She swayed in her chair, the wee swaying with her.

'Do you want some water?' I asked. I had to say something, though not being able to find the stairs, I didn't know how I would manage a drink.

'That would be lovely,' she said, 'you nurses are so kind.'

In desperation I went over to the reception desk. 'That lady's not feeling well,' I advised. 'Could she have some water?'

One of the receptionists looked up; she had the face of a tiger whose tail has just been trodden on. 'You'll have to find one of the nurses, we just deal with the paperwork. I've already got too much to do.'

'Where will I find a nurse?' I asked.

'They're all busy in the clinics but you might find one of the cadets.'

I knew I shouldn't have asked. 'Where?'

'Upstairs in medical records,' she advised.

Chapter 4

Inspection Day

As I got off the bus on Wednesday morning, I was undecided whether to get straight back on. There had been a family conference over the evening meal the night before. Playing with a bread roll (I was off stew), I'd dabbed a wet hanky to my red eyes.

'You can always try again when you're eighteen,' Mum had advised sympathetically.

Dad was more angry. 'It was a daft idea anyway. Fancy working somewhere that makes you that miserable. There's plenty more jobs.' Which wasn't strictly true for a sixteen-year-old, ex-secondary-modern schoolgirl in 1964. It was the factory, up t'mill, a shop, a typing pool or a wedding ring and baby, advisably in that order. To aspire to be a nurse was quite upmarket, an ambition not to be thrown away after just two days.

Vale had been having similar thoughts but she'd told Brian, her boyfriend who rode a motorbike, wore leather and said she'd never stick it anyway, so she might as well jack it in now. Two days into our nursing careers, Salt and Pepper were ready to get out of the cruet. We had sore hands, aching feet and growing inferiority complexes. I was having nightmares about Sister Mandrake, in which she sat on a steeple-high pile of X-rays that she wouldn't let me have, or kept a ringing telephone under her cap, while Vale was sticking pins in a doll which she said resembled Sister Tissleton.

After a restless night I'd decided to rough it out until Friday and review my options over the weekend, but my feet were not eager as I headed for the hospital. I managed to sign in on time and, in step with a muttering Vale, we hurried up to the locker room.

'This is typical,' she growled. 'We work this end of the hospital but we have to gallop up to the other end to put on our overalls, then gallop back again just to be insulted by some dragon in a frilly cap. If they had any common sense, we'd be allowed to come ready dressed, but oh no, that might make life a bit easier for us. That would never do!'

She was in an especially bad mood that morning and I worried that she might end up throwing her tin of Gumption at someone before lunch. It wasn't helped by the smoke-filled cadets' changing room, with the flaking paint and dead-end lockers. Vale fought to get her key to turn in the rusting lock. 'This damn thing belongs in a junk shop,' she said, giving it a couple of kicks that frightened it into opening.

I'd discovered my locker hiding in a dust-filled corner. It was a rust-bucket, more brown than green, which wobbled when interfered with. Only a faded six remained of its number, the one and four having disappeared over the decades it must have lingered in the changing room.

The cadets milled around, struggling to get a turn at the small mirror, which was so ancient that the under surface showed through, making it appear to be covered in speckled blobs. The central blob resembled the heel of Italy and tended to appear just over the nose area. Each time I looked in it, I was frightened I'd caught some hospital skin disease which started by eating away at the nasal tissue.

The cadets were gathering, as Wednesday morning was 'inspection day'. I'd only found out about this weekly ritual humiliation when I'd been going off duty the previous evening as Thompson had pulled on her cloak. 'Oh, it's inspection tomorrow morning so make sure you put on a clean overall and do your hair special tidy, or you'll cop it.'

'Inspection?' I'd asked, puzzled as usual.

'Miss Pettigrew's cadet parade, every Wednesday morning. You'll see.'

'Do you know anything about this inspection?' I asked Vale, as we were working on scattered bits of hair. Vale's doughnut had taken a battering from the morning breeze and she was trying to win a small corner of the mirror to jam the untidy strands in place.

'Didn't know a thing about it until you said. No one tells you a damn thing in this place.' She pushed the end of a tail-comb under her golden heap and I thought, not for the first time, what a pretty girl she was. I wondered why she wanted to be a nurse when she could have done something much more glamorous, like modelling. 'I see you've shed the seams,' she murmured with a smile.

Mum had been under strict orders the day before and had searched the market for a stall that sold seamless black stockings. With relief I had put them on that morning. We were smoothing down our new, stiff overalls. 'What sort of material do you think it is?' I asked Vale.

'Something cheap but hard wearing.'

'How are you two getting on?' said a voice behind us. It was the Nightingale, Leslie, with that same smug look she'd worn the first morning. I was just about to say that I'd spent two of the most awful days of my life, when she added, 'I've been having a super time. X-ray is wonderful, the staff are really nice and Mrs Waring is teaching me all about X-rays. I make her tea and she always gives me a cup and she feeds me chocolate biscuits. I'm going to get quite fat if I'm not careful.' I gave Vale a look as Leslie continued to gush.

It was ten to nine when the cadets started to move out *en masse* from the changing room. This was the first time that I'd seen them all together and, as we straggled up the staircase and out into the sunshine heading for the administration block, we resembled a river of custard. Thompson fell back a little and nodded at my cloak, which swung over an arm. 'You have to fold it so your name tag shows. She's very particular about name tags is Miss Pettigrew.' I thanked her for the advice; she was trying to be helpful, which was more than could be said for the rest of the senior cadets.

We retraced our steps of Monday morning but instead of turning towards Matron or Miss Patton's office, we went up a short flight of stairs, down a passage and through a door marked STORAGE.

'Typical,' Vale muttered, 'to have to meet in a junk room.'

It was a large storeroom with two walls piled from floor to ceiling with boxes and some spare bed heads propped against a couple of new mattresses. It was just before nine as we packed in, assembling in a semi-circle before a table and chair which awaited the assistant matron. Everyone was putting finishing touches to stray hairs, yanking overalls and lining up name badges. Silence fell as she entered; like a general ready to survey her army she settled herself behind the desk.

'Good morning, cadets.'

'Good morning, Miss Pettigrew,' we chorused, like first years at morning school assembly.

She was a scrawny little woman, nudging fifty, with

intense blue eyes which scanned us like an owl after prey. She wore a maroon uniform with long sleeves and a white lace collar. Her stringy, greying hair was pulled tightly back from her lean face and vanished under a severe frilly cap. The inevitable brown folder was opened. 'The six new cadets must receive their vaccinations; these will be done in the outpatient department tomorrow. You will go during your afternoon break. Pick up a form from my office before you go.'

Being pointed out as the 'new cadets' drew every eye in our direction and I had a picture of Thompson and Barnes at second lunch, flicking ash off their cigarettes and saying, 'That new cadet, Salt, is a real ninny. She can't do anything right, not even answer the telephone and Sister Mandrake detests her.'

Miss Pettigrew moved on to her next point. 'I've had reports of cadets wearing their cloaks indoors. I have told you repeatedly that cloaks must be carried inside the hospital buildings. I even had one report that a cadet was seen outside the hospital gates in a cloak.' Everyone looked innocent.

'Also,' and she paused for effect; what terrible crime had we now committed? 'There have been instances of cadets answering the telephone incorrectly.' I could feel the blood starting to creep up my neck. 'If you are called upon to answer a telephone, you say the name of your department or ward number, then "nursing cadet" and your surname.' I was sure she was looking at me and the sweat spread across my forehead. Sister Mandrake had put the scalpel in. Her frown deepened as she closed the folder. 'Is there anything any of you wish to bring up?' Breakfast, I thought, but there was a predictable silence.

She came out from behind the desk and, beginning at one end of the semi-circle, she worked her way along. Her eyes started at the hair, worked their way down the overall and finished off at the shoes. Then she went back to the cloak, checked the name and indicated for the cadet to turn around. Back of hair, collar and down the overall to again finish at the shoe heels. 'Round!' she ordered and finished by inspecting hands and fingernails. I was intrigued as I watched her move from cadet to cadet. As she reached the fifth in line she paused and raised a wooden measuring gauge. This had a flat leg which rested on the ground, an upright ruler and another wooden projection which stuck out at an acute right angle. She stood it on the floor and the projecting piece sat about five inches below the hem. 'Nursing Cadet Hymes, you have turned this overall up.'

'It must have shrunk,' said the offending Hymes, as a few of the cadets stifled giggles.

Miss Pettigrew snorted. 'Don't tell lies, Hymes, this isn't the first time I've had to tell you about the length of your skirt. The hem should be not less than six inches from the ground and yours is nearer twelve! And you work on a men's ward! Really, cadet!' Hymes tried to look repentant but failed, and the rest of the cadets had great difficulty controlling their laughter. The assistant matron was not amused and she gave us all a scowl. 'It is not funny, cadets. A lot of bending is required when you are working on the wards and it is important to maintain your decency. It would be terrible if you were to show a suspender or a glimpse of knickers.'

Along with the majority of the cadets I was ready to explode but Miss Pettigrew could see nothing funny and continued to scowl as she turned back to Hymes. 'This is your last chance. You will go straight to the sewing room after inspection and have your hems attended to. If I find your skirts short again, you will go to Matron.'

Up the line she came, until she reached Leslie. 'Are you settling in, Cadet Nightingale?' she asked.

'Oh yes thank you, Miss Pettigrew, I'm really enjoying

it.'

'And what about you, Cadet Salt?' she inquired as she reached me. Oh, the things I could have said, the mouthful of misery I could have cast into her teeth. The humiliation, fear, puzzlement, the daily dilemmas, the feelings of inadequacy; but I choked them all down and muttered, 'Yes, thank you, Miss Pettigrew.'

'Your hair is on your collar, have it cut before next week, Salt,' she commanded as I twirled.

She moved along until she reached Vale. 'Are you settling in, Cadet Pepper?'

I could imagine what was going through Vale's mind but she kept it under her bouffant. 'Yes, thank you, Miss Pettigrew,' she echoed.

'Where is it you're working?'

'Casualty,' said Vale. I saw the other cadets exchange glances.

'How long have you been employed at this hospital, Pepper?'

'Two days.'

The assistant matron swung her frown from Vale and cast it around the semi-circle. 'Two days, and you are already calling the accident and emergency department, "Casualty"!' Obviously Vale had committed a cardinal sin but the other cadets were to blame. Miss Pettigrew screwed her mouth into a disgusted pout. 'How many times have you been told? This hospital has spent thousands of pounds on new signs, new direction markers and new stationery to change the name to accident and emergency and, after all that, a cadet who has worked here just two days has already picked up the habit from those around her of calling it casualty!' She stopped and glared at one of the senior cadets. 'Atkinson, you are working on accident and emergency.'

'Yes, Miss Pettigrew,' said Atkinson. I was sure she was

mentally calling all the plagues of Egypt down on Vale's head.

'Tell Nursing Cadet Pepper why the name was changed.'

'To stop patients coming to the department with minor ailments or conditions which should have been treated by their GP,' chanted Atkinson.

'Exactly.' Miss Pettigrew returned to Vale. 'The name of the department is accident and emergency. Don't let me hear you call it casualty again. Do I make myself clear, cadet?'

It was apparent that Vale couldn't see what all the fuss was about and she made a poor job of looking contrite. 'Yes, Miss Pettigrew.'

A few minutes later it was over. No one said anything until we were out of the building, when the bundle of yellow split into groups as we hurried off to our work places. Since Vale and I were both working in the same area of the hospital, we fell into step.

'What a palaver!' said Vale. 'It felt like a slave auction. I kept expecting her to check how good my teeth are. Have you ever seen anything like it?'

'When she was going on about suspenders and knickers, I don't know how I kept my face straight.'

'Silly old bat, a good flash of knickers or underpants would do her good. Fancy telling you to cut your hair. It's worse than the army. She better not start on my hair or that's the final straw, I'm off!'

'Salt, there's a gentleman to go to X-ray,' were Sister Mandrake's first words to me that morning. This was a new challenge. For two days I had been perfecting my cleaning duties, thankful for a good grounding in domestic science at my secondary-modern school. These were the days when the average girl was prepared to be a skilled, conscientious housewife, and during my first school year I had learnt every cleaning technique from scouring cupboards and floors to polishing brass, wood and silver. I could starch and iron with the best, and no stain was beyond my abilities to remove. I had also, since my arrival at Benny's, started my education in detection and decided that should my nursing career end in disaster, I might try the police. But to be trusted to escort someone to X-ray was surely a step in the right direction. With visions of lending a comforting arm during a gentle stroll across the tarmac, I headed into the waiting room.

The room was in the grasp of its usual morning turmoil. Mr Dawkins, a pale, middle-aged man with thinning hair and moustache, was sitting patiently in a wheelchair, one of his legs propped on the footrest so it stuck out like a railway signal.

'Are you my carriage driver?' he asked.

It appeared that I was. For the first time in my life, and with my vast two-day experience behind me, I was now required to push him in his chair to X-ray. I tried to appear confident. 'Yes, I'll soon have you there. What happened?'

'Daftest thing nurse, I fell over the cat. Next thing I knew, mi' leg was broke.'

'Well, let's get moving,' I said, taking up position behind the back bar and giving a hearty push. Nothing happened. I pushed again.

'I think you have to take the brake off, Nurse,' he advised.

'Of course.' I slid my fingers down the back, along the arms, under the seat, round the wheels and back up the rear where I found a small button. Relieved, I pressed. The back of the wheelchair came away in my hands. My patient, taken unawares, started to fall back. I grabbed, he yelped. Frantically I steadied him, pushed the seat back upright, until it slipped back into position.

I was trembling and we hadn't even moved. 'That was a near do, nurse,' said my patient, who was living up to his designation. 'I think the brake's somewhere at the top of the wheel, that black knob,' he indicated.

'This is a new model, I'll soon get the hang of it,' I assured him. I slid the knob back, and we were off!

My first task was to manoeuvre him out of the waiting room. A 1960s' square-bottomed wheelchair was quite a size. The same vehicle with the leg rest poking out was another two foot longer. After two attempts, we managed to break free of the wall but then steered into a line of packed chairs. There was much shuffling out of the way and bag and child moving. Broken legs were desperately dragged out of danger, and wounded arms and collar bones shrank away as I projected my misguided missile towards them. 'Got square wheels, hasn't it, nurse,' joked my very patient patient, as the base of the footrest plus his bare toes bumped into a young girl's ribs.

'Ouch!' she bellowed.

'Ouch!' he echoed.

'I'm so sorry,' I said, apologising to everyone in sight.

'Not passed your driving test yet,' laughed an elderly lady, who was sitting in the gangway and had hurriedly jumped out of my way. Fearing I might up-end them, two of the walking wounded on crutches held open the waiting room door and I edged through. The corridor filled with the crowd waiting for the plaster room lay ahead. There was just enough room to drive a laden wheelchair between the parked immobile, each with a limb stuck out. I inched along, my patient smiling benignly at those we passed who automatically shrank nearer the wall.

I was just about to congratulate myself when the last wheelchair in line decided to move. The brake had not been put on securely and, as the woman occupant took it upon herself to struggle into her coat pocket for a hanky, she jogged her transportation into my path. The collision brought a scream from her and a high-pitched yelp from Mr Dawkins.

I fluttered around, terrified Sister Mandrake might be on the prowl. I made more apologies, soothed the lady back into position and made a hasty retreat. Mr Dawkins, looking even paler, smiled. 'You're doing grand, nurse. Have we far to go?'

I struggled through the door and managed to break out into the sunshine with no further trouble. I had to push him along the side of orthopaedic, then down the ramp, across the yard and, since it was a fine day, head around the buildings to the front door of X-ray. My spirits rose and, for the first time since I'd donned my yellows, I started to feel like a proper nurse. Visions returned of my gentle figure drifting from bed to bed, checking my fob watch (when I could afford one), pressing the pulse and resting my soft palm on a fevered forehead.

The ramp leading down into the main yard lay ahead. 'Lovely day again, nurse,' said my patient. 'Shame you got to spend it pushing about an old duffer like me.'

'Oh, it's a pleasure,' I assured him, as we started down the ramp. It really wasn't that steep. More slope than hill, a slight gradient not a mountain and yet, as the wheels hit the top of the slope, my vehicle suddenly felt extremely heavy and I started to feel control slipping away. I hung on as my patient, realising his impending peril, grabbed the chair arms as if in an ejector seat.

We started to slip down the ramp. I dug in my heels and swung backwards, arms outstretched, legs braced, my backside sinking towards the tarmac, but I could feel the wheelchair gathering speed. I pulled back with every ounce of strength I possessed as we jerked from side to side for a couple of yards. We gained pace and I realised I had two choices: carry on and risk catapulting my wounded patient into the hospital yard, where he might end up with a second broken leg, or take one of the pansy beds that lay on either side of the ramp.

The metal rail, four foot from the tarmac, ran on either side of the ramp. I steered the inside front wheel into the soil and the wheelchair slewed sideways, tipping at an angle. My patient ducked to avoid decapitation from the railing; he was now lying flat in the chair, his head down by the arm, one leg dangling, the other hovering in mid-air. A fraction of a second later, the back inside wheel hit the soil and the wheelchair tilted. My patient slipped, heading for the pansies. I did a falling snatch like a cricketer after the ball. We ended up in a clutter of yellow overall, arms, legs and crushed pansies. My battered patient was whimpering, I was apologising and thank goodness a couple of ambulance men were running to help.

Wheelchair, patient and me were carefully extracted from the pansies and deposited in the yard. 'You short of work, love?' one asked. 'Trying to break a few more bones? You must want a bit of plastering practice.'

I was terrified I'd hurt the poor man. 'Are you alright?' I kept asking. 'Are you sure?' I pressed, as he assured me he was fine.

'Wait till I tell the wife I've been in the flower bed with a pretty young nurse! She'll be fair jealous.'

'Where you off to, nurse?' asked one of the ambulance men.

'X-ray.' I was rubbing a bruised shin and trying to scrape the soil off my shoes.

'I think we better give you an escort, love,' he said, as they took over the rear of the wheelchair and started to push it towards X-ray. 'You might end up in the boating lake next.'

It was a blessing this was the 1960s, before the 'sue-at-the-drop-of-the-hat' culture, or I could have ended my nursing career within days. The ambulance men left us in the X-ray waiting room. 'Now don't you go pushing him

71

down the toilet,' said one, grinning as he put the brake on.

'You need danger money, mate,' said the other. 'See if you can get her to push you into the dark room, as a consolation prize.'

***

It was mid-way through Thursday morning when I started serious work on my escalating telephone phobia. After my first experience, I had avoided Sister's telephone like a time bomb but now it rang with a demanding clamour and no one else was taking any notice. I waited another few seconds, praying that someone would turn up, but apart from a couple of patients the corridor was bare. Her office door stood open and I stretched out a reluctant hand, picking up the receiver as one would a stinging nettle. At least I got my script correct.

'Hallo, orthopaedic department, Nursing Cadet Salt speaking.'

'I want to speak to Sister Mandrake,' said an important-sounding voice.

'Who's speaking, please?'

'Just get Sister Mandrake.' Someone had gone off script and it wasn't me, but my courage was failing and I dare not ask again.

'I'll go and get her. Please hang on.' I was off on the obstacle course, up the corridor, bypassing the wounded, through two doors and into the clinic. The senior orthopaedic consultant surgeon, accompanied by his secretary, registrar, houseman and a collection of other doctors, were examining patients. Sister Mandrake was busy supervising, and Barnes was the tidy-up-behind-them-and-run-urgent-messages cadet. A dignified hush hovered inside the clinic, with just the clipped correct English of the consultant breaking the silence. His entourage hung on his every word, and the tiny lady with the pain in her hip who was lying on the examination couch eyed him with a look reserved for God making Adam's rib into woman.

I arrived in this distinguished gathering, feeling like a vagrant at the mayor's ball. Sister Mandrake was in the centre of the crowd. Trying to be as unobtrusive as possible, I made my way through the white coats, until I arrived at her elbow. She ignored me for a couple of minutes then, with that look on her face, she whispered, 'What do you want, Salt?'

'There's someone on the telephone for you.' I knew what the next question was going to be.

'Who is it?' she hissed.

'She wouldn't tell me but she insists on speaking to you.'

Sister Mandrake gave me a look like a gorilla with painful piles. 'Go and find out who it is and what she wants.'

I left in a hurry, nearly knocking over one of the unsuspecting doctors. Back out of the clinic, through two doors, past the wounded to the phone. The unknown woman had been waiting nearly four minutes and her temper was growing. 'I'm very sorry, but Sister is busy in the clinic. Could I have your name and take a message?' I was quite satisfied with my speech. I hadn't stammered or got muddled and I couldn't have been more polite.

My efforts had gone unnoticed. 'I wish to speak to Sister Mandrake, now!' she bellowed. I dropped the phone like a hot potato and dashed off, side-stepping the wounded, nearly knocking myself unconscious on one of the doors, and back into the inner sanctum. For the second time I pushed through the throng to Sister Mandrake's side.

The angry gorilla's piles had clearly grown worse. 'Well?' she hissed.

'I'm sorry, but she won't tell me who she is. She must speak to you.' By now I was attracting some attention from the great man who, I felt, wanted to swat me like a fly. His secretary was looking faintly shocked over her spectacles and the remaining doctors were shuffling uncomfortably.

Sister Mandrake brought her face close to mine, giving me a strong whiff of toothpaste and onion. 'Go-and-take-a-message.' She spoke quietly and slowly, as one would to a child with learning difficulties.

For the third time I retreated, out of the clinic, through the doors, down the corridor and past the wounded. The phone lay waiting, a ticking explosive about to detonate. I was shaking as I picked it up and at first the words wouldn't come. 'I really – sorry – am,' I managed, 'but Sis – Mandrake Sister – come can't, to phone, message me.' It was no good, I'd lost the script.

The voice on the other end stung. She'd been hanging on the phone approaching seven minutes and all she'd managed was to speak to this daft nursing cadet, who couldn't even put one sensible word after another. Suddenly I recognised the voice and I could see Granny sitting behind her mahogany desk, wondering where nursing was heading if I was its future. 'This is Matron speaking. Could you please bring Sister Mandrake?' she purred.

With wobbly knees, I journeyed back. I collided with a chap on crutches and fell over a wheelchair, before making my grand entrance into the clinic. This time they were waiting for me. The great man fell silent and all eyes focused on me as I made my way across the clinic floor. The doctors parted and the secretary removed her glasses for a better view. Even the little grey-haired lady on the couch looked at me expectantly, wondering what momentous tidings I was carrying. Sister Mandrake glared; by now the gorilla had a severe case of indigestion as well as piles.

I took centre stage like an actor in a bad play, with clammy palms, knocking knees and a mouth like the inside of an old glove. 'It's Ma - Ma - Ma - Matron.'

Sister threw the file of notes she was holding onto the couch. 'Why didn't you say that in the first place?' she spat. 'Do excuse me, sir.' And with a swish of starch she was gone.

I spent the remainder of the day between the linen cupboard and the sluice, where I felt a measure of safety. Thompson dragged me out to take some specimens to the laboratory and I dawdled there and back. I daydreamed about what else in this difficult world I could do; surely my meagre talents could find better employment? I wondered if I was suited to hairdressing but, reviewing my mop of unruly curls, I concluded that if I couldn't even keep my own hair tidy... Window dressing? That was a possibility; surely even I could put bra and pants on a mannequin? I did play with the idea of acting, picturing myself strutting the boards, being showered in bouquets and rapturous applause, perhaps even appearing in films. I was busy signing autographs when I arrived back to the reality of orthopaedic and nearly knocked over Sister Mandrake outside the plaster room.

The clinic was over and she'd just popped out of her office for something, which was certainly not me. The shock of having this odious yellow overall blunder into her knocked her frilly cap sideways. I blamed her white hair clips; she mustn't have jammed them in firmly enough.

The gorilla had calmed down a little with the departure of the consultant and the comfort of her late afternoon tea. She resembled a cod out of water as she sucked in and blew out, hunting for words. Sadly the cod turned shark; she'd had enough of me, and I dreaded to think what her next report to Miss Pettigrew would be. There was a strong possibility that I wouldn't have to quit to pursue my future path as a Hollywood starlet because I would get the sack.

'You will have to improve dramatically, Cadet Salt, if you wish to continue working in this department,' she spat. 'If you think you can manage it, you can take away my tea tray.' She watched as I picked up the tray from her table, the china vibrating in my trembling hands. I felt her eyes boring into my spine as I walked out, heading for the sluice.

Once out of her sight I calmed down a little, glanced at the clock and noted it was 4.15. I wondered if I could make the washing up of a cup, saucer and plate with two crumbs on it last until five. With great precision I filled the washing-up bowl, worked the suds up into delicate heaps and plunged in the cup. It was very pretty china, with rosebuds and vine leaves. I would always drink from something like this when I was a star. I would have my china specially made to my own design and refuse to take tea in anything but my own personal cup. Perhaps I would have my initials interlaced around the rim in pure gold. I noticed the saucer had lost a little of its gold leaf; perhaps it was a cheap second. The plate didn't even match; this would certainly never meet my future standards. I stood before the footlights, blowing kisses to my fans, roses falling at my feet. 'Thank you, thank you,' I trilled. 'Bravo! Bravo!' they bellowed.

I rubbed the dishcloth carefully over the soapy crockery as I drifted, in a gown of shimmering sequins, down the red carpet. I stopped as an eager autograph hunter pushed her book under my diamond bracelet. 'Could you sign your autograph, please Miss Salt?' she drooled. 'We used to work together.'

I slid a monogrammed silver pen across the page, scrawling an illegible signature. The gorilla cooed, transformed into a cute monkey willing to please. Her squinty little eyes and crinkled mouth gazed up at me in adoration. 'It was when you were at the hospital,' she hinted.

I pictured myself leering down at her, flashing my diamonds under her nose as I answered in a silky whisper, 'I'm afraid I don't remember you.'

Just then I heard the phone ring, I spun round to get the tray, touched the china plate with the edge of the dishcloth. It wobbled, tilted and slid and, with a magnificent crash, hit the sluice floor. It was such a good thing it hadn't matched.

Chapter 5

Tizzy

'Have you ever ridden an elephant?' Vale asked. We had struggled through to Friday morning and were on our way up to the lockers. My arm was still aching from the injections which had dared to take five minutes longer than my prescribed break and had drawn another reprimand from Sister Mandrake.

Vale's question took me aback and I wondered if she'd decided on a new turn to her career. I couldn't see her working at the zoo shovelling elephant dung, so it had to be the circus. Was she planning to run away? And, horror, did she want me to go with her? I'd never seen myself tightrope walking or being the target for knives and the trouble with elephants, though I was sure they were very nice when you got to know them, was that they were so tall. I got dizzy standing on a chair.

'Well, I did have a go at the zoo when I was about six but I screamed so loud they took me off. Why?'

'I'm going to ride an elephant and I wondered if you'd fancy joining me.'

'When's this all going to happen?'

'Tomorrow afternoon,' she announced. 'We've had such

a pig of a week, it'll be fun.' It wasn't quite the word I'd have chosen but I didn't want to risk our new friendship. I was sure Vale must already think me a wimp. She got angry, I got nervous; she got mad, I got frightened.

'Who do you know with an elephant?'

'The circus is coming to town tomorrow. Brian knows the boss, he worked for them last time they were here. They want an attraction to lead the parade and he suggested me in my new nurse's uniform, sitting on an elephant'

I gasped. 'You're going to wear your overall?'

'Why not?'

'We're not even supposed to wear them outside the gates, let alone wear one to ride an elephant. Anyway, you said you wouldn't want anyone to see you in it.'

'Oh, I'm going to take one home tonight, turn it up and put a few sensible darts in to give it some shape. Add a belt and it'll be okay. Once I've done my hair and put my face on, I shouldn't look so bad. What do you think?'

'If anyone finds out there'll be hell on.'

'I don't see how they'll know. I'm a good bus ride away from Thorpe.' Vale lived in a small mill town up against the Pennines called Moresbry, which was a half-hour bus journey from Thorpe.

'Come with me, it'll be a scream.' Scream was most likely the right expression. I wasn't sure which I was more afraid of: being caught wearing my overall outside hospital premises or the idea of swaying around like Tarzan's Jane on an unpredictable monster. I hunted for excuses.

'I don't know if I could do it, I'm terrified of heights.'

'Tell you what, you can walk in front and help guide it.'

'In my yellow overall?' I asked timidly. 'Can't I wear my best dress?'

'Come on, Salt, rules were made to be broken. It's a good job you've met me, you need taking in hand.'

'What if they find out and we get in trouble?'

'They won't find out, and if they do we'll plead ignorance. They won't believe me but you can look very innocent. Go on, give it a go.'

I found myself agreeing and realised that Pepper was going to be a delightfully bad influence on my future development.

During my morning in orthopaedic, I planned how to sneak an overall into my bag and whether, with my weak abilities in needlecraft, I could transpose my sack into a stylish outfit. Hopefully it might rain and I could hide it under a coat. That way I might look presentable and also I wouldn't be picked out as 'that cadet in a yellow overall leading an elephant'.

That brought me to the elephant. I might actually be safer on its back. Once I'd climbed up, I could always keep my eyes closed and hold on tight. If I was leading it, I'd be in line with those great legs. What if it took fright and trampled me? I'd be rushed to casualty, sorry accident and emergency, perhaps with a broken arm or ankle. Sister Tissleton would be in attendance. 'This can't be one of our nursing cadets?' I heard her say. 'How dare she wear her overall outside the hospital?'

I'd never met Sister Tissleton but I felt I knew her after Vale's vivid description. She'd most likely have to cut the overall to get it off me, parting the yellow cloth from the blood. I'd be missing one uniform; how would I explain to Miss Pettigrew? Then the next morning I'd be a patient in orthopaedic, sitting in one of the chairs parked outside the plaster room. 'This just serves you right, Salt,' Sister Mandrake would say. 'To think you could lead an elephant. You can't even steer a wheelchair, let alone wash a pot without breaking it.'

I was plotting ways of extracting myself from the grip of Pepper and her big ideas when Thompson broke in abruptly on my thoughts. 'Are you hiding in the linen cupboard again, Salt? There's no clinics this afternoon so you better learn a few things. There's a change list due in a few weeks and me and Barnes will be off onto the wards. You'll be the only one who knows the ropes when the new cadets arrive. Sister Mandrake will expect you to know what you're doing.' I had a feeling Sister Mandrake was going to be disappointed.

'We'll start with what happens on day patient morning. As the patients arrive, you show them to a bed. Draw the curtains round and ask them to get undressed and put on a theatre gown. You know, you're lucky working on orthopaedic. There's no student nurses, so we get to do heaps more than any of the cadets in the other departments.' I made a mental note to try and feel lucky. 'Ladies leave on knickers, men underpants,' she continued. 'Each one has to have a plastic name band put on their wrist and their temperature and pulse taken. Have you ever taken a temperature or pulse?' she added. I shook my head. 'Right,' said Thompson in businesslike manner. 'This is a thermometer.' She extended a thin glass tube with a metal piece at one end. 'First you need to know how to shake one down.'

She made it seem very easy as she talked me through the procedure. 'You hold the thermometer by the glass end; it's the metal bit that goes under the tongue. Grip the thermometer securely between the thumb and first finger, hold tight and at the same time let your wrist go limp so that the mercury falls as you shake.' With a few quick flips of her wrist she shook the thermometer and then rolled it across the back of her hand. 'Yes, that's down. Can you see the black line, up the centre?' Predictably I couldn't see a thing. Next she popped it under my tongue, waited four minutes, took it out, gave a brisk wipe with a swab, and rolled it to read. 'You're normal,' she announced. I didn't know whether to be relieved or disappointed, I was just ready for a good dose of flu. 'Now, see if you can shake it down,' said Thompson.

I managed the 'hold the thermometer firmly' but the 'let the wrist go limp' instruction seemed physically impossible. My hand and wrist moved up and down, stiff and unyielding, the mercury stayed solid on 98.4. Time and again I tried, Thompson shaking her head. Feeling desperate, I gave the thermometer a final fling; the wrist went slack, so did the fingers, and the thermometer went spinning away to shatter on the floor. I looked aghast.

Thompson was quite nice about it. 'Don't worry, we all break one when we're learning.' I brought the brush and shovel and Thompson hunted out a fresh thermometer. 'Remember, fingers firm, wrist slack.'

For the next half hour I shook, flapped and rolled, strained my eyes to see the 'thin black line' and never saw a thing, gripped and shook the thermometer until my fingers and wrist ached – but the mercury never moved. Thompson somehow kept her patience and I was sure she would make an excellent nurse. Her resolve did crack a little when I sent the second thermometer crashing, but she made a marvellous catch when the third went sailing through the air. I wondered if she'd been good at netball at school. 'I think you better take the thermometer home and practise,' she said, shaking her head.

We just had time for a few pulse-taking sessions before she went for afternoon tea. I actually found her pulse: I could feel a gentle throbbing under my fingers, and proudly told her she was making twenty beats a minute. She informed me I must be missing some as it should be around seventy, which I thought was a bit unjust when I'd managed to feel something at least. When I had a go at my own I couldn't feel a thing but, since my arm and feet were still aching, I was sure I was definitely alive. I resolved to practise both temperature and pulse-taking over the weekend. Surely I now had a good excuse to free myself from the elephant adventure but when I saw Vale at afternoon break, she was full of it and, like tumbleweed, I was blown along by her plans.

'You'll have to come home with me tomorrow. Bring your overall. You are going to turn it up tonight?' I nodded. 'I'll do your hair and you can borrow some of my eye make-up and lippy. We haven't to be there before four, so we've plenty of time.' She paused to sip tea. 'I've had a hell of a day. God, I hate Sister Tissleton! I was cleaning this cupboard under the sink in the main treatment room and she was watching me the whole time. I could feel her eyes drilling into my neck then suddenly she pounced. "You've missed a bit, girl, that disinfectant bottle has a dirty stopper." She gave me such a start, I dropped the damn bottle and the disinfectant went everywhere. "Butterfingers," she shrieked, and I spent ages mopping up. She's completely mad. Everyone says she is; your Sister Mandrake's a sweet old pussy cat compared to Tissleton.'

It was just after five when I trailed out of the department behind Thompson and Barnes. I'd been wondering what happened on Saturday morning. Since no one had said anything, I thought I'd better ask. Barnes looked down her nose. 'Orthopaedics closed at the weekend,' she said.

'So do we open up and have a good clean?'

'You are thick, Salt,' said Barnes sarcastically. 'It's closed, not open. Shut. Got it?'

'So what do we do?'

'We spend the morning on the wards. I'm on men's medical, Thompson's on women's orthopaedic.'

'What about me?'

'Oh, you spend the morning in casualty, getting to know dear Sister Tissleton,' she spat.

'You poor sod!' said Vale when I told her. With these comforting words ringing in my mind, I took the bus into

Thorpe. Mum was delighted that I'd brought one of my new uniforms home and, as she was much better with a needle than me, offered to do the alterations. Though she did have some reservations about me and an elephant,

'I'm going to help the man lead it and it's very tame,' I assured her.

'Will you be on the telly?'

'God, I hope not! It's only just a small-town circus, it happens every year. We're only going because Vale's boyfriend Brian knows the circus owner.'

'That's a shame,' said Mum. 'How about if I come and watch and bring the camera.'

I had visions of my proud mother working the crowd and telling everyone about my amazing new nursing career. Knowing her (there was a lot of Vale in her make-up) she'd chat to all the clowns, knife-throwers and the lion tamer, and end up riding the elephant herself. 'It's quite a bus ride up to Moresbry and you know how busy you are on a Saturday. I'll take the camera and get someone to take my picture.'

'Oh no, I wouldn't miss this. You around an elephant I must see.'

I spent a restless night; Vale's stories of the horrors of casualty and Sister Tissleton gathered to haunt me. I woke up in a cold sweat with the vivid picture of this leering giant of a woman trying to stuff a tin of Gumption down my throat.

As I went to work my first Saturday morning, my bag was heavy with my remodelled overall, hair rollers, grips and other hairdressing essentials. I didn't have any hope of talking Vale out of the adventure but I prayed for rain, then no one would see even a flash of yellow. Sadly, the sky was cloudless and it promised to be beautiful day.

'How did the uniform turn out?'

'Mum did the honours. It looks quite nice apart from

the colour.'

Vale nodded. 'I've mopped that colour off the floor a few times this last week. You'd be amazed how much vomit someone can bring up, it looks like a bucketful when it's all swirling around the floor.' As my meeting with Sister Tintwistle drew nearer, I felt like adding to Vale's bucket.

We'd reached the main door with the big A&E sign over it. As usual, even at nine in the morning the place was busy. Most of the chairs were occupied with an assortment of the wounded. There was a couple of screaming children, plus four others who looked exceedingly fit and were playing hide and seek around the waiting room.

'We go in here,' said Vale. She showed me where to hang my cloak and we gave our hair a tidy; at least there was a good mirror on the wall. Vale gave me a quick guided tour as we headed for sister's office. 'Medicine room, plaster room, examination cubicles, main treatment room, small ops – and this is the lion's den,' she said as we paused at a door marked SISTER. 'Good luck. I'll try and help if you get stuck. Just make sure you always have a dishcloth and a tin of Gumption in your hands,' she added, as she knocked.

'Come!' yelled a voice from inside. Sister was busy trying to fish an over-dunked chocolate biscuit out of her teacup as we entered. Intent on her task, she ignored us and we exchanged looks as she slopped around with a spoon, swearing fluently the whole time. Eventually she gave up and, spinning her swivel chair to face us, bounded to her feet like a kangaroo.

She was the tallest woman I had ever seen and her frilly cap floated just a few inches below the lampshade. Her hair was straw yellow and more fluffy than curly. It bushed out like an over-brushed doll and I was fascinated by how she managed to keep her cap in position. Her face was a pasty colour from too much make-up and her green eyes glared behind large, brown-framed spectacles. She bent over us like an ostrich about to peck and I shrank back involuntarily. 'Who are you?' she shrieked. (I was to discover she was almost incapable of speaking in a soft tone, each announcement coming out like a railway tannoy.)

'Nursing Cadet Salt. Reporting on duty, sister.'

'Where've you come from?' I wondered if she thought I was an undercover agent, sent by some foreign power to discover where she kept her chocolate biscuits.

'Orthopaedic.'

She looked me up and down. 'You're no use to me. Just here on a Saturday morning, no use at all! Pepper!' she yelled.

'Yes, Sister,' said Vale.

'Find her something to do, keep her out of my way. I've got your cleaning list here somewhere.' She hunted around her overflowing desk, looking at and discarding various bits of paper. Eventually she found the list under her swimming teacup. It was well-splashed and most of the ink was smudged. She tossed it to Vale. 'No time for idle hands. Get busy, girl, and take her with you.' Feeling like a bag of mucky laundry, I slid after Vale.

'Is she always like that?'

'Oh she's in a good mood this morning. You want to catch her on a bad day, she's like a dog with rabies.'

Vale tried to smooth out the illegible, soggy list. 'I can make out "sinks" and "cubicles", but what the heck does that say?' said Vale, shuffling the list under my nose.

'She's a terrible writer.'

'Don't let her hear you say that. She's always on at the doctors for their handwriting and hers is worse than any of them.'

'I think it says cut-hordes, and something about blessings. Is the vicar due?'

'Got it,' said Vale in triumph. 'Cupboards and dressings, but which cupboards and what dressings I haven't a clue.'

'Is there anyone we can ask?' Surely there must be someone sane on the department.

'We'll try Gert.'

'Who's Gert?' I asked.

'The male orderly. He's a real old woman so everyone calls him Gert, at least behind his back. It's Bert or Mr Leigh to his face. Come on, let's try and find him.'

We located Gert in the main treatment room. He was cleaning a dirty trolley which was overflowing with blood-soaked bandages. When he spoke, his voice came out in a high-pitched soprano. 'What's the matter, love?' he inquired.

Pepper pushed the list at him. 'Tizz gave us this and we can't make head nor tail of it.'

Gert smoothed out a small crease in his jacket and moistened an eyebrow. 'Shocking hand, her ladyship, a monkey could write better. Let's see.' He held the list up to the light, frowning. 'Haven't a clue, deary, but I know what she expects the cadets to do every Saturday morning.'

'You're a life-saver,' said Vale.

'Well, she has all the sinks scrubbed, taps polished and the under-sink cupboards cleaned. Some brave soul has to go into her office and clean the telephone – she has a thing about the telephone being disinfected once a week. Then you have to go round all the cubicles and make sure the trolley wheels and rail bars are clean. Oh, and don't forget the shelves, light fittings and cubicle curtains. Then the dressing drums have to be packed and the large cupboard in the small storeroom has to be emptied, scrubbed and refilled. And if you've finished all that before you go home, come and find me and see if anything else needs doing.'

I felt tired just listening; no wonder Vale had been complaining all week. For the first time I began to appreciate what Thompson had meant by being lucky to be on orthopaedic.

Vale took charge. 'My hands are past help so I'll do the sinks, cubicles and her damn telephone. You can pack the drums and do the storeroom cupboard, that should keep you out of her way most of the morning.'

'Pack the drums?' I queried.

'Come on, I'll show you.'

We bustled off to where we'd hung our cloaks. There was a door in the corner of the room which led into a tiny end storeroom. A pile of round metal drums, each about a foot high, were on the table and boxes piled up against the wall. Vale expertly snapped open a drum, which was secured by special clips. I was impressed; I'd have spent ages just trying to work out the entrance code. Then she reached for two boxes from the heap, one of square, cotton dressing pads the other of cottonwool balls. 'Pile of pads all the way around the inside of the drum, then fill the empty space in the centre with cottonwool balls. Fill four drums – that should be enough. It doesn't take long but you take your time and it should last you through 'til break at ten thirty. I'll come and get you.'

It was the equivalent to the orthopaedic laundry cupboard, a safe refuge away from Sister. Shut away in my tiny haven, I immersed myself happily in drum-packing. It was very quiet in there and the hustle and bustle of the main department might not have existed. I worked away, opening boxes and carefully arranging the swabs and wool balls.

I was on my last tin, making beautiful heaps as I aligned my swabs in miniature tower-blocks. My wool balls looked like gentle masses of soft, snow and I drifted away, wondering if I might take up skating and become an Olympic gold medallist. I saw myself gliding swan-like between snow-covered mountains, across a silver frozen lake, as the crowd applauded. The cameras were flashing and I was busy picking up flowers thrown onto the ice, when the door burst open and I gazed up at Sister Tissleton.

'What you doing in here, girl?' she spat. The spray hit me on the forehead, a warm, sticky baptism.

Speechless, I gulped, hands filled with swabs, thinking what a daft question. I wish I'd had the nerve to say something like 'deep-sea fishing' or 'baking bread'. When I did manage to find my tongue, I muttered, 'Tins, filling, Sister Swab.'

I was sure her hair puffed out even further as her cap danced up and down. Because of her tremendous height, I was fascinated to see a cobweb detach itself and settle like grey lace across the frills. 'Tins!' she shrieked. 'Tins should be done by now. Slacking girl, holed up in here like a rabbit. Pepper's gone on errands and there's cleaning not finished. Come on, girl, out! Out now!'

I threw the rest of the swabs into the tin, slammed down the lid and followed, trembling. She talked the whole time, marching with me in her wake, a general about to go into action. 'The treatment room sink is a disgrace, there's cubicles not done, vomit to be mopped and laundry to put away. And—' with this she suddenly slammed to a halt, so that I narrowly avoided colliding with her white, starched apron '—my telephone needs decontaminating. NOW!' she yelled.

It was like plunging into battle, with every cubicle filled. There were folk on trolleys and in wheelchairs, very like orthopaedic but with a good splattering of blood, grizzle and vomit added. I grabbed a dishcloth and a tin of Gumption and attacked anything that looked dirty. Soap suds bubbled from the sink and draining boards, and I took a dry towel to the taps, trying in vain to make them shine.

As I dashed around in a cleaning frenzy, Sister whipped about, giving orders in her shrill scream to Gert, an assortment of nursing staff and various fraught-looking doctors. Gert hurried past with an armful of sheets, his eyebrows soaring into his hairline. 'Tizz is in a right state, she's got her bridge this afternoon, and she wanted to get away early but there's a road smash come in. Very inconsiderate of them to crash on her bridge day.'

Finding a bottle of disinfectant, I slipped into Sister's office, relieved there was no one there. The phone was a solid affair, heavy and black, with a stained metal dial. Once I hooked the receiver off its stand, a bored voice from the switchboard said, 'Which number, please?' Startled, I dropped it and it fell with a clang onto the floor.

'Sorry, I was just cleaning the receiver,' I muttered having retrieved it, thankfully un-smashed. For the next ten minutes I cleaned, dried and polished the wretched thing, which looked no different at the end of my ministrations. Convinced I was spending Saturday morning in a mad house, I dashed back to the main treatment room, Gumption at the ready, praying that Pepper had returned. But I met Sister, head-on. 'What are you doing, girl?'

'I've just cleaned—' I got no further.

'You shouldn't be here, you should be on your break. Can't you tell the time? After ten thirty, cadets break. Go, girl, go and don't be long.'

I threw down the cloth and Gumption and fled. There was no sign of Pepper in the dining room and most of the other cadets had been and gone. I bolted down a cup of tea, grabbed a biscuit and wondered if I should take up smoking. Most of the cadets smoked like chimneys, which was hardly surprising if they'd spent time with Sister Tissleton.

'God, I'm fed up! I've been back and forward like a pit pony to the lab and X-ray, and now she's dared to say I've been too long and I've missed my coffee.' Pepper was busy scrubbing when I got back. 'Isn't it awful? Do you wonder I'm pig sick? It's only the thought of riding that elephant that's keeping me going.'

Which brought me back to the elephant. I plunged back into the sink with visions of Sister Tissleton swaying along through the jungle. She was so tall that jungle creepers twisted around her and she was swept away, crying as she went: 'Have you disinfected my telephone, girl?'

'Have you disinfected my telephone, girl?' I dropped the Gumption with a splash, as my daydream became reality.

'Yes, sister.'

'I never saw you. Bet you've never been near it. Full of germs, it is. Cadets! I spend all my time telling them what to do and do they listen? No! Expect to be nurses, not even fit to be cleaners most of them. Phone, girl, phone.' After this high-pitched tirade, she spun on her heel and was on the move towards the over-flowing cubicles.

For the second time I shot into her office. I took the spotless phone off the rest, assured the operator I was cleaning it and didn't need a line, and proceeded to disinfect, dry and polish. I was rapidly coming to the conclusion that telephones and I were destined for an uncomfortable relationship.

It had quietened down a little and surely there was nothing left to clean, so I headed back to the storeroom. Peace descended as I closed the door against the turmoil and confusion of casualty. I repacked the final tin, which was in a bit of a mess, then turned to the tall, thin and mainly glass cupboard. It was filled with odd-looking instruments, which I supposed must have some weird and wonderful use. I was busy working my way down from the top shelf when the door burst open once more.

'This is where you're hiding,' shrieked Sister Tissleton. I jumped with fright and dropped the handful of metal forceps I'd been holding. They scattered over the floor, clattering and spinning away like ninepins. 'Those are delicate surgical instruments, girl, not tennis balls. Ham-fisted, that's what you are. Ham-fisted. Good job you weren't holding a baby. If you want to work in my department, you'll have to buck up your ideas. Skulking around like a ferret. Can't abide ferrets, nasty, sly little things,' she ranted on.

I wasn't sure how we'd got on to ferrets. I was scrabbling around the floor, retrieving forceps, profoundly wishing I was a ferret and could give her a good nip on her ankle.

'But I was—' As usual I got no further.

'No excuses, girl. The sinks are dirty again, that's if you ever cleaned them in the first place. The cubicles are a disgrace and you still haven't disinfected my telephone!' It was a wonder the woman hadn't a perpetual sore throat. Once more our procession went from the storeroom, through the department and into the main treatment room, but this time she was determined there would be no more indolence where her infected telephone was concerned. 'Cloths, disinfectant and Gumption, girl,' she demanded, pointing at the sink. 'Come!'

She led me into her office like a lamb to the abattoir. Under her piercing eyes I cleaned the wretched telephone for the third time that morning. I could feel her hot breath on my neck as I removed the receiver and told the operator for the third time that I didn't want a line but was cleaning the phone. The woman on the switchboard must have thought there was some terrible epidemic brewing in casualty and I heard her say, 'What again, dear?'

I disinfected, scrubbed, dried and polished the hated thing. Sister watched every rub and dab, and I couldn't help thinking it was a pity that she'd nothing better to do. I was almost afraid to finish as I gave it a final buff. 'No need to make a meal of it, girl, no wonder you never finish a job if you take this long just to clean a telephone. If you'd done it the first time you were asked, there'd have been no need for me to remind you.' She glanced at her watch. 'Twelve o'clock already, that gives you an hour. Sinks, cubicles, cupboard!' she bellowed as she marched away.

Gert was busy plastering a leg when I returned to the treatment room. 'How you getting on, deary?' he asked. I shook my head, bewildered. Hands full of plaster, he wandered over. 'Don't worry, the road accident has cleared, nothing too serious, and the rest of the walking wounded are getting sorted. She'll be off to her bridge at half past. You just look busy so she can see you, and we'll have a cuppa when she's gone.' He washed his hands under the tap and, in tones reminiscent of Vale, complained: 'It doesn't matter how much hand cream I use, this plaster is terrible for my skin.'

As Gert predicted, Sister went off in a rush at 12.30. As her car was seen drawing away from the staff car park, the whole department drew a collective breath of relief. Staff Nurse Fraser was left in command. She was small and sweet, the antithesis of Tizzy. Gert had the kettle on and mugs, milk and biscuits came out of the cupboard – not Sister's reserved chocolate ones; even Staff Nurse and Gert, were not that brave.

'You two girls have been running round all morning,' said Staff Nurse, 'and you even missed your break, Pepper. Soon as you've finished your tea, off you go and enjoy your afternoon. Have you anything special planned?'

Vale looked innocent. 'Oh, nothing special.'

'Have a good time. You'll most likely enjoy putting your feet up.'

Vale nodded, sipping tea. I knew that in her mind she was already hoisted high, waving to the crowd, swaying to the lumbering movement of the great beast. I pictured myself, trying to keep one step ahead of those great feet.

A massive dark grey trunk was nuzzling my cheek and threatening to wrap itself around my red, sweaty neck. As elephant saliva, or whatever came out of an elephant's trunk, splattered my new yellow overall, I had this vision of gazing at the assembled crowd and seeing the dark, enraged features of Sister Mandrake.

Chapter 6

Ethel

'Brian and his mate, Jed, are coming to pick us up,' said Vale, as we hurried up to the locker room. We'd got off fifteen minutes early, which meant we had a head start on the other cadets. 'I've got us a cap and apron each,' she added.

'Where did you get them from?'

'Beryl Bates, one of the students on casualty, she thinks it's great. She wanted to come and watch but she's on duty this afternoon.'

'You didn't tell anyone else, did you?'

'No and Beryl promised to keep it quiet. Don't worry, Salt, it's going to be fun and no one will ever know.'

We pushed our dirty overalls into the lockers and got changed. Vale marched ahead gabbling happily about elephants, while I tagged along trying to get a word in. Brian and his mate were waiting outside. I'd never met the famous Brian, who was a few years older than Vale, but I'd heard a lot about him. He was sitting astride a powerful motorbike, revving noisily. He was a big, beefy chap, handsome in a grizzled sort of way, with a mass of black curly hair. Vale expertly cocked a leg over the pillion and, with sudden dread, I realised I was expected to pile on behind Jed.

Jed looked like Al Capone with attitude. He was big and greasy, with a boxer's nose and a scar curling down his cheek. I couldn't help wondering if he kept a flick knife in the pocket of the black leathers that enveloped him. Chains decorated his chest, and DEATH was picked out in silver studs on the back of his jacket. His motorbike was black and silver, with a large skull and cross bones painted on each side.

'You ever bin on a bike?' He spoke in a low bass; I assumed his vocal chords had been damaged in some punch-up. I shook my head, wondering if it was too late to back out. 'Climb on,' he growled, so I cocked a black-stockinged leg over the seat, showing a good piece of knee and thigh in the process. The seat was broad and hard and brought back memories of uncomfortable school gymnastics. I sat back, feeling awkward, the word DEATH looming at me from below Jed's wide shoulders.

He revved violently. 'You'll have to hold on, wrap your arms round,' he yelled, slamming down the accelerator. With a deafening veeerrrruumm!!! we were off. These were the days before compulsory helmets and the movement took me by surprise. I shot forward into the studs, my nose burying itself into the A. I clung on like a drowning sailor clutching a life-raft as we roared away from the hospital. I dread to think what speed we were doing and prayed no convalescents were taking a quiet stroll.

The stud was making an uncomfortable dint in my nose and stray strands of his hair were disappearing into my nostrils. I came up for air and risked a quick glance. We were just in the process of overtaking a red bus but, since another was coming in the opposite direction at the same time, all I could see was an explosion of red as we blasted through the gap, taking the white line.

We raced through the remains of the thirty-mile zone but, as we hit the green belt, Jed crunched his foot even harder on the accelerator. 'Come on, baby,' he roared, giving it full throttle. I was relieved when I realised he was talking to our hell-driven chariot. 'Baby' responded with a race-track rev. I opened half an eye to see a haze of green dashing past. If it hadn't been for the sensation that I was part of a rocket experiment, I could have believed that 'Baby' was stationary and the world itself was hurtling along.

The stud was rapidly becoming part of my nose. I couldn't move my head, I was too terrified. I realized I'd clamped my jaws so tightly that they were aching and any remnants of a hair-do were long gone. I saw the outskirts of Moresbry loom ahead. It was a strange little town, tucked away on the edge of the Pennines, unsure whether it was an urban development or the remnants of an over-sized village. There were a couple of cotton factories limping along against increasing cheap imports, and an array of shops, but it was also trimmed with small family farms, horse stables and boasted a market.

Jed never braked; he was clearly not into speed limits. I wondered if there might be a police car lying in wait; perhaps he was on their 'most wanted' list. I imagined the whirl of blue flashers, a high-speed chase through the back streets, him cornered, me in tow behind a waste-disposal bunker. They'd assume I was his moll, we'd be taken-in for questioning. 'I'm only here to lead the elephant,' I heard myself saying. I'd read that a petrol station had been held up the week before and I was sure Jed fitted the robber's description. Perhaps they'd think I was the 'small one with the balaclava'. I was being led into the dock between two hefty prison warders when the bike shuddered to a halt.

Brian and Vale had just arrived. Their bike was parked ahead and Vale was shaking out her blonde tresses which seemed strangely unaffected by the wind-blown journey. She must have been well lacquered. I swung a trembling leg over the seat and hit the pavement like a space man touching earth. My legs felt like blancmange and every piece of me seemed to be vibrating. Queasily I wobbled towards Vale. I heard Jed say to Brian, 'I think Baby were a bit sluggish today. Perhaps I got a blockage?'

'Great, isn't it?' said Vale. 'Me and Brian went to Blackpool at top speed last weekend. What do you make of Jed?'

I searched for an apt word as my legs became accustomed to the ground, and I realised I was going to live to see the afternoon. 'Different.'

Vale led me down a short path between two colourful but unimaginative flower-beds to her front door. She lived on one of the new council estates on the edge of Moresbry. It was a neat little house, stacked with patchwork cushions, lace runners and embroidered chair-backs. 'Mum's into craft,' Vale said, throwing off her coat. 'Put the kettle on, Brian,' she ordered, as I followed her upstairs.

We spent the next hour with hair-dos and make-up. Our shortened yellow overalls acquired white aprons, which had been crisply starched. I noticed that Vale's yellow had been chopped by nearly eighteen inches, and was now a rather cute mini. She had a flare with hair and she expertly rollered and back-combed, using my natural curl in ways I'd never dreamed of. A violent lacquering followed, until my locks were set in place like cement. Hair done, she brought out her over-stuffed make-up bag; Vale was a great one for facial improvement. I was decked out in mascara for the first time and my already long eye-lashes wafted like curled brushes. The final touch was a white starched cap to which Vale had added an exotic, circular brooch.

'Well, it is an Indian elephant,' she explained, as the cap

was set in place.

When we looked at ourselves in Vale's full length mirror, the effect was quite amazing – but I couldn't help thinking that we looked more suited to the naughty pages of some men's magazine than the side of a sickbed.

We came downstairs to admiring applause and whistles from the men. Jed edged near, offering whisky from a flask; he'd most likely been well over the limit on our journey. I settled for tea and a plain biscuit, deciding I needed a clear head before meeting an elephant. The sun shone with that golden brightness that it can manage, even in Lancashire when it tries, and I had no excuse to bury myself in my navy-blue mac. 'It's only a short walk,' said Vale, as we stepped out of her door decked in glamour-yellow.

We walked at a brisk pace past council houses, shops and a terrace of older property. As we headed past a row of detached properties in the prosperous end of Moresbry, I wondered if someone important from the hospital lived here and might be watching, ready to relay news of our enterprise to Matron.

The circus was busy setting up in a large field against the road. The big top was already up and there was a good scattering of lorries, animal carriers and caravans. Brian and Jed had arrived ahead of us and were laughing with a strange pair of little men, Pat and Pete, who were clowns. We went over to them as Jethro the ring master, started to get the parade into some order.

Mr Prothereo was the elephant trainer. He said he was Italian but I was sure I detected a hint of Lancashire. He was a tall, emaciated man who looked as if a stiff Pennine breeze would easily sweep him away. He sported a sparkly blue and silver outfit. 'Thees is Ethel, my leeedle eelephant,' he announced.

Ethel was busy eating whatever 'eelephants' eat, unfazed by the activity around her. She was attached to a metal strut by a small chain round her ankle which I felt was there merely for show than any real chance of restraint. My gaze travelled upwards as I was introduced, until my neck was bent right back. She happily shovelled more food into her small mouth with her curling, versatile trunk. Her tusks had been removed leaving small stumps, but it was her eyes that intrigued me: they were tiny. Beady little orbs peeped from a colossal head, out of place on such a massive creature. I was sure she gave me a wink as a ladder was brought for Vale.

Quite a crowd gathered as the yellow-clad mahout climbed to her important seat. Whether they were there to see if she managed to reach her lofty perch without disaster, or the men were interested in looking up her skirt as she climbed, I wasn't sure. Typical Vale, she boldly attacked the ladder, making her ascent in style. A miniature howdah had been provided, with a flat seat but without the ceremonial canopy. It was trimmed with crimson tassels and had a couple of hand holds. Unlike horse riding, where the legs went a-straddle, Vale had to curl her legs to one side, similar to the statue of the Little Mermaid. It all looked very precarious to me, and I was glad I'd resolved to stay earth-bound.

My relief was short-lived when Mr Prothereo, now decked in a very imposing, tall, spangled hat, took me by the arm. 'Come, preety ladee nurse, holdee Ethel's trunk, shee reel queet.'

I decided he meant quiet. Ethel gazed down, nodding her head. I reached out a tentative hand. 'Shee not a crocodeel,' advised Mr Prothereo, pushing my timorous fingers and palm down onto her trunk. Ethel took no notice, she just swayed like a big hay stack in the breeze. 'I walk thees side, you outher,' he continued. 'Don't worreee, Ethel like nurses.'

The parade was ready. As the main attraction, Ethel led

the way followed by the band, a jolly bunch in red and gold uniforms with lots of braid and tassels. They made a lot of noise to some vaguely recognizable tune, overpowered by the drummer who whacked the skins with gusto. Then came the ringmaster, very dashing in purple and sporting a high hat with an enormous feather. He was followed by an assortment of clowns, jugglers and an alarming fire-eater. A cavalcade of six white horses brought up the rear and I wondered why, oh, why, Vale had not elected to ride a horse, I'd have been quite content to tote a bag of oats.

To much cheering from the remainder of the circus people and a few onlookers, we made our way across the field. I had no time to look up and see how Vale was managing, I was much too busy trunk-holding and making sure I kept ahead of the capstan-thick legs that plodded steadily, a short distance behind.

Mr Prothereo was enjoying himself, waving and singing in tune with the band. He kept taking off his hat, and doffing it to the ladies. Occasionally he patted my hand. 'Enjoy yourseelf, smeel, preety nurse.'

We reached the gate onto the road where the police were waiting to hold up the traffic. A panda car went ahead of us as we entered Moresbry. I was still not convinced I wasn't going to be trampled into the tarmac, and I wondered if Ethel was afraid of anything like barking dogs or sudden noises. One thing was certain: if Ethel took it into her mind to stampede, not Mr Prothereo, Vale and certainly not me, would be able to stop her.

The crowds started to build as we turned towards the town centre. Lots of children were waving little come-to-the-circus flags and a host of multi-coloured balloons. There was a good police presence to keep the crowds in order but the boys in blue were obviously enjoying themselves. I had relaxed a little and was managing the odd wave and smile. I was also getting used to the horny feel of Ethel's trunk, which hung between me and Mr Prothereo. We swayed along to the cheering crowd and the rhythm of the band.

We were halfway down the high street, well into our journey, which would finish with a right turn round the market then back to the field. I'd just spotted Mother with her camera, elbowing her way through the crowd. I tried to smile sweetly as her finger clicked on the shutter; I supposed she'd have great pleasure having prints done at Christmas. 'This was our Susan, the day she led the elephant through town.' I could see her writing to Aunty Mary in Canada and Cousin Rachel Down-under.

I suddenly became aware of a wet, rough, hairy sensation working its way upwards from my ankle. It paused around the knee, inspecting, then continued to investigate. I glanced down to see Ethel's inquisitive trunk edging its way up my skirt. I slid a hand down the trunk, vainly trying to push it away. I might as well have been trying to push Ethel up a mountain.

'Mr Prothereo!' I hissed but he was busy, hat in the air, blowing kisses. He wasn't even touching Ethel's trunk, sure that she knew where she was going. Ethel certainly *did* know: up to my stocking top, and enjoying every second. While I pushed and struggled, trying to maintain some measure of dignity, the soft end of her proboscis slopped its way over flesh and knicker leg. The struggle was turning into a scuffle as I frantically hung onto my skirt while Ethel poked around. I'd been prepared for a trampling but not amorous advances on the high street, and I was rapidly losing the fight. I yelled for Mr Prothereo, my pleas drowned out by the band. He was signing autographs, I was thrashing about caught between trunk, skirt and stocking. Amidst the commotion, I could see pointing fingers and people roaring with laughter; they most likely thought it was part of the show. I hoped Mother was no longer capturing every moment for posterity.

'Naughty Ethel!' I chastised, both hands now around her trunk which had attached itself firmly to the bottom of my knickers. We were still heading forwards while the wrestling match continued. I felt my knickers starting to travel down. I clung on with one hand to the knickers and with the other I slapped at Ethel's trunk, hoping to dislodge her hold. My yellow overall was hitched up, showing my white slip and a good piece of upper leg. 'Ethel! Get off!' I bellowed. 'Mr Prothereo!'

At last he heard and, with complete unconcern and a huge laugh, he gave Ethel a slight slap on the upper trunk and produced some greenery from his pocket. Ethel made a quick decision that she preferred food to knicker and promptly let go. My relief was short lived though for, as soon as she'd finished her meal, she decided to have nurse's cap for afters and whipped my head-dress away with a flurry. It was not as interesting as knicker, but she was going to make the most of it. She held it high, waving it back and forth, to the delight of the crowd which clapped and cheered her on.

I was left dancing around, vainly trying to grab my crown from her grasp. The more I jumped, the higher Ethel displayed her trophy. The more she waved her prize about, the more the crowd shouted their approval. My stiff hair-style had been virtually glued to the cap so quite a few hairs had gone with it; the remainder stuck out in all directions, leaving me looking like a Zulu warrior. Finally, Ethel twirled the cap around a few times then sent it spinning into the centre of the crowd. No cricketer scoring a six could have caused a greater sensation as the children scrambled about, fighting to seize the prize.

Having been nearly ravished by Ethel in the centre of Moresbry, I was feeling decidedly fraught. My leg top was damp and sticky where I'd been inspected and my hair looked as if I'd been caught in a whirlwind. I took a quick glance up to where Vale was sitting pretty, waving and blowing kisses to the spectators, having a wonderful time. My eye flicked across the waving children, mums and dads – and fastened on a face. It was one of those faces that is familiar but the owner's name floats just out of reach.

As we continued down the high street and rounded the market, heading back to our set-off point, I hunted around for a name. The circus field lay ahead, my elephant leading was nearly done when, with a cold feeling of despair, I found the solution. I saw her mouthing 'notes' across the orthopaedic clinic: it was Sister Phipps.

'Are you sure it was her?' Vale asked. 'People look different out of uniform and you don't know her very well.'

I knew she was trying to convince herself, not just me. I was beginning to have doubts and it was only a quick glance; it might have been someone who looked like her. I wasn't that good on faces. I remembered the time I'd twittered on to this man, sure he was our ex-minister, only to recall with a sick feeling, an hour later, that it was the milkman.

'Perhaps I was wrong but I knew her from somewhere.'

'It might have been someone off the market or a shop you go in, or even a patient from this last week.'

We'd left the elephant and Mr Prothereo on the field. It was difficult to say which of them was the most difficult to leave. Vale had found it far harder to climb down than get up, especially since Ethel kept whirling her trunk around, eager to help. Eventually, after much bribing with titbits, Ethel quietened a little and, with a number of eager young circus men helping, Vale managed to dismount. I was clearly a big hit with Ethel (just my luck to have an elephant after me), who made a big show of her goodbyes. She had another poke with her trunk and managed a slobber down my neck and through my hair. The cap was long gone, most likely some sticky child's circus souvenir. I hoped Vale's friend, Beryl, wouldn't mind one of her caps going on permanent loan.

After we finally disentangled ourselves from Ethel, Mr Prothereo was very demonstrative with his thanks and praise. 'Lovlee, breeve nurses,' he kept saying; perhaps he really was Italian. We left clutching a free circus ticket, small reward, especially if we both ended up being sacked.

Back at Vale's house, I pushed my yellows away and handed back the apron. At least my overall would let down again. Vale had taken the scissors to hers and it was past help; it would never pass Miss Pettigrew's inspection and would be a definite candidate for 'a glimpse of knickers'. 'I'll manage with one less,' Vale assured me. 'I'll keep this one for going out dressed in uniform, it tarts up quite well.' She really was incorrigible.

I'd been offered a lift by Jed but, having had one narrow escape, I'd decided my nerves couldn't stand the strain. I didn't fancy another journey pressed into the stud. Jed and Brian had been full of praise for our afternoon adventure and Jed had been dropping broad hints about 'being between girlfriends'. I didn't rise to the bait.

As I travelled home on the bus, I had time to wonder if either of us would ever get to wear our yellows again. If it had been Sister Phipps in the crowd, she'd surely be on to Miss Cooper-Ffinch first thing Monday morning; at the very least she'd tell Sister Mandrake and she'd be so glad to be rid of me, she'd have me off to Matron in a flash.

Mum was ecstatic when I got home, and thought the best part of the afternoon had been seeing me fighting Ethel off my stocking tops. 'I've got some great pictures,' she confided.

Monday morning found me a bundle of nerves. I met up with Vale as we signed in. She'd taken advantage of the free circus ticket and been reunited with Ethel at the Sunday matinee, to rapturous applause.

'Mr Prothereo invited me into the ring,' she said, 'and this gorgeous strong-arm man called Freado tossed me up on his shoulder. Brian was really jealous. I was only sorry I hadn't got the uniform on.'

As I pulled on my yellows in the changing room, none of the cadets mentioned our weekend's adventure. One girl said she and her mum were going to the circus that evening and Vale gave me a mischievous wink. As I trod after Barnes and Thompson on my way to orthopaedic, my heart was pounding. 'You'll feel a bit more confident, it being your second week,' said Thompson.

Sister greeted us with her usual welcoming frown. 'Cadet Mellor has resigned, that leaves me one junior cadet short. You'll have to learn much quicker, Salt.' She gave her usual string of instructions, turned on her heel and was off. I wondered what had happened to the mysterious Mellor; she'd been off sick when I'd arrived and now had departed. If her introduction to nursing had been anything like mine, I wasn't surprised.

I'd not seen Sister Phipps, who was busy in the inner clinic. I was soon caught up in the frantic pace of my second Monday. The main improvement was that at least I knew where a few places were, and I was beginning to become familiar with the mystical inner running of the department. It was not until I was asked to take some X-rays into Sister Phipps that I began to feel like Shadrack being ordered into the fiery furnace.

I slipped into the hush of the clinic. The registrar, with a couple of junior doctors, was busy examining a freshly de-plastered leg. Sister turned as I entered and, holding out her hand, mouthed 'X-rays' then dismissed me with a nod. I didn't know whether to feel relieved or apprehensive; perhaps she and Sister Mandrake were waiting until later to confront me. I pictured myself summoned to the office when the department had quietened for my crime to be laid bare. Perhaps they'd already spoken to Matron, and the order to attend 'the presence' was just a phone call away.

I met Vale at morning coffee which, as usual, we drank in a rush. I was becoming accustomed to swallowing scalding fluids and gobbling down biscuits or cream crackers so quickly they hardly touched the sides. One eye was fastened on the clock for by the time we reached the dining room, queued and were served, barely five minutes eating time remained before the dash back. This was to have a permanent effect on my eating habits, leaving me incapable of enjoying a hot drink unless it is one degree below boiling, and my ability to wolf down snacks would win any fast-eating competition.

Vale whispered. 'Did she say anything?'

I shook my head. 'I think we've got away with it. Did anyone say anything to you?'

'No.' We heaved a sigh of relief and burst out laughing. 'You've made a big hit with Jed. He keeps asking Brian where you live and if you've got a boyfriend.'

'I don't think he's really my type,' I put in quickly.

'I know he looks like a gangster but he's quite nice when you get to know him.'

The week galloped on at its usual frantic pace. I'd just about cracked 'shaking the thermometer down', and discovered where to locate the pulse. Thompson was quite happy with my progress but had me down as a 'slow learner'. I was now working my way up to urine testing and was introduced to the intricacies of the various solutions and the Bunsen burner.

Every investigation involved adding a number of drops of some weird and wonderful solution to a measure of urine, then bubbling it up over a Bunsen burner. The smell of sizzling wee regularly filled the sluice. As I bent to my task, I must have resembled an eccentric scientist hell-bent on destroying the planet. I developed a flare for this rudimentary chemistry and towards the end of the week I was becoming quite adept. I think Thompson was relieved that at least I'd picked up something quickly. I discovered it was a wonderful place to hide, even better than the linen room. If I was discovered awash with wee, I looked both terribly busy and efficient and, since it was a specialised and time-consuming job, no one could find much reason to pick on me.

The worst labour of my day was sister's tea tray. After my first week's accident with what I was assured had been Sister Mandrake's 'favourite plate', it had become the job I dreaded most. The sluice doubled up as kitchen, and it seemed odd to prepare tea and biscuits a foot away from where a smelly assortment of bodily waste was tested. Luckily a tin of Gumption a week went into sink cleaning and since neither sister had succumbed to any terrible stomach disorder, they were either immune or the germs were better trained than to dare attack Sister Mandrake's innards.

The tea making was the easy part; it was the timing – getting it onto Sister's table; the taking it in and later retrieving it – that caused the headaches. If the tea arrived early, it was stewed and cold by the time the Dragon was ready to partake; if it was late, it was because I had no sense of time. If the office door was closed, it sometimes meant she was there and didn't want to be disturbed. On the other hand it could mean she was relaxing, waiting for her beverage. If I knocked, I might be greeted with her thundering to the door to tell me she was busy and to come back later. If I didn't knock, she would invariably seek me out, with the demand: 'Are you going to bring my tray sometime before midnight?' I would hover outside her closed door, knuckles poised, undecided what to do. Sometimes I crept away in despair then had to keep nipping back and forth wondering what to do for the best.

Having once got the wretched tray onto her table, that was only half the problem solved. I had to go through the same performance to retrieve the thing and see it washed and cleared away before the 'witching hour' or she would be after me again. I came to the conclusion that the vanished Mellor had suffered a mental collapse between the closed office door and the tea caddy.

Vale was still suffering loudly under the chaotic madness of Sister Tissleton and every day she had a new tale to tell. 'You'll never believe what the old bat did this morning!' or 'I'm sure she's getting worse, do you know what she said to me today?' became two of Vale's opening phrases whenever we met. After my first Saturday on casualty, I was prepared to believe anything and to make matters worse, as the week advanced, my next Saturday loomed.

It had reached Friday and even though I had only been a 'yellow' for less than two weeks, it felt like forever. I'd adjusted to being almost constantly on my feet and was just about keeping the blisters from the new shoes under control. I'd resigned myself to being part cleaner, part whipping-girl, part diplomat, part nervous wreck and a tiny part trainee nurse, with the hope that 'things could only get better'.

I'd participated in two of Miss Pettigrew's inspections and come to realise that it was a highlight of the week. Not only did it keep me out of the clutches of Sister Mandrake, but it was like being involved in a comic opera. The biggest trial on inspection morning was to keep a straight face and to convince Miss Pettigrew that we were taking her words of wisdom with total seriousness. Her gem that week had been, 'Do make sure, cadets, that you wear a suitably firm bra. It's very unladylike for you to bounce about when you're on duty.'

As I signed on, two of the senior cadets were just ahead of me. They treated me to cold stares, which was quite unusual as they tended to ignore the junior cadets completely. I trailed in their wake towards the changing room, wondering what the day would bring and trying not to think about tomorrow.

I slipped into the changing room, which was busy with cadets in various stages of undress. Some found the overalls so hot at this time of the year that they peeled down to knickers, suspender belt and bra – but they were careful not to show any cleavage; others kept on underskirts before donning their yellow coverings. My entry into the changing room caused a lull in the conversation and I wondered if perhaps a bird had pooed on me, or I was developing some nasty spots that might be infectious. I hoped it was spots; they would give me an excellent excuse not to appear in casualty the next morning.

Baffled, I turned my locker key and had a quick glance in the small mirror I kept there; sadly no spots. I slipped the overall over a thin summer dress and attacked my wayward locks. I noticed Leslie looking in my direction and whispering something to her neighbour. The stares from various cadets continued and I started to feel my neck getting red and the sweat started to prick. Whatever was the matter? I ran through the possibilities. I had no gory past which could have suddenly been discovered and, as far as I knew, I hadn't upset anyone in the last few days apart from Sister Mandrake.

I looked round for Vale but she was either very early or on the verge of late. Just the morning I could have really done with her support. I knew what she would have done and when Hudson (she of the laundry) passed me by with what looked like a sympathetic smile, I decided to grasp the nettle. 'Is something up?' I asked innocently.

'You are brave,' she whispered. 'I do hope you don't get into trouble.'

Brave and *trouble*, they sounded ominous. As my sweating grew worse a horrible thought began to nag at me, in the shape of an elephant.

Leslie gave me a superior look; she'd obviously been practising for when she was a senior. 'I wouldn't be surprised if you were dismissed, Salt. I would have expected anything of Pepper but I thought you had more sense.'

I decided to play dumb. 'What are you on about?'

'Circus. Elephant. Ring a bell?'

I gulped. How had everyone found out? I was sure that if Sister Phipps were going to tell, the roof would have fallen in before now. So who was it?

Thompson was heading over. 'You're a dark horse, Salt, or should I say a dark elephant? I didn't think you had it in you.' A few of the senior cadets cracked out laughing. 'It's a scream. I'm longing to see Miss Pettigrew's face next inspection. You and Pepper will be the star criminals and old Patton will be having a fit,' she continued. 'That's if you're still here come next inspection. You're bound to get sent to Matron.'

'However did you get in with the circus?' asked an unfamiliar cadet, one of the 'I never normally speak to juniors' brigade'.

'Brian, that's Vale's boyfriend, knows them.'

'But fancy wearing your yellows outside the hospital. It's a cardinal sin to even go home without changing. But to lead the circus around Moresbry... Talk about asking for the chop!'

'We didn't think anyone would find out,' I said.

'Not much chance of that. Where did you get the aprons and caps?'

'Vale borrowed them.' There were more giggles.

'Where is your co-criminal?' asked Thompson.

'Perhaps she's chickened out, I know I would. Mind you I wouldn't have been as daft as to do something like that anyway,' said Barnes.

Far from chickening out, Vale suddenly arrived, moaning about the alarm clock and the bus. 'Well, speak of the devil,' said Thompson.

'What's up?' asked Vale as she dashed to her locker, tearing off clothing.

'They've found out,' I gasped, 'about Ethel.'

'Ethel?' queried Vale, her mind obviously not in gear.

'Ethel?' chorused the cadets. 'The elephant was called Ethel!' More howls of laughter.

'Elephant!' Vale stuck her head round her locker door, a look of alarm spreading across her face.

'Fancy calling an elephant Ethel,' said Thompson, laughing.

'How d'you find out about the elephant?' asked Vale, one arm in and one arm out of her overall.

'Aren't you wearing your micro-mini uniform with apron, cap and exotic brooch today?' asked Leslie, with a sneer. 'I wouldn't like to be in your shoes,' she added as she breezed out with her followers.

'How did they find out?' asked Vale again.

'I don't know, someone must have seen us,' I said.

'All of Thorpe, Moresbry and the surrounding area's seen you,' said Thompson, pushing the weekly local newspaper under my nose. There on the front page in glaring newsprint ran the headline: 'Nurses Lead Nellie Into Town!' Below it were two pictures. The smaller one showed Vale atop the elephant, waving to the crowd; the second much larger picture showed me, frantically trying to stop an inquisitive trunk going up my skirt. The byline read 'Naughty Nellie and the Nurses'.

'She was called Ethel,' was all I managed to say.

Chapter 7

The 'Trump'

Sister Mandrake was in her office with Phipps when we reported on duty; her face could have withered a petunia. A copy of the *Thorpe and Moresbry Reporter* sat on her desk. She dismissed Thompson and Barnes to their duties and fastened her scowl on me. 'You are to report to Miss Patton's office at ten, Salt. As for this,' she continued, waving the newspaper under my nose, 'if you took more notice learning how to do your work, and less of making a fool of yourself in the centre of Moresbry, you might one day make a nurse. Go and clean the sluice and help Digby in the plaster room – and tidy yourself up before you see Miss Patton.' As usual Sister Phipps didn't speak but I thought she looked slightly sympathetic as she made a great show of tidying the desk.

I didn't remember cleaning the sluice, it passed in a haze of worry and regret. The tears were not far away and when I saw Digby's fatherly smile, they gushed out like a geyser. 'Don't take on, pet,' he consoled. 'Yer didn't know yer were doing anythin' wrong. Mountain out of a mole-hill, just like this lot 'ere.' He found a large white hanky and put a comforting arm around my shoulder.

'I – I – I'll get – the sackkk', I sobbed.

'No way, not over an elephant. Anyone'd think you'd killed someone. Come on, love, cheer up.'

'Do – do you think, I'll be – be sent to Matron?' I spluttered, between blows into his handkerchief.

'What if you do? It's not th' end of t'world. Just look sorry.'

I was busy dabbing and wiping as Digby added: 'Smashin' pictures of you an' Pepper in t'paper. Right pair of bobby-dazzlers, you two.'

I left the department at 9.45, giving me fifteen minutes before execution time. I met Vale coming out of casualty. Unlike me, she was her usual bright and breezy self. 'You've not been crying have you, Salt?' she asked.

The tears were still just over the horizon and I didn't trust myself to speak, but managed a nod. 'Great!' she announced. 'You turn on the waterworks and they're bound to take pity on us.'

'Aren't you bothered?' I whispered.

'Well, yes, but the last time I cried was when this kid thumped me in the playground when I was six. I bit him and ended up standing in the corner all afternoon. I was that mad that teacher had taken his part, I just howled.' I laughed at the thought of this small, blonde-haired horror, her teeth full of child, stamping angrily in a corner of the schoolroom.

As we neared the administration block and the impending interview, I started to feel bilious. Vale spat on a finger and started rubbing at her eyes. 'Do I look weepy?' she asked with a wink.

Our terrible crime was too severe for a mere assistant matron like Miss Pettigrew to deal with. We were to see Miss Patton, the sour, suet pudding from our first morning. Vale knocked but no one answered. We waited with growing apprehension. 'Should you knock again?' I asked.

'We're not that eager for court martial, are we?'

'Perhaps she didn't hear and she'll think we're late.'

'Silly old bat should get a hearing-aid,' said Vale. 'She's doing this on purpose to build up the tension.'

'If she does it for much longer, I'll have to have the toilet.'

'You realise we're missing morning coffee. She couldn't have seen us in hospital time. We even get told off in our few minutes' break.'

'What did Sister Tissleton say?' I asked.

'It was quite jolly really. As I walked into Cas everyone piped up "Nellie the Elephant", and Gert said if I wanted a set of frilly knickers for next time, he'd make me some. Then Tizzy arrived with the news about me having to see Miss Patton. "Since you are a circus performer, girl," she said, "you can get the stepladder out and clean the top of all the curtain rails."'

My reply was cut off as the door opened and Miss Patton's cold stare fastened upon us like frost. Her chill words 'Follow me' were the foreboding of doom. Like two killers on our way to the electric chair, we trailed behind her. The only things missing were prison guards and an Alsatian. I realised we were on our way to Matron and at that moment a firing squad would have been preferable. We passed two student nurses on our short journey who cast compassionate looks in our direction.

We stood silently in the hall outside Matron's office, where we'd been joined by a pained-looking Miss Pettigrew. She looked worse than I felt and I had a sneaky suspicion she was in more trouble than us. Miss Patton tapped on the sacred door and she and Pettigrew slipped inside when the green ENTER light flashed on.

'Don't worry,' Vale whispered. I swallowed and stole a look at the great Benjamin Hale's portrait that frowned down upon us. As the minutes ticked away, I had an imaginary conversation with Big Ben, explaining that all I'd done was lead an elephant. 'What a disgraceful exhibition!' he thundered, standing before me, playing with his gold half-hunter. 'If you wanted to be an elephant trainer, you should have joined the circus. I wouldn't even let one of my mill girls muck around with an elephant, let alone a gal who's hoping to be a nurse.'

I threw myself on his mercy. 'Please, Mr Hall, your worship, all I've ever wanted to be is a nurse. I'm sure I'll make a good nurse, I'll never go near an elephant again,' I implored.

The factory smoke billowed in the background and the hooter went as the workers spilled out of the mill. 'Perhaps you're better suited to the loom, girl.'

'Spare me the mill. Please, sir, not the mill.'

'Salt, Pepper, Miss Cooper-Ffinch will see you now.' Miss Pettigrew broke into my daydream, just as Big Ben was about to pronounce my fate. Gritting my teeth, I walked with shaking knees and a full bladder into Matron's office, remembering that it was only a few short days since we'd been here before.

She sat tight-lipped behind her table, which served as a barrier between herself and minor mortals. The newspaper lay before her and she raised her eyes from its contents as we entered. Miss Patton stood to her right as second assassin, Miss Pettigrew to the left. It was reminiscent of school, and being sent to the head. Vale and I stood side by side, literally 'on the carpet'. The monarch of Benjamin Hale surveyed us with distaste.

'Cadets,' she asked, 'what explanation can you offer for this appalling behaviour?'

I felt that 'appalling behaviour' was a bit over the top. She made it sound as if we'd ridden through Moresbry naked except for a frilly cap. I was incapable of words:

sobs, sniffles, begging, these I could have managed but sensible explanations were beyond me. It was left to Vale to try and save us. 'We're very sorry, Matron,' she said, putting on her most repentant little girl voice. 'But we didn't realise we were doing anything wrong.' I nodded as a tear escaped; Vale would be proud of me.

'Surely you couldn't think that such behaviour is acceptable for a nursing cadet at Benjamin Hale?'

'It was only an elephant, Matron,' said Vale.

'Which you' (she chose her words with care) '*performed* upon in your overalls.' If the circumstances hadn't had been so career threatening, 'performed' would have been worth at least a giggle. Vale had just perched, looking pretty, not stood on her hands or tucked her feet behind her ears. I'd merely led the thing and been sucked and slavered over. If anything had performed, it was Ethel. We'd been quite restrained.

Matron picked up the local rag and waved it like a sword. 'Also, you defaced your overalls by adding apron, cap and some common ornaments. You have brought disrepute upon yourselves and this hospital. Such actions are intolerable.'

Another tear escaped; we were obviously for the chop. The mill loomed ahead but even that was closing down so my cotton-manufacturing career would be short lived. There were shops, of course; quite a few from my secondary modern had headed in that direction. My only experience of the retail trade had been as a Saturday girl in Woolworths. I kept jamming the till and had an awful time adding up in my head all the shillings, pence and halfpennies and I was sure that Woolworths had lost pounds during my employment. Perhaps I could go to night school and gain some qualifications, but what sort of a reference would we get from Miss Cooper-Finch? Dire, if Sister Mandrake was consulted.

Vale must have also seen the approaching axe and, in true George Medal mode, she decided to take the full blame. 'It was my idea, Matron. I talked Nursing Cadet Salt into it. I am truly sorry.'

Her grit gave me courage; for better or worse we were in this together. 'We were equally to blame, Matron. Please – forgive – us,' I spluttered, before dissolving into sniffles.

She placed the newspaper on the table and edged it away as if it were contaminated as she fixed us with a severe gaze. 'Nursing cadets are never to wear their overalls outside hospital property. As cadets you are not entitled to wear caps, and aprons are only worn by senior cadets on the wards. Jewellery of any description is never worn with your overalls. Even off duty and out of your working clothes, as employees and possible future nurses of this hospital, you are expected to conduct yourselves with decorum. Do you understand, cadets?'

'Yes, Matron,' we chorused.

'The only reason I am not going to dismiss you' (at this point I let out the breath I'd been holding) 'is that this is only your second week in the hospital and I feel that you were not correctly informed about the rules and what is expected of you.' As she said this, she cast a quick glance in Miss Pettigrew's direction. She was patently the lieutenant who'd let down the general by not giving accurate information to the troops. I had a feeling that Pepper and I had provided material for many an inspection-morning lecture, and it would be a long time before we'd be allowed to forget our wicked escapade.

'I am giving you both a verbal warning that such behaviour will never be overlooked again. You are on a three-month trial and if you break any further rules, or if I have any reason to reprimand you again, you will be instantly dismissed with no reference. You may return to your duties.'

She nodded her dismissal and with a final, 'Yes, Matron. Thank you, Matron,' we fled.

We didn't speak until we were outside the administration block and well out of earshot. 'Good grief! You'd have thought we'd been arrested for indecent exposure,' said Vale. 'And did you see the look she gave poor old Pettigrew? I bet she's having her ears chewed.'

'She'll take it out on us, we'll never hear the last of it.'

'When she said we'd been performing in our overalls, I nearly cracked out laughing. Whatever did she think I could do on top of Ethel? I was too busy making sure I didn't fall off. And you got a bath.'

'Well, at least she didn't sack us.'

'Most likely frightened we'd go back to the papers. I can just see the headlines,

"NURSES SACKED FOR RIDING NELLIE".'

'"SALT AND PEPPER CAST OUT OF CRUET".'

We both started laughing with relief. We'd got away with it.

We were a few days' wonder, drawing some sarcastic comments and much hilarity. True to our expectations, we were the main topic for Miss Pettigrew's sermon at the next inspection. She had obviously caught the rough edge of Miss Cooper-Ffinch's tongue, and she was determined that the lesson would be pressed home. As the cadets gathered, she marched in like a ship's captain about to set up the whipping gate for some rebellious sailors.

'Cadets Salt and Pepper, step forward,' she ordered, before launching into a tirade of denunciation and ending with the warning that: 'These two junior cadets have only narrowly avoided dismissal. Let this be a lesson to you all.' If we'd been novice nuns, we'd almost certainly have had to kiss her feet, say a hundred Hail Marys and take only bread and water for a week.

I was a minor personality at the fracture clinic for a

few weeks. One morning an elderly lady with her arm in a plaster cast announced to the heaving waiting room, 'That's that little nurse who had trouble with the elephant.' I received a round of applause and an oily youth asked if I fancied 'riding him'. I gave him a look that would have curdled milk and his mum gave him a quick clip round the head.

Sister Mandrake detested me before my 'scandalous behaviour'; her opinion of me confirmed, I began to realise that no matter what I did, she would never like or trust me. Between her and my regular Saturday Gumption-scrubbing sessions under the tyrannical reign of Tizzy, who pecked, poked and screamed at me and Vale all morning, by the fourth week of my excursion into nursing, I was wishing Matron had sacked us. Sacking would have taken the decision from me; now I was back in undecided mode, swinging from 'I can't stand another day' to 'I've always wanted to be a nurse, so I'll put up with anything.' Vale was in a similar frame of mind and each meal time found us swapping horror stories and wondering if tomorrow would be the day we'd quit.

I had found a new ally. Tucked away in a discreet corner behind the reception desk was a door marked PRIVATE. For the first few days I'd assumed it led to a store cupboard. It was only when I nearly opened it by accident, hunting for a fresh supply of X-ray forms, that Fran warned me. 'Don't go in there whatever you do, that's Trump's lair.'

'Trump?'

'Miss Abigail Trumpton, OSAO.'

'Whatever's one of them?'

'Orthopaedic Special Appliances Officer, and a bitch of the first order! That office is her territory and she guards it like a bull on heat.'

'I've never seen her, doesn't she ever come out?'

'She arrives about 8.30, takes all her breaks in her office

and slips away when she's checked the coast is clear. I see her about once a fortnight when I catch her in the act of escaping.'

'Goodness, is she very shy?'

'She's very peculiar. You keep your distance, Salt. You've enough problems with Sister Mandrake without antagonising the Trump.'

There was a small letter box in the Trump's door and all requests for appliances were posted through it. Once a week the appliance man would come to measure and fit the odd assortment of spare bits which could be attached to the human frame to make life easier for those who'd lost something. He was the only person I ever saw go through the door. He would knock, then slide in and vanish for about an hour.

'What do they get up to?' I asked Fran.

'Who knows? Perhaps they have a bit of reckless slap and tickle on her desk. I have seen him straightening his tie, when he comes out.' We roared with laughter. I'd never seen the weird Trump, but the idea of her and the appliance man 'physically occupied' in her den was delightful.

'Mind you, he'd have to be hard up to pursue the Trump. They most likely share tea and home-baked coconut macaroons. I have her down as a dedicated home baker.'

As my luck would have it one morning, about a month after my venture into orthopaedic, I was given a large envelope by Sister Phipps.

'OSAO,' she mouthed. Fran was busy sorting out mixed-up appointments, and both Thompson and Barnes were employed doing important tasks for Sister.

Trump's letterbox was located at knee height. I knelt down and tried desperately to fit this over-sized envelope through the small aperture. I'd no idea what was in it but it wouldn't fold and, try as I might, it was impossible to post it through. I wondered if it was important, perhaps some vital bit of new anatomy which someone was eagerly awaiting. I stood, undecided if I dare knock. My door and telephone phobias had grown out of all proportion; I now jumped like a rabbit whenever the phone rang and entered closed doors as if a rabid wolf waited beyond.

After a few false starts, I tapped gently, pressing my ear against the door to listen for any answer. Nothing. I tapped a little louder. Nothing. Was she really there? It wasn't the appliance man's day and since she was rarely seen, she might be taking a few days off or away with the flu. I made a third attempt, fairly loud. Still nothing. What if she was dead? In fact she could have been dead for a few days and no one would know, until some abominable smell started to filter through the letterbox. Bearing this in mind, I knelt down again, and lifted the flap. Gingerly I stuck my nose through and took in a deep breath. There was certainly a funny smell and, not knowing what dead body smelled like, I took a second lung full to be sure. At that point the metal letter-box flap decided I'd abused its goodwill for too long and sprang shut. With a yelp I pulled away, nursing a battered snitch, just as the secret door opened.

My first view of Trump was a length of grey stocking, which poked beneath a dark green hem. From my prone position at her feet I was also treated to a brief scrutiny of pink underslip and lace-edged knickers. Trump liked her fancy underwear. Trying to gain composure and rubbing my nose which was throbbing, I struggled to my feet and found myself looking down on a diminutive, angry lady of advanced age. She was dressed in a tweed costume over a vivid pink blouse. Her thin hair wisped over an oval crimson face, dark brown eyes and a short strip of mouth. I noticed she wore heavy make-up, lots of blusher, powder and bright red lipstick. But the overall impression was of a tired woman, edging towards retirement who'd had a raw deal from life.

'Was it you that knocked?' she demanded. Her voice was educated but husky and sounded like she'd been talking all day and run out of spit.

'I'm sorry to disturb you but Sister Phipps gave me this.' I poked the bulky envelope towards her, swaying as I added, 'It wouldn't fit through your letterbox.'

'What's Sister Phipps doing with my correspondence?' she croaked. 'She knows my department is totally separate from orthopaedic. She's no right to interfere with my post.'

'I don't know,' I said. I was starting to see the world in strange black-and-white mode, with shooting stars jumping in and out of my head. My nose felt like I'd been a couple of rounds with a boxer and I had a horrible feeling I was going to pass out.

'It's marked "appliances". Even Sister Phipps should be able to see that, and all post marked appliances comes directly to me.' She ranted as I rocked, seeing her going in and out of focus.

'I'm very sorry,' I said, 'but – I think I'm going to faint.' With this, I staggered forward into her den. The outline of a leather chair loomed and I just managed to slide into it before I succumbed. I didn't actually pass out but was aware of this small woman fluttering about. My head was pushed down gently, then a cool flannel and a cup of water appeared. Gradually I started to see colours and the world stabilized. I sipped the water, and pressed the flannel against my pulsating nose.

'Is it that time of the month, dear?' she asked. 'When I was your age I used to have terrible attacks. I was always being picked up off the carpet. My mother had me back and forwards to the doctor but he said it was something I just had to put up with, and I'd most likely grow out of it. But I didn't. Men don't understand, they don't have to suffer each month. Would you like a sip of brandy? I always keep some in my cupboard for medicinal purposes, but I could get you a little.'

She blathered on like a tiny crow who's recently learned to fly and wants to tell the whole world. She was busy pouring a good tot of brandy into a glass when I managed to speak. 'I caught my nose in your letterbox.'

She paused, bottle in one hand, glass in the other. 'Whatever were you doing with your nose in my letterbox?'

Well, I could hardly tell her I was sniffing to see if she was dead. 'I thought I smelt gas.'

'Oh, there's no gas in here, even the electric is old-fashioned. I need rewiring but nobody bothers about my little office. Look at that light fitting,' she said, pointing to the ceiling socket where an ancient green lampshade surrounded the bulb. The wire from ceiling to bulb was threadbare. 'A death trap, that's what this office is, but do they care? Of course not. I ask and ask for repairs, new plugs, sockets, but deaf ears, that's all I ever get, dear. Are you feeling better?' I nodded as she pressed the brandy into my hand. 'Better take a sip, dear. Do you think you should go to casualty? So nasty, bumps on the nose. I fell over a pavement last winter, they don't look after the pavements. I was very lucky not to fracture my skull but I gave my nose such a knock, it went all black and swollen.'

I was starting to feel overwhelmed. I wasn't used to concern in orthopaedic and even Digby, who was my favourite occupant of this strange realm, didn't chatter quite as much. I couldn't understand Fran's description of this grumpy, silent woman who hurried past without a word. My first impressions of the Trump were of a fussy, worried, chatterbox.

I was a bit concerned about the brandy. I had the feeling it would most likely do me good but I wasn't used to alcohol and wondered if it would go to my head. If Sister Mandrake smelt booze on me, I'd be back off to

Matron in a flash, with no explanations accepted. I had a quick vision of me holding on to Miss Cooper-Ffinch's mahogany table, swaying in between hiccups, blurting out, 'I got my nose caught in a letterbox and I just had a little tot to bring me round.'

'I feel much better now, thank you, Trum – Miss Trumpton,' I said, edging out of the chair.

'Well, if you're sure. I don't see much of the staff, not that I want to see that awful Mandrake woman, she's an ill-mannered tyrant. And that Phipps isn't much better, stealing my mail.' Gazing into Trumps eyes, I realised I had met a kindred spirit.

From that day Trump's office became a safe haven whenever the going got bad. We seemed to click immediately. I was a good listener, and she loved to talk. She was the most badly done by woman on the planet and she made my circumstances seem quite easy by comparison.

It appeared that everyone in the hospital had it in for her. Her mail went missing, her equipment either wasn't delivered or broke down and no one cared. Her stationery went astray, or was incorrectly printed, or badly packed and damaged. Her typewriter was elderly and she couldn't get a new one issued. I would often find her frantically changing ribbons and hand-winding long banners of inked tape from one spool to another.

The smell which had so alarmed me was a combination of damp and pencil peelings. Poor Trump was 'riddled' with damp. 'Look at this wall,' she would say. 'Saturated. It's unhealthy and I'm expected to work in here. I can't even put card or paper against that wall or it all goes musty, and I'm expected to sit in here day after day. It's little wonder I'm never well. I've asked them to re-house me, there must be an office somewhere in the hospital that's not used, but no, I get no co-operation from anyone. Mr Parnossis has tried, but he hasn't got an office at all. A shared desk, that's all he gets, and the begrudging use of a clinic room once a week.' Mr Parnossis, I realised was the appliance man and, 'A gentleman, there's not many around these days. It's disgusting the way that Mandrake woman treats him, and he's so skilled he can fit a leg on anyone.'

Trump possessed a beautiful fountain pen but her real love was pencils. She had a box of them on her table, sharpened to different lengths. A barrelled pencil sharpener took pride of place on her table and she was always busy winding, reducing her latest pencil to a long strip of wooden shavings. This led to a heap of discarded pencil threads piled up beneath her winder, like a miniature wood pile awaiting some chilly elf to come along and build a bonfire. The shavings were always escaping onto her carpet and since she never allowed a cleaner in, ('Confidential my work, dear, I don't want some domestic poking around in my drawers,') she was forever crawling around with a brush and pan, gathering up tiny wooden droppings.

The rest of Trump's office was a delightful muddle. The table, window sill and every spare piece of floor was piled high with files. The room was overflowing with false legs, arms, boxes filled with wigs, braces, special boots and other appliances. She had a cupboard which was a veritable store house, containing everything necessary for high-tea. She regularly supplemented it with tins of cakes, biscuits and delicious scones. Fran had been right about her home-baking skills and, as I rapidly became her main confidante, I was treated to a share of the goodies.

She lived alone with two cats, Merlin and Puss. She was as badly done by in her private life as her working one. She had terrible neighbours who were a constant cause of distress, her car was always breaking down and the garage cheated her. She'd had workmen at the house who'd made an awful mess fitting new windows, robbed her blind, and the council wouldn't repair a leaking sewer.

Then she wasn't well; she should have retired, but who would do this thankless job if she didn't? She was a martyr to her feet; the chiropodist had been at them for years but they were no better. What with her corns and bunions, fallen arches, crooked toes and hard skin, it was amazing she managed to walk at all. She also had 'tummy trouble', 'ladies problems down there' and an awful back. In fact, my first worry that she'd dropped dead was quite near the mark; she was always telling me it would be a miracle if she survived the day.

Fran was amazed that not only was I allowed easy access into Trump's den but that I'd actually made a friend of her. The one piece of gossip Fran had was for me to look out for Trump's ring and a small picture that she was supposed to keep on her desk.

'I heard she'd been engaged to a soldier but he was killed on D-Day. She never married but has always worn his ring and kept his photo,' Fran confided. 'Sad, isn't it? Perhaps that's why she's so odd.'

The more I got to know Trump, the less odd she seemed. I felt she was lonely and eccentric and had a severe persecution complex, but she was kind and genuine, qualities that were in short supply at Benjamin Hale. She did wear a sweet little ring, which I would sometimes see her twirl while we were chatting, but if she had her sweetheart's picture I never saw it, and I never asked.

***

I had found one last sanctuary, a top-secret hideaway known to few and rarely visited. I'd been on an X-ray hunt and returned with a good heap of films ready for the next day. Only one had eluded me, though I'd found the number in the reference index. I was becoming like

Sherlock Holmes when it came to ferreting out missing items.

The main X-ray file room was a rambling annexe attached to the rear of the X-ray department. After working out the illogical way that the numbers ran (A091100 for some reason coming after B101100), I could now take my list of prey and triumphantly reappear clutching the required heap. But when I found a number with no reasonable link with the others, I had to admit defeat.

Fran laughed and pressed a small, rusty key into my palm. 'Basement,' she said. 'You'll enjoy it down there, as long as you don't mind spiders.' There were many doors in orthopaedic and, by my third week, most had given up their secrets. Only one was always kept locked: a blue, anonymous door that would have passed for a broom cupboard. It was halfway along the short corridor which led to the back door and it hid the basement staircase.

Keys were not my strong point and it took me a while to work out the combination. The door creaked open. Cobwebs trimmed the corners; Sister Mandrake's cleaning regime obviously did not extend down here. A steep, stone flight of stairs lay before me. I flicked on the light, which came from a shadeless bulb heavily laden with dust. Worried a patient might fall down the steps, I pulled the door closed and carefully negotiated the steps.

It was like the entrance to a crypt. Step by step, I made my way down to a short passage which led to another door. This door was stiff and its ancient paint had long since rubbed away. It had a big old-fashioned glass knob and groaned like an arthritic rhinoceros. A substantial basement room lay beyond, which must have run nearly the full length of orthopaedic. Lit by two dim bulbs, it was filled with rack upon rack of antiquated X-rays. I was sure they had been there since the early days of Madame

Curie; I almost expected to see her ghost slipping in and out of the aisles with a spider entwined in her greying hair.

Luckily I have never been an arachnophobe and had been drilled with the 'if you wish to live and thrive, let the spider run alive' rhyme since childhood. I was quite content to let them patter around as long as they didn't bother me. It was their place of residence, I was only passing through.

My biggest worry was mice. Now mice were a different prospect, mice had long tails, beady eyes and scuttled with menace across the floor. There wasn't even a chair to jump on so, with mice in mind, I headed into the basement, one eye on the door ready to make a hasty dash at the first squeak or scurry. A careful reconnoitre reassured me there were no obvious signs of habitation, though it would take a few visits to build up my confidence.

It took some time to work out the filing system, or rather not to. Many of the X-rays were older than me and I was sure that a lot of the enclosed black-and-white negatives had no living claimant. Thousands of the dead had left a lasting memory of the shape of their pelvis or the sad degeneration of their vertebrae locked in the orthopaedic basement. Anything (or anyone) could have been hidden down there, in the secure knowledge that ninety-nine per cent of the hospital inhabitants didn't even know the place existed. And the few who did made only brief visits.

I discovered the required X-rays housed in faded brown envelopes and from that day the basement became my last place of retreat. On occasion, I had a valid reason to vanish on a treasure hunt but sometimes I could stand no more. I found it easy to secrete the key and, since no one used the back door which doubled as a fire-escape, the corridor was usually deserted. After a stressful session of door-opening and phone answering, which invariably led to being on the receiving end of Sister Mandrake's sarcasm, I would grab a chocolate bar from my bag and go to share it with the spiders. I had discovered the soothing virtue of chocolate in junior school and found it still acted as both a pacifier and a channel for optimism.

It was late Friday afternoon, about an hour before I was off duty. The clinics were finished for the day and Sister and most of the staff had gone home. I was putting the final touches to the cleaning and wandering around the waiting room, counting the minutes before I dare leave. 'Hi, Salt, you in charge?' I jumped at Vale's voice. 'Goodness, you have a nice quiet time, no patients, no Wizzy Tizzy. I don't know what you complain about, it's bliss here.' She slumped into an empty chair and slipped off a shoe. 'My feet are killing me. I've been dashing about like an Olympic sprinter.'

'Believe me, it's not often like this. The Dragon and her mates have gone home.'

'Where's Pinkie and Perky?' We'd taken to calling Thompson and Barnes by these nicknames.

'In the ward, doing something terribly important and complicated.'

'Cupboard cleaning?'

'Most likely, but filled with breakables.'

'Wouldn't dare let you near then, Salt.'

'No chance. Did you want something or have you escaped for a natter?'

'My dear, there is no escape from casualty. Every errand is ordered, every movement ordained. No, I am here on a mission. The doctor wants some ancient X-ray, and I was told they might be in your basement.'

'I'll need to see your identification and special pass before you're allowed down in my cellar,' I said sternly, as she produced a pink tongue.

I got the key and, Vale in tow, headed for the door. The combination proved difficult but after three attempts and an extra kick, it groaned open. Vale sniffed and looked down into the darkness below. 'I don't like the look of that. Those steps are a death trap, there isn't even a handrail.'

I flicked on the light. 'Come on, it's not that bad. Just take the steps carefully and hold onto the wall.'

Automatically I closed the door behind us and we made our way down into the bowels of orthopaedic. Vale shivered as I opened the inner door leading into the storage room and she let out a yelp as I put on the light and the spiders hurried for cover. 'Hell! I hate spiders. What a creepy hole, it's like a dungeon. You don't honestly like coming down here, Salt? You must be crackers.'

'Oh it's lovely, and no Sister Mandrake,' I assured her, as we made our way through the stacks, hunting for the numbered X-ray she was after.

'Come on, be quick, I can't stand it down here. Oww! There's a spider in my hair, oooooooohhh!!' Poor Vale started beating at her fair locks, sure some ghastly thing had got tangled inside. 'Can you see anything?' she wailed, as I inspected the blonde mass under a dusty light.

'I can't see a thing, you must have imagined it. There's a bit of cobweb here,' I said triumphantly as I extracted an old blob of web.

'Yuck! I'm off, I'll wait upstairs for you,' she shrieked, making a dash for the bottom door, slapping and beating at her scattered tresses. I heard a crash, bang and scream, and turned round to see her prostrate on the concrete floor. In her headlong rush she'd caught her foot, thrown out her hands to save herself and crashed into the door, slamming it shut. She'd ended up sprawled on the floor, thrashing around at what she believed to be an attacking hoard of spiders.

My horror at seeing my bold friend in such obvious distress was only matched by the frightful realisation that I had never before closed the bottom door from the inside.

I worked at the rusty knob, trying to propel it first one way then the other. My ministrations had no effect and the awful truth dawned. I realised with a cold feeling of dread that we were imprisoned in the orthopaedic basement.

Chapter 8

The Basement

'We can't be shut in.' Vale was back on her feet, straining at the door. We tried a joint effort, four hands locked around the knob, hanging back, swinging like a pair of frantic monkeys. We tried kicking, wriggling, jiggling, but it was wasted endeavour. 'Let's shout,' said Vale, as she dodged another spider.

'There's no one to hear. The place is deserted apart from Pinkie and Perky, and they're at the other end of the building.'

'Perhaps they'll come looking for you.'

'No chance.'

'Well we can't stand here and do nothing.'

'I'm open to suggestions,' I said, giving the door a final tug, but it was stuck like glue. Unlike Vale, I wasn't bothered about our crawling companions. I'd become used to them, as long as they didn't try to get down my neck. 'I think the cleaners arrive later on, but I'm not sure when.'

'They're bound to hear us.'

'I don't know if the sound will carry through two doors and up a staircase.'

'We'll be missed, they'll send out a search party.'

'We're hardly marooned on the moors. My mum will be in a state but I expect she'll blame you and think we've gone off together. She won't start panicking until late. What about your mum?'

'Out, not due back until midnight.'

'Brian?'

'Working away until Monday.'

I was starting to feel like a mummy in a pyramid, shut away from the world until some archaeological professor started digging. I pictured him, clad in sand-coloured shorts, his voice shaking with excitement. 'The door! It leads down. There are some stone steps. Another door!' His comrades would crowd behind as he cut his way through the thick cobwebs. He would take a crowbar, tracing the door shape, prising away the rust. Inch by inch, it would screech on its hinges. Fascinated, they would enter to see two skeletons, still dressed in their faded yellow overalls. 'It must be the cadets who went missing all those years ago,' he would say, while the others shook their heads. He was picking up my skeletal hand when Vale's voice broke into my imaginings.

'There's a tiny window up here.' I jumped as the professor dropped my bones, and trailed to the far end of the basement. 'Perhaps we could smash it and yell. Surely someone will hear.'

The window was little more than a grille, about six inches square. Only a dim glow struggled through; the spiders had long-since woven a thick, webbed curtain across the pane. I'd never noticed it and I tried to work out where it faced. 'It must be just above ground level around the back.'

'Give me a leg up.' Vale was all action, anything to take her mind off spiders. We cleared a pile of obsolete X-rays onto the floor and she started to clamber up the shelves. The unit was not used to being abused and it rocked ominously.

'Be careful,' I advised, giving her bottom a push. Vale pulled herself up while I held on to two rounded buttocks. She teetered half way to the ceiling and scrambled higher, managing to get her nose up against the dirty window. 'I can't see a thing,' she shouted, rubbing at the glass. 'I think there's some netting on the outside.'

'Can you break it?' I yelled up her skirt. She was hammering a fist into the glass, causing it to rain lacy threads and dust.

'Have you got a hammer?'

'I don't normally carry one.'

'Funny. Can you see anything lying around?'

'I've got a pencil and a couple of paper clips.'

'Think positive, Salt.'

'Can you hold on if I have a hunt?'

'Yes, but don't be long, I've already broken a fingernail.'

I freed myself from my position as the ladder. Vale braced, like a mountain climber half way up the Annapurna. I started a dusty hunt under and over heaped shelves. I scoured the floor for anything that looked remotely dangerous but I found nothing apart from a discarded button and an old wine gum.

'Get a move on, Salt, I can't hang on much longer,' Vale shouted.

'I can't find anything. You'd better come down before you fall.'

'This is ridiculous. Hallo! Hallo!' Vale's fist drummed to little effect on the window. 'Halloooooooooooo!!' There was a scream, then a whoosh as the shelving decided to part company with the wall. I yelped as a heap of ancient X-rays tumbled gleefully towards me. One shelf clattered into the next, causing a domino effect as thousands of large brown X-ray folders and accompanying dust headed for the floor. Vale followed them backwards.

The light bulb swung violently with the shock of the explosive movement, casting eerie shifting shadows across the basement. Spiders scuttled for cover and I was sure I heard a squeak. Vale ended up sprawled like a drunken duck, half submerged in X-rays. Terrified she'd killed herself, I clambered over the confusion. She was cursing fluently.

'Are you alright?'

'I think I twisted my ankle,' she said, giving it a rub. 'There must be some way out of this damn place.'

'Let's have another go at the door and try shouting.'

'What time is it?'

'You know I'm waiting for Christmas to get my fob watch, but it must be five.'

'Do you think Pinkie and Perky will have gone without you?'

'Bound to.'

'Let's shout, and see if anyone hears.' We settled down to yell and hammer. Like inmates of the Black Hole of Calcutta, we banged and bellowed.

'It's quite exciting, isn't it?' I offered.

'Salt, your idea of excitement is really strange.'

'My life was quite boring before I met you.' I settled down for a rest on a pile of scattered films. 'I bet I get the job of tidying this lot up. Sister Mandrake will play hell when she sees the state of this room.'

'What a jolly time you'll have, alone down here with the spiders. Please don't ask for me to help.'

I reached for a hanky and had a good blow, trying to rid my nose of the dust. 'Hey, I've just remembered, I've got a chocolate bar in my pocket.'

'Salt, you're a life saver. I'm starving.' Like castaways, we made ourselves comfortable as I shared out the meagre resources of my larder. Vale made sure her seat was free of crawlies and kept her skirts well bunched up under her. 'I don't fancy an uninvited guest creeping up my knickers.'

We made every mouthful count, savouring the rich taste, picking chocolate crumbs off our palms, licking every last grain off our fingers. The only trouble was we could have done with a cup of tea to wash it down.

'Now what?' Vale asked.

I was out of ideas and so, for now, was Vale. We wondered how long it would be before a search party was launched. 'They knew in casualty. You were off searching for old X-rays in orthopaedic; when you don't turn up, they're bound to start looking here.'

Vale didn't look so confident. 'Yes, but how long will it take? Staff Nurse sent me for the X-rays and she was about to go off duty.'

'When's she back?'

'She's not, it was her last day. She's taking maternity leave.'

'Oh.' The skeleton loomed. 'What about the doctor who wanted them?'

'A locum, just filling in.'

'Don't tell me, it was his last evening and he's going on holiday.'

Vale nodded. 'His plane leaves tomorrow for Bombay, he's going home.'

'I wonder if the cleaners are in yet. Let's have another yell.' We spent more fruitless minutes banging and shouting, resulting in nothing but bruised knuckles and hoarse throats.

Vale limped back to her seat. 'How often does anyone apart from you come down here?'

'Now and again the cadets from outpatients turn up.' We made conversation for a while, each of us trying to keep calm. Becoming used to our presence, the spiders began to close in. Many had been disturbed by the toppling shelves and I had a sneaky feeling they were bent on revenge for their squashed relatives. A particularly vindictive specimen decided to climb up Vale's leg. She shrieked and dashed to the other end of the basement. The spider crawled away disgusted.

'I wonder how long the air will last,' said Vale. 'I don't know which is worse, the thought of suffocating or being eaten by spiders.'

My stomach churned; the only consolation for our predicament was that I wasn't alone. 'They'll see our bags and cloaks, they'll still be where we left them.'

Vale brightened slightly. 'But they won't know we're down here.'

'No, but they're sure to search orthopaedic and casualty.' It was a small sliver of hope and it kept us going for a while. We decided to hope for the best. Every so often we had another shout but our confidence was diminishing.

'How did you get a name like Vale?' I asked. The name had intrigued me from that first day. If I was doomed to fade away slowly in the orthopaedic basement, I was going to get as many questions as possible answered before I went.

Vale laughed. 'Have a guess.'

'Your mum hoped you'd be a nun?'

'Come off it, Salt, could you see me as a nun?'

'Well, your mum might have been religious when you were born.'

'No chance. Try again.'

'Grandma's name?' Vale shook her head. 'Somewhere your mum used to live?'

'No. Have another go.'

'How about where you were conceived, some peaceful dale, with the birds singing.'

'You're a romantic, Salt. Give up?'

I nodded. After another spider battle, Vale settled down to tell me the tale. 'Don't ask me if it's true, but this is the way Mum tells it. She was working in the mill and the mill owner's son was getting married. Mr Truet, the mill owner, was a very generous man and to celebrate his son's nuptials, he threw a party for his workers. All the girls went and this lad brought a bottle of vodka. Well, Mother got very tipsy and young Mr Truet, Fred, offered to drive her home in his car. She vows she doesn't remember much about the night but nine months later she had me.'

'So you're dad was Fred, the mill owner's son.'

'Fred denied all and Mum ended up marrying Bill from down the street.'

'So Bill became your dad.'

'No, Bill was killed when I was only three months and mum married Sam.'

'Dear me. So Sam became your dad.'

'No, Sam went off with the fair when I was five.'

'It's like a Catherine Cookson novel but I still don't see where Vale comes into it.'

'Mother had a long, painful labour and she was pig sick by the time she'd had me. She says that afterwards she lay there trying to decide what to call me. After much pondering she came up with VALE: Vodka Accidentally Lands Embryo.' Our laughter filled the basement.

'You made that up, I don't believe a word of it.' Her only answer was a wink.

I had no idea how long we'd been there. It felt like half the night had passed but a faint oblong of dim light struggled through the tiny window. I guessed perhaps two hours had gone, so it was possibly sometime after seven. The cleaners must be in upstairs but another bout of yelling brought no response. We prowled around our prison, clambering over the confusion on the floor. We had a further go at the door, straining our arms as we hung back like deep sea fishermen hauling in their nets but nothing moved, nothing changed.

'What's that?'

Vale shot in the air and landed on a battered pile of X-rays with a yelp, clutching her ankle. She gathered her skirts up tight around her knees. 'What! It's not a rat, it is? That would be the final straw. Where is it?'

'No,' I said, 'I meant that on the wall.'

'Is it alive?'

'No.' I scrambled past her to the mottled off-white wall where the shelf unit had come away. It was filthy; it must have been years since the shelf had been moved. 'There's something here on the wall, behind the muck. At least, I thought I saw something.'

'As long as it's not moving I don't care.' As Vale remained bundled up, ready to ward off attack, I tried to brush the webs aside. 'Tell me it's a secret door leading out.'

'I think it's something almost as good.'

'What is it?' Vale demanded.

'It's a fire alarm.'

'What?' Vale braved the spiders and came to join me. 'Do you think it still works?'

'There's only one way to find out,' I said. The glass was a dirty brown, with the red FIRE almost rubbed away. I took off a shoe and, hopping on one leg, banged away with the heel at the glass. It took about four whacks before the glass shattered. I pressed the small red button and prayed. We stood listening, Vale perched on top of a pile of X-rays, me holding on to her as I swayed on one leg. I struggled back into the shoe and we headed to the door.

'Can you hear anything?' I asked.

'Not sure. What's a fire alarm sound like?'

'I think it's like a bell, a bit like school, but it keeps on wailing.'

'Will they know where the alarm was set off?'

I shook my head. 'No idea, let's hope so.' Our knowledge of hospital fire procedures was nil, another of the many necessary items of information no one had bothered to tell us.

'I think I can hear something,' said Vale. 'A bit like a kettle whistling in the distance.'

'That's it, we'll have the fire brigade here in double time. They're bound to make hospitals a priority.'

Vale sighed with relief. 'The first man through that door gets me. I want a fireman's lift out of this crawly den, a hot cup of sweet tea and lots of sympathy.'

'I hope they look down here.'

'Don't start with the pessimism. We're going to hammer and yell our lungs out. Firemen are trained to listen for maidens in distress.'

We plunged into serious bellowing and attacked the door with fists and my shoes – Vale wouldn't take hers off. 'Do you think this will warrant another session with Matron?' I asked.

'We didn't get stuck down here on purpose. I think they should be extra nice to us, we could have come to a nasty end and I'm injured. Anyway, at the moment I couldn't care less, I just want to be out. Come on, Salt, shout!'

Never did two girls make so much noise. No football supporter could have done a better job; our team would have romped to victory if we'd been cheerleaders. My throat felt sore with all the screeching and my shoe heels were decidedly the worse for wear, but for ages it seemed as if we were straining our vocal chords for nothing. Then we heard a shout. 'Is there anyone down there?' Never was a male voice so welcome.

'Yes! Yes! We're here!' Our shouting went up a decibel and we banged those shoes like sinners trying to escape through the doors of hell.

There was the sound of heavy footsteps and with scuffling outside the door. The knob wriggled round but the door stayed closed.

'Hang on, I'll have you out in a tick.' We heard a clang and scraping as a crowbar was applied to the door frame. Gradually it started to move until a set of big fingers appeared then, with a reluctant jar, the door creaked open. A hunky shape filled the doorway: it was our hero complete with masterful grin and fireman's helmet. 'Hello, girls. Now, what are you two doing down here?'

'Getting out fast,' said Vale. 'I've hurt my ankle and I think I feel faint,' she added, settling gracefully into his arms, blonde hair rippling down in a confused tumble. He scooped her up and in true film-star fashion she curled her arms around his neck and snuggled up against his coat buttons, as the 'frail' female she was. 'We've been trapped for hours,' she whimpered, 'and I'm sure the air was going.'

'Don't worry love, you're safe now,' he reassured her. 'You hold on tight and I'll carry you.' He cradled her in his great beefy arms and set off back up the stairs, shouting to the other firemen who were standing at the top. 'There's two nurses down here but they're okay.'

'I was nearly eaten by spiders and I fell off a shelf,' murmured Vale. ('And chipped a fingernail,' I added silently.)

'Can you manage, nurse?' he added over his shoulder to me as he carried his beautiful burden up the steep stairs.

I was hopping around, trying to get my battered shoes back on. I cast a final look around the basement, horrified at the mess, then flicked off the light-switch and followed. 'Oh yes, I'm fine,' I said.

They took us to casualty, where we created a minor sensation amongst the night staff. It appeared there'd been quite a commotion when the fire alarm went off. The emergency procedure swung into action and everyone was prepared for evacuation. Fire escapes were opened, staff and patients mustered, and everyone was about to pile out into the courtyard. On the chance that one of the wards was on fire, the turntable ladder and three fire tenders had been despatched, so the place was swarming with firemen and red engines.

The fireman carried Vale all the way into casualty, me in tow, and laid her down like an injured starlet on a cubicle bed. The doctor and night staff nurse clustered round. 'She fell off a shelf trying to open a window, a real brave lass,' said the fireman.

'Thank you so much for rescuing us,' said Vale, fluttering her eyelashes. 'It was really frightening down there.'

'I'm just glad you're both alright.' Gosh, he was handsome: six foot, broad, great big brown eyes and a smile to die for. 'Well I best be off,' he added, slipping away reluctantly. 'Has she got a boyfriend?' he whispered to me.

'Yes, he's an all-in-wrestler and very jealous.'

'Pity,' then he was gone, back to his fire engine, leaving me standing at the invalid's bedside, looking dishevelled in a mucky uniform, dirty shoes and with skinned knuckles. Vale was booked into X-ray as her ankle was a little red. 'Better make sure nothing's broken,' the doctor said, with a comforting beam. 'Will you be able to take her?' he'd added to me, pointing to the wheelchair.

I was about to display my own injuries and ask about the calming cup of tea, but it appeared I was now designated porter to ferry the injured heroine. Vale thought it was hilarious and giggled all the way, giving instructions and sticking her arm out to indicate a right or left turn.

'Steady on, Salt,' she yelled, as we gained speed down a corridor. 'I'm in a delicate state.'

'What about me? I look like I've come down a chimney.'

'You will go delving around in the under crofts of the hospital and lure me down into your den. I might have nightmares about spiders for weeks.'

'More likely gorgeous dreams about muscular firemen.

That one was really disappointed when I told him you had a boyfriend.'

'He was a dish. It was like being carried by Tarzan.'

'I bet there's nothing wrong with your ankle.'

'Salt, fancy doubting me! I might even manage a few days at home with my ankle on a cushion. Think of it, a few days away from the Gumption and Tizzy. Paradise. I hope you bring me some grapes.'

'You're a fraud.'

She revelled in the attention, even though (to her great disappointment) nothing was broken. 'A nasty sprain,' was the doctor's diagnosis, 'but you must rest it for a few days.' Eventually, an hour later and well bandaged, Vale was sent home by ambulance, clutching a sick note.

She waved as the ambulance doors swung to. 'See you in a week, Salt, unless you fancy coming sick visiting.' I was left to make my way alone back to the locker room to change in the semi-darkness. It was approaching nine and, by the time I'd pulled off my filthy yellows and slipped into my own clothes then trailed back through the hospital to the bus stop, it was not far off ten, dark and starting to rain.

'Wherever have you been?' was Mum's greeting, adding, 'off somewhere with that new friend of yours. I hope you haven't been on that motorbike.'

'No, Mother, I've been locked in a cellar,' I muttered and spent the remainder of the evening explaining how, why and when, only having to repeat it all when Dad came in from the evening shift. It was the general agreement that I 'really shouldn't have to go poking around in cellars'.

'What do they think you are, a miner?' put in Dad, adding, 'I always said it was a daft idea. Any time you want to pack it in, it's okay with me.'

There was an ominous note pinned to the signing-in book on Monday morning: 'Cadet Salt to report to Miss

Patton'. Dreading what might be awaiting me, I knocked on her door, wishing my fellow cellar-rat was standing beside me. 'Come in, Salt,' she said. Was that a slight smile? 'Do sit down, dear.'

I nearly fell into the chair with shock as she continued, 'Are you alright after your ordeal?'

'Yes, thank you, Miss Patton,' I managed,

'You might have been there all weekend. Thank goodness you had the presence of mind to ring the fire alarm. Although it caused quite a fuss, you didn't have any other option.'

'We only found the alarm after the shelf fell down.'

'Yes, and Cadet Pepper hurt her ankle. She could have been killed. When I think what might have happened…'

She was genuinely concerned; I suppose it was the latent nurse awakening in her. She must have been kind and considerate in some distant past or she'd never have taken up nursing. Or perhaps it was the thought of all the paperwork she would have had to sort out if Pepper and I had ended up injured or dead. I wasn't sure.

'Are you certain you didn't hurt yourself?' she added.

'No, I just got a bit dirty.'

'Well, that's a relief. Do be more careful in future, cadet. You better get along to orthopaedic and give Sister Mandrake my apologies that you are late.'

I slipped out of her office, feeling bemused and distinctly important. She cared. It was the first time since I'd arrived at Benny's that I actually felt a part of the staff and not some counterfeit in a yellow overall. I was 'one the cadets', a very small part of the hospital, but a part all the same.

I was half an hour late on duty and a small portion of my mind harboured the hope that Sister Mandrake might also be concerned about my well being. As usual, my hopes were crushed. 'Really, Cadet Salt, of all the stupid things to do, getting yourself locked in the cellar. You know that door sticks. I thought even you would have had more sense.' I'd found her in her usual Monday morning mood, menacing like a storm about to break. 'That cellar looks like a rugby team has been in it. You'll have to tidy it up and sort and restack all the X-rays. You can do that whenever the department is quiet, but for goodness' sake tell someone when you're going down there in future.' I trotted at her side as she marched around the day patients, giving orders. 'Do get some work done, Salt. The urines are waiting, there's notes missing and the sluice is a tip.'

The only comment I got from Thompson, as she lined up the assortment of wee bottles was: 'Really, Salt, we have such trouble keeping up with your escapades. Elephants, now the fire brigade – whatever next?'

'She'll most likely blow the place up,' Barnes added sarcastically, as she sailed passed the sluice door with an armful of sheets.

A hospital, I was slowly learning, was like a village, especially a relatively small local hospital like Benny's. Most people knew each other, if not by sight, certainly by reputation. Gossip spread like a forest fire. It was the standing joke that if you sneezed at one end of the hospital, everyone knew you were sickening for flu at the other end before the day was out. I was again the centre of attention at Miss Pettigrew's weekly cadet gathering. This time the lecture centred around telling other members of staff where we were going and being especially careful about doors and cellars and, in typical Miss Pettigrew manner, she said, 'Do remember, cadets, you are expected to behave like ladies, not monkeys.' With visions of Vale swinging from the top shelf, I somehow managed to keep a straight face.

I never got sympathy and was stupid to expect from the Dragon, but I did receive some from the Trump. She brought a special cake she'd made to a new recipe, and oooh'd and aah'd all the way through my tale, which I had to repeat four times. 'You could have both died down there, my dear,' she sympathised. 'But that Mandrake woman wouldn't have cared. She doesn't care about anyone, she's evil. Do you know what she said to me the other day?'

I was curled up in a chair, safe for a short while. I shook my head as I sipped tea. '"Miss Tumpton," she said, after all these years, and she can't even pronounce my name, just like her. "Miss Tumpton," she said, "there's a prosthetic leg sitting in my office. I have quite enough to do without dealing with spare legs and arms which should come to you. Please collect it as soon as you can."'

It was my turn to oooh and aah. We fellow sufferers must stick together. 'The cheek of the woman. It's not my fault if the hospital postman is that stupid that he mixes up the mail. It's that new chap, Arthur, I don't think he can read. That's the third time this week he's mixed up my post. I've been waiting for that leg. I was going to phone up about it and there it was, sitting in her office all the time. It's a wonder she didn't hide it. She's done that before. A few months ago, I was waiting for a special neck brace. I phoned and phoned and they kept saying they hadn't got it and she had it all the time.'

I tended to let poor old Trump witter on. She had no one else to talk to and she was so badly done by, I often felt she would explode if she couldn't unburden herself on me. I licked the last crumbs of chocolate off my fingers, knowing the moment when I must leave the peace of the Trump's office for the trauma of the department couldn't be delayed much longer.

'If that woman once gets her hands on my support stockings, I'll never see them again. You take care now, dear,' she added, as I slipped reluctantly back into the fray.

Vale returned the following Monday, ankle intact. I had a sneaky suspicion that the 'sick week' had been an unexpected holiday. She assured me she had lain in agony on the couch and oh no, she was in much too much pain to have gone out with Brian on the bike. When I pointed out that I had arrived on Thursday evening, weighed down with grapes, and found her out, she denied it vigorously. 'Must have limped off to the quack,' she assured me, adding, 'but you might have left the grapes.' I said I'd eaten the lot on the journey back on the bus to Thorpe.

'Pig!'

'I decided I deserved them more than you. After all, I've had dear Sister Mandrake all week, plus I've had to cope with Tizzy's madhouse on Saturday morning.'

'How did you manage?' she asked. I pulled a face which I hoped conveyed the nerve-wracking experience.

'Don't forget to report back on duty after being off sick,' advised one of the senior cadets. Vale and I looked puzzled. 'Whenever you've been off sick or away on holiday, when you get back you always have to go and see Matron and report yourself back on duty.'

'Why?' asked Vale.

'It's the done thing and you'll cop out if you don't.'

'Do I have to make an appointment?'

'No, just turn up outside her office before you go to Cas and join the queue. When you go in, you just say, "Nursing Cadet Pepper, reporting back on duty after illness, Matron".'

'What a performance, it sounds a complete waste of time.'

'It's good manners.'

As we parted for our various departments Vale, as always, had the last word on our recent escapade. 'What do you get if you cross a spider with a fireman, Salt?'

'I dread to think.'

'Eight strong arms! Don't worry, Salt me old buddy, we'll try for a strapping copper next time.'

'Next time!'

Chapter 9

Problems with Laundry

The first week in September saw a minor landmark in my nursing career. Not only had I survived two full months at Benny's, but I was now officially the 'senior' cadet on orthopaedic, much to Sister Mandrake's disgust.

In the last week of August, a change list was displayed. These insignificant looking pieces of paper were the herald of happiness or despair to our massed ranks. They appeared every four months, with the occasional reshuffle in between. Those cadets who had arrived at the magnificent age of seventeen anxiously looked for confirmation of their first step onto the wards. These fortunate yellows would be showered with advice. 'Oh lucky you, you're going to 3. Charlie the Charge Nurse is a real sweetheart but keep on the right side of Beryl the cleaner.'

'You poor sod, you're on 6, Sister Pearce is a tyrant!'

'Ward 7 is awful, you spend the whole day cleaning.'

'Sister Travers on Ward 15 is completely paranoid,' and so on.

Vale and I looked with dying hope but our names were not listed. 'Four more months with Tizzy,' groaned Vale.

'I'll be as daft as her at the end.'

If I was not moving, Barnes and Thompson were. I would not be sorry to see the back of them, especially Barnes, who had made me feel inferior and stupid since my arrival. Thompson had tried to be patient and had persevered to knock me into shape, ready for their departure. I had a basic grip of the inner workings of the department and if I had learned one thing to perfection, it was how to irritate Sister Mandrake.

The day the list was posted 'that Mandrake woman' as the Trump called her, had summoned me to her office. Sister Phipps sipped her morning coffee, idly dunking a digestive. Sister Mandrake eyed me with distaste. 'You'll have seen the change list?'

'Yes, Sister.'

'I've already complained to Miss Pettigrew that I'll be left without a senior cadet but it appears there's nothing she can do about it. Barnes and Thompson are already overdue transfer to the wards. They're both excellent cadets and, after the training they've received here, they are well on the way to becoming very good student nurses.' She paused for effect, her scowl growing darker.

'So, I am left with you!' I felt like the runt of the litter who really should have been drowned at birth. Sister Phipps looked apologetic; I noticed she had lost the biscuit and was poking about with a spoon, trying to secure the soggy remains. Sister Mandrake continued, 'There will be two other cadets joining you. Miss Pettigrew has agreed I can have Cadet Nightingale from X-ray; I believe she shows outstanding competence for a young cadet. Also a new cadet, Broadbent, will be starting on Monday. She is seventeen, and will commence training as a student in the New Year but since she has no departmental experience, she is being placed here until Christmas.'

She took breath while I absorbed the information.

The thought of the 'brilliant nurse Nightingale' coming to orthopaedic wiped out the pleasure of seeing the back of Pinkie and Perky. Leslie had worked her way right up mine and Vale's noses. 'I will expect you to show the new cadets what to do. I will not have the smooth running of this department disrupted. I'm sure Cadet Nightingale will pick up the routine rapidly and I hope that Broadbent, in view of her age, will learn quickly.' I could see she was choosing her words as she continued: 'You have not covered yourself in glory since your arrival at Benjamin Hale, Salt. I have found you slow to learn, vague and lacking in confidence. You have a long way to go if you ever expect to start nurse training. Unfortunately, I will have to depend on you in the coming weeks.' She let out a sigh. 'Should I find you incapable of the responsibility required, I will have you replaced.' With this withering comment, a positive boost to my self-assurance, I was dismissed.

Leslie had been animated, like a child about to be let loose in a chocolate factory, from the moment she'd found out about her impending move. 'You've been so fortunate, Salt, working on orthopaedic. You do lots of procedures, testing urine, taking temps and pulses and even proper bed making. All I did in X-ray was file, run errands and make tea. It's going to be such a change. Of course, I already know how to take and record temperatures,' she added. 'And I'm always checking my own pulse.' I remembered my three broken thermometers, strained wrist and undetectable pulse; our upbringing had obviously taken a different route.

'Why are you always checking your pulse, Leslie?' I couldn't resist asking; perhaps she had a heart defect.

'I've done first-aid classes since I was small and it's one of the routine things we learn. I'm also proficient with bandages, burns, sprains, fainting, mouth to mouth, and stings.' As she rambled on about her prowess, I made a mental note to put Leslie down as 'Sister's official tea maker'.

'What's Sister Phipps like?' she added.

'Quiet.'

I'd decided that for Leslie's first morning she could run round after notes and manhandle the Gumption. As senior cadet I would do the important bits, though it would mean working with Sister Mandrake. I would welcome the day patients, make sure all their paperwork was correct, test the wee and sort them out for theatre. I would be calm and efficient, no longer a mere appendage to the orthopaedic staff but the cadet with the experience.

When we reported on duty, Sister Mandrake was tied up on the telephone so we presented ourselves to Sister Phipps. 'Show Cadet Nightingale around,' she whispered. 'Broadbent isn't here yet.' I gave Leslie the quick tour and introduced her to Digby and Fran. I expected Broadbent was going through the 'new cadet' routine and would show up later.

We were heading into the day ward and I was busy issuing instructions, which she was jotting down in her little notebook, Leslie was into notebooks. I tried to imitate Thompson and be politely patient. I was just saying, 'And after you've made sure all the notes are available, you'll need to scrub the sluice, it gets in an awful mess,' when Sister Mandrake waylaid us in the doorway.

'Have you shown Cadet Nightingale around the department, Salt?'

'Yes, Sister,' I replied, in what I hoped was a professional manner. I was just about to add that she was on her way to reception, to see if Mrs Hughes wanted anything finding.

'Good,' she broke in. 'You'd better get round to reception, there are a number of X-rays missing. Sister Phipps has specimens for the laboratory and the plaster room sink is a disgrace. Oh, and watch out for Cadet Broadbent.' With what actually resembled a smile, she turned to Leslie. 'Cadet Nightingale, you can stay in the day patient ward with me this morning. I believe you can already take temperatures and pulses.'

'Yes, sister,' purred the little weasel. 'I can also make hospital beds, but I've never tested urine.'

'Don't worry, I'm sure you'll soon pick it up. I'll test them today while you watch, and you can do them next time.'

With Leslie in tow, she sailed up the day ward to sort out the patients. I didn't know whether to scream or cry. The script was not going according to plan. The unfairness of it, the rotten, insensitive meanness of it, hit me like a hammer. I wanted to stamp. I wanted to go after her, spin her round and shout into that nasty, toad-like face that I was the senior cadet. I was the one who'd suffered for the past two months. I was the one who'd learnt how the department ran and I was quite capable of helping in the day ward. I could now take temperatures (even though I had broken three thermometers along the way). I could find a pulse, though I didn't bother checking my own on a regular basis, and I could test wee, even if it came in a scent bottle. For a painful thirty seconds, I hovered in the ward doorway as Leslie and Sister slipped behind a set of bed curtains. Seething and hurt, I spun on my heel and headed for reception.

'What are you doing here?' asked Fran.

I was almost beyond speech. I just about managed to whisper, 'Sister Mandrake sent me.'

'I thought you'd be queen of the day cases today.'

'She's got Leslie Nightingale in there instead.'

'Bitch!' hissed Fran. 'It's just like her to play favourites. Never mind, Sue, you go and hunt these X-rays, get you out of her way for a bit.'

I could only manage a nod, as she added, 'Cheer up, love.'

I picked up the specimens and, swallowing deeply, I was outside, glad of the fresh air. As I scooted round to the laboratory and X-ray, my mind was not on my tasks. I was building a mental bonfire, piling up files and wheelchairs, adding a few beds and the plaster-room sink. Then right on the top, tied to her office desk, I secured my guy: a sour, orthopaedic department sister. With glee, I poked a flaming brand into the bottom of the heap and happily watched her evil smirk disintegrate as she roasted.

Later in the morning I was just finishing off the hated sink under Digby's sympathetic smile when the door opened and a pale face, followed by a crisp, new yellow overall, looked in. 'Hallo,' said a hesitant voice. 'Are you Cadet Salt? I've been told to find you.'

'That's me,' I answered. 'Chief Gumption wielder and official cadet of dirty sinks.'

'Oh,' said the new yellow, taken aback. I gave her a welcoming smile. It wasn't her fault that Sister Mandrake was a bitch and Leslie a sneaky, sucking-up little rat.

'Sue Salt,' I said, extending a soapy, red palm. 'Welcome to the mad house.'

Wendy Broadbent was a neat little thing, looking younger than seventeen with her wide innocent smile and green eyes. She reminded me of a rabbit caught by surprise in a car's headlights. She wore her dark hair up in a bun and, as with all new cadets, her overall hung on her like a yellow shroud. If anything, Wendy looked worse than most because she was so tiny, just topping five foot, and the overall seemed to drown her. Her shoulders and waist were lost in the floppy shift, which bulged at the front, hunting for a forty-inch bust which she clearly didn't possess.

For the second time that morning, I did an educational

tour around the department. Unlike Leslie, Wendy did not make notes and looked even more terrified than I'd been that first day – and that took some doing. We went on a lost-note hunt and came back via the lab and Cas. I started to feel a little better as I passed on my knowledge of hospital geography to the bemused new girl.

Leslie greeted us on our return. 'Sister Mandrake says you have to take Broadbent to first break and also to first lunch.' The cheek, passing on her orders. The only consolation was that, being on first break, I'd catch up with Vale. I'd been expecting, as senior orthopaedic cadet, to be at second sitting. I guided Wendy to the dining room, where we met up with a harassed Vale.

'You might have Mandrake but at least she's sane. Tizz is completely batty. She's found a tiny piece of muck that she swore was a mouse dropping. "Mice, girl, we've got mice!" she boomed. She's had me crawling round every skirting board and hole, mouse hunting. Me, mouse hunting!' Vale gave Wendy a nod. 'You want your head examining. Go and find a nice clean shop to work in, anywhere's better than this place.' We were busy rushing down boiling tea and ginger biscuits. 'Anyway, what are you doing on first break? I thought you were chief cadet over in the bones department?' she asked.

I gave her a brief run down on the morning's happenings. Wendy was very quiet, obviously overawed. 'You poor sod,' consoled Vale, as I told my tale of woe. 'First Mandrake, now Leslie as well. Mind you, I found out a few titbits about dear Leslie, and you haven't got a hope.'

'What?'

'Comes from a long line of Nightingales. Mother's a deputy matron down in Manchester, father a doctor, two sisters in nursing and a brother training to be a heart surgeon. Plus God knows how many aunties and cousins all up to their armpits in bandages and surgical spirit.'

'She never said.'

'Plays her cards close to her chest, our Leslie. Most likely her mum and old Mandrake are bosom buddies. Give it up as a lost cause, Salt, and just keep out of their way.'

Vale's words proved to be prophetic. Leslie speedily became Sister Mandrake's right-hand cadet. Not only was she personally groomed to assist in the day care ward, but she was soon invaluable within the clinics. As Broadbent and I rushed around finding mislaid X-rays, hunted through filing cabinets for redundant notes, dashed back and forth to the laboratory and scrubbed everything in sight, Leslie was never far from Sister Mandrake's elbow. If I went into one of the clinics with messages or forms, there she was, next to the consultant, looking after the patient or passing vital equipment.

Wendy took over as tea cadet, until I found her weeping about the ordeal. If anything she was more frightened of 'that Mandrake woman' than I was, and she was treated even worse. The choice comment reserved for her was: 'You don't have the brains of a ten year old, let alone a girl aged seventeen who's due to commence nurse training in the new year.'

'Don't let her upset you,' I advised. 'She thrives on being caustic.'

Towards the end of that first week, Wendy confided, 'I don't really think I'll be going into PTS. I only came to work at the hospital to be near Charlie.'

'Charlie?' I asked, 'is he your boyfriend?' She nodded but when I tried to find out more she clammed up, and I was left to ponder who the unknown Charlie could be.

I did have one piece of luck to offset that miserable week. It was the Wednesday weekly cadet inspection. Miss Pettigrew's lecture for that week had been about fingernails. It was difficult to judge which was the greater crime, the long manicured type which could scratch some helpless patient and harbour millions of germs, or the well-bitten variety like mine which looked unsightly and showed lack of self-control. 'Your hands are regularly on show in all areas of your work,' she advised. 'It's essential that your nails are short and well manicured. A neat set of fingernails leads to a neat nurse.'

'And just think where those fingers go,' whispered one of the senior cadets, who'd been airing her expertise that morning in the locker room about how to push a suppository into a fat backside.

The lecture over, we were dismissed. As I turned to leave, Miss Pettigrew held me back. 'Nursing Cadet Salt, just a minute.' As always when singled out for attention, the last few days whizzed through my mind as I hunted for misdeeds. Since I never did anything right for Sister Mandrake, I was prepared to be reported and only amazed that I wasn't permanently standing in the corner.

'I want you to take over as laundry cadet,' she advised. 'This will entail you opening up and running the laundry room on Wednesday afternoon and Saturday morning each week.'

I could have hugged her. No more Saturday mornings in Cas, plus a full afternoon away from Sister Mandrake every week. I'd no idea what the laundry cadet did, but it had to be an improvement on dashing around casualty each Saturday with a tin of Gumption.

'You pick the key up from the porters' lodge in the lower hospital and take it back when you close up. The laundry will need sorting and everyone who picks up their clean linen has to sign the book. That's about it, Salt,' she finished, though I felt she wanted to add, 'even you can manage that.'

I felt like skipping from the administration block down to orthopaedic that morning. Vale and Wendy were waiting, worried that I was in trouble. 'That's a doddle of a job!' said Vale. 'And since we start college next week, that means you'll only have to work in orthopaedic Monday and Tuesday and half-day Wednesday, and no Tizz on Saturday. You've actually got lucky, Salt.'

'About bloody time,' was my reply.

If I was expecting regret from Sister Mandrake at having to forego the pleasure of my company each Wednesday afternoon, I was in for a disappointment. When I told her of my new appointment, she merely curled a lip and muttered, 'I'm sure we can struggle along without you, Salt.'

'Sarcastic bitch!' was Vale's comment.

'I'll be all alone,' said Wendy. She didn't count Leslie as either ally or protector. They'd hardly exchanged a word since she'd had arrived; Leslie was much too busy being 'the right-hand yellow'.

'You'll have to manage next week when we start college. You really will be alone Thursday and Friday.'

Wendy looked slightly green. Since she was only going to be a cadet for a few months, it had been decided that there was no point her going to college with the rest of us. I wondered if she would head in the tracks of the vanishing Mellor. 'Charlie says it's only for a few months,' she said, brightening.

I was airing my opinion of 'little Broadbent' to Vale as we walked up to the changing room on Friday morning. 'I thought she was going to faint yesterday when Mandrake pitched into her. She jumps whenever she hears her voice. I wish her Charlie, whoever he is, would talk her into quitting before she makes herself ill.'

'It's a wonder "her Charlie" hasn't told Sister Mandrake where to put herself,' said Vale, with a mysterious smile.

'I'm sure the Dragon wouldn't take a jot of notice of some young porter, or whoever he is, telling her anything.

More likely get him sacked.'

'Well, she might be able to get him sacked but not for giving her a mouthful.'

I looked puzzled. Vale had obviously tapped into the grapevine. 'What don't I know?'

'Who Charlie is.'

'Well?'

We'd just entered the hospital corridor. Vale leaned closer and whispered, 'Mr Charles Stanton Bree, Senior Charge Nurse, Ward 3.'

I stopped in my tracks. 'A charge nurse!' I gasped.

'Shush!' warned Vale. 'It's supposed to be a secret.'

'Then how did you find out? It must be a rumour.'

'It's true. I've seen them together.'

'Where?'

'I had to go with a patient to X-ray and I saw them as I was coming back.'

'Saw them doing what?'

'Snogging,' said Vale, with a small note of triumph.

'Good grief! He's old enough to be her father.'

'He's nearly old enough to be her grandfather,' Vale added.

'Are you sure they were snogging? I mean, she didn't have a fly in her eye or something?'

'It doesn't take a big sloppy meeting of lips to get a fly out of your eye. No, my trusting Salt, they were definitely at it.'

'But she's as timid as a mouse,' I said amazed. 'Perhaps she's got a crush on him, a bit like a pupil–teacher sort of thing.'

Vale laughed. 'I had one hell of a crush on the PE teacher but sadly I never got to grips with him. Our little Wendy isn't as innocent as she looks.'

'He's obviously taking advantage of her, it's disgraceful.'

'Come off it, Salt, don't be a prude. Perhaps it's love.'

'Love my foot, she's a fool.' I tried to get my head round this amazing news. I'd only seen Charlie Bree once; he was handsome in a middle-aged, distinguished sort of way. Greying at the temples, a kind, fatherly face, no paunch – but as a boyfriend for a seventeen year old, it was unbelievable.

'Are you going to ask her about him?' said Vale.

'She's always going on about Charlie. She worships him but she clams up if I ask anything.'

'No wonder. If it got out that he was having it off with a cadet, they'd both be out on their ears.'

'They might not be "having it off", perhaps they're just friends.'

Vale snorted. 'Salt, you're a gem. I can see I'll have to sit you down for a quiet word about the birds and the bees. Trust me, oh my naive mate, they don't get together to discuss his etchings. They're at it.'

I bowed to her greater experience and wondered if I should tackle Wendy, or leave well enough alone. With the first Saturday of my elevated position to laundry cadet looming, and our first session at college following in the next week, I decided to leave the problem for the time being.

For the first time since my arrival at Benny's, I did not dread Saturday morning. The thought of not having to scuttle around Cas with the crazed Tizzy on my tail was wonderful. In many ways, my removal from Cas was a pity. The accident and emergency department lived up to its name and, under different circumstances, would have been the best place possible as an introduction to hospital life. No one knew from minute to minute what would come through those battered swing doors, and all sorts of nursing experience was available within its confines. Even Vale, on occasions, had been present at life-and-death situations but her abilities had never had any chance to develop, as Sister Tissleton had rapidly despatched her to clean. That was the trouble: Tizzy looked upon cadets as additional domestics so gave them no chance to learn anything except how to wield a dish cloth and scrubbing brush. I pitied Wendy, who was being plunged in at the deep end that morning. Vale had promised to look after her but if Wendy's reaction to Sister Mandrake was anything to go by, she'd no chance round Tiz.

I had to collect the linen room key from the porters. I signed on, and headed up the main corridor to the porters' booth. It was a semi-circular, reception-type cubicle, half glazed, which fronted onto a small back room. The booth was empty, so I pressed the button which should summon a porter.

After repeated button pressing no one had appeared and I was growing desperate. Miss Pettigrew had impressed on me the importance of opening up the linen room promptly at nine. It was now nearly ten to, and I still had to trek up to the changing room then all the way back to the administration block. The linen room was on a small corridor half way between Matron and Miss Patton's offices. Whatever it was doing there, I didn't know. It would have seemed logical for the clean linen to be picked up from the vicinity of the laundry.

I looked with increasing agitation into the empty booth and saw a small cupboard on the wall with KEYS written in bold red. There seemed no choice so, hoping I wasn't going to be caught in the act of trespass (everyone was very territorial in Benny's), I inched through the side door. I swung open the cupboard door and was delighted to see a small brass key announcing LINEN ROOM. But, as I was lifting it off the hook, without warning the cupboard jumped off the wall and hurled itself at me. I ended up on the floor in a pile of debris. As the cupboard fell from the wall, it bounced off my head and landed on a wheelchair which upended and clattered into a table. Overcome by this full-frontal attack from a combination of cupboard, chair and cadet, the table collapsed, throwing the porters' tea-cups, teapot, sugar basin and milk across the booth.

I staggered up, deciding I needed danger money to work at Benny's. No porter had appeared during the disaster; where were they all? Was there a strike that no one had thought to mention? Not quite cutting a straight line, I slipped out through the door and, casting a quick glance about, decided to escape.

Staff nurses, students, cadets, auxiliary nurses and ward orderlies all collected their linen from the hallowed room. The main delivery came from the laundry on Wednesday and this had to be sorted. On Saturday it was just a matter of opening up and keeping everyone happy. It was obvious that I was going to fail on both counts. It was ten past nine when I reached the administration block and headed to the linen room. There was a very irritated queue, ten deep.

'You're late,' said the staff nurse in the lead. Those behind her shuffled forward like a crowd of mutineers, muttering threats and casting black looks in my direction.

'Bloody cadets,' I heard a pimply ward orderly say.

'Sister will be in such a foul mood if I'm not back soon,' muttered a brown-belted second year student.

With profuse apologies, I grovelled round in my copious pocket for the key. Some people are put on this earth to open any door that comes their way; not me. Keys have been my downfall on numerous occasions. We had an elderly, castle-sized key for our front door at home. The combination to this varied from three turns left, two turns right, a jiggle and a kick, to repeated turns and obscenities as frustration grew. I stood on many a wet day, struggling unsuccessfully to break the code, with the rain dripping off my nose.

I pushed the key with difficulty into the laundry room lock but got no further. It refused to turn. The impatient crowd took turns, the men (who would never let a mere key defeat them) taking a lead. The key was forced in and out, yanked backwards and forwards, and the door was given a few hearty shoves. Nothing. More 'laundry-picker-uppers' had arrived, thronging the corridor. I heard anxious voices from the rear of the queue demanding, 'What's the hold-up?'

'I've only got five minutes,' trembled a small voice. 'Sister will play hell if I'm late back.'

'I must have a clean apron, I've got to see Matron on Monday,' said another.

'This is ludicrous!' A furious looking staff nurse, who was all bust and bustle, pushed her way forward. 'I have far more important things to do than waste my time standing here.' She seized the key and jammed it back in the lock. Her man-sized fist pushed it reluctantly right, then left. She got her shoulder to the door and heaved. 'Are you sure you've got the right key?' she demanded.

I was now on unsafe ground. No one had actually given me the key. 'It says linen room,' I said. She nodded and continued banging and generally abusing the lock, which still refused to budge.

'It's the wrong key,' said a quiet, knowledgeable voice from three back in the line. It was a student nurse, wearing a blue first-year belt. 'I was laundry cadet for three months and the right key says NURSES LAUNDRY ROOM. That key is for the cleaners' and porters' linen room; they gave me the wrong key once.'

The news was passed down the irate line, like Chinese whispers. 'She's got the wrong key.'

'It's not the right key'

'The key's wrong.'

Head to head, cap to cap. Mutters and curses and

unpleasant looks were cast in my direction. Worried eyes searched watches. In despair, most of the line began to disperse.

'I can't wait any longer, Sister will have my guts.'

'I'll be in awful trouble with no clean apron.'

'I'll blame the laundry cadet when Sister says my cap's dirty.'

'I wouldn't mind, but a baby sicked all over me last night and this uniform stinks!'

My first morning as designated cadet in charge of laundry for nearly the whole hospital – and I'd messed up! I didn't think it would be possible but at that moment I wished myself back in casualty, running around with the Gumption. Only the furious staff nurse had stayed the course. 'Well, I'm not budging,' she announced. 'I refuse to work in a filthy uniform because of your inefficiency. You can just go back to the porters' desk, and get the right key.'

'Yes, Staff Nurse,' I said. Back across the car park, over the road, past the nurses' home, in through a back door and down into the lower end of the hospital. My mind raced much faster than my legs; I started worrying how I was going to get the right key without admitting that by finding the wrong key, I'd wreaked havoc in the porters' lodge. I resolved that honesty was not the best policy. I got on well with the porters and I didn't want to get on their wrong side by admitting I'd entered porter-designated territory without permission. There was a good chance that each porter would think the other one had given me the wrong key and merely exchange it without argument. Having made my plan, I was quite proud, feeling that Vale's training in duplicity was paying off. Just a few weeks before I would have owned up, but I was now learning the art of deception which was essential for survival in Benny's.

I arrived back at the porters' booth, to be greeted by the

police. A small crowd had gathered including porters, a group of cleaners, an ambulance man and a few nurses. 'What's up?' I heard one ask.

'Vandals,' a nurse announced, 'or a robbery, they're not sure which. It seems the porters were only away for a few minutes and when they came back everything was tipped up and keys and things thrown all over.'

'Terrible, isn't it? No respect some people, fancy vandalising a hospital. Whatever next?' I felt like I'd been dunked in cold water as I pushed my nose through the gathering.

'Were there any witnesses?' asked one of the cleaners.

'No, they're that quick these teddy boys. Steal yer' teeth, if yer' mouth's open.'

'Do you think it were teddy boys?' asked her friend. 'Perhaps it were a drunk out of Cas.'

'Bit early for a drunk.'

'Some folks are drunk any time. My auld feller, he likes a tipple with his breakfast.'

'That's not all yer auld feller likes with 'is breakfast, is it, Mavis?' There was general laughter as my cold water was turning into a hot flush.

I managed to reach the counter. The head porter was in deep conversation with a couple of policemen who were busy taking notes. 'Do you think anything's missing,' I heard one ask.

'Difficult to say with all this mess, but I don't think so. We keep anything valuable locked up in the safe round t'back. There might be a key missing, we keep lots of them here.' The policeman continued to take notes. 'Mike's checking.'

Mike had a line of keys laid out across the counter. There was a good assortment of Yale keys and varying sizes of larger keys. Each held a tag but reading upside-down wasn't my strong point, especially when I was trembling like a jelly. I knew Mike quite well. He had steered me in the right direction on a number of my 'hunt-the-department' expeditions, and had provided at least one cup of tea well laden with sympathy. He continued sorting through the keys, like a jailer intent on keeping the inmates locked up. I screwed up my courage. 'Mike, love, I've got the wrong key. Can I have the one for the nurses' laundry room? There's a hell of a queue and they're all carping.'

He glanced up from his task. 'Bad do this is, Susie. Can't turn yer back for a minute, without trouble. I'd like to get my hands on the little blighter that's made this mess. Screw his neck I would.'

'Awful, isn't it?' I consoled, hoping I looked genuinely concerned. 'You won't get into trouble, will you?' I asked, a sudden pang of guilt stabbing at my conscience.

'No way. I had to take a patient to X-ray and George was off down Ward 4. Can't be everywhere at once.'

I heaved a sigh of relief; at least I wasn't about to get anyone sacked. 'Which key you got?' he asked.

I handed it over. 'He's a daft bat that George, giving you the wrong one, yer first morning as well. This is the one you want.' He held up my much-needed treasure. 'You feeling alright, you look a bit peaky?'

I was thankful I was not in handcuffs; peaky I could manage. 'I've just dashed down from the admin block.'

'Anytime you need the key, if there's no one here you'll find it in that box on the wall. Well, it was on the wall before these damn vandals pulled it down. You just help yourself,' he said.

'I'll do that,' I said as I hurried away.

Chapter 10

Hettie and Herbert

We started at the college of further education, which was a short bus ride from Benny's, the following Thursday. It was a modern building and my first experience of anything resembling a skyscraper. It soared eight storeys high and had lots of glass. It was set in its own grounds and boasted flower beds, lawns and a tennis court. It had only opened a few months earlier and we were forever being informed how fortunate we were to be able to study in such convivial surroundings. For most of us, the smell of newness was unknown. Both of my past schools had been elderly and creaking at the joints. My primary, on the backstreets of Thorpe, had not even had indoor toilets, and I had bitter memories of dashing across the pitted playground to the 'outside lav' in all weathers. Our house was late nineteenth century; in fact, apart from Vale's fairly new, faceless council house, I'd never set foot in anything in mint condition.

There were fifteen first-year cadets. Apart from those who had arrived the same day as Vale and me, there was a bunch who'd trickled in between Easter and June and a few who had appeared since July. This latter group, being our juniors, were treated to our wisdom and guidance.

The pre-nursing department was the domain of a husband-and-wife team, who went by the unfortunate names of Mr and Mrs Smallcock. Hettie Smallcock was the ugliest woman I had ever met. She was sallow and greasy, with great horn-rimmed spectacles and pimples. She had the most appalling dress sense and regularly appeared in a combination of puce-green skirt, bright yellow blouse and shocking pink cardigan. Hettie was into cardigans and had an amazing assortment in varying degrees of technicolor. Hettie taught English, anatomy and hygiene, the latter being a contradiction in terms, as at times her halitosis was quite overpowering.

Herbert Smallcock, whose name naturally left him open to snide remarks, was the typical absent-minded professor. He was nearly bald, with just a few strands of hair combed over his pate; these had a habit of wafting backwards, making him look lopsided. He had a narrow face, pinched mouth and wispy moustache. He always had this sort of doleful bloodhound droop, and we immediately dubbed him hen-pecked. I only ever saw him in the one suit, a run-down affair with cigarette ash brushed into the lapels and reinforced leather on the elbows. He taught mathematics, science and biology.

The third member of the team was Sister Prewitt, who taught physiology and nursing. She was a dumpy woman who threatened to burst from her bulging uniform, but she disproved the theory that fat people are a jolly bunch. Prewitt was stern, with a sarcastic tongue and unpleasant nature. I pitied the patients who had ever been at her mercy and I couldn't but help wonder how nursing, which was supposedly such a caring profession, seemed to attract such a bitter bunch of women. Was it because they had never married? Most older nurses trained in the era when nursing was a lifelong vocation, leaving no room for husband and children. Perhaps their gentle, compassionate side was reserved for their patients.

Our only other teacher spared us two hours every fortnight. This was Mrs Bowers, who taught invalid cookery and dietary matters. I was never quite sure what use it would be in my future career to know how to make egg custard and since my efforts would have poisoned the healthy, let alone the sick, it was a good job I never had to demonstrate my meagre abilities.

The nursing department was on the top storey which, if nothing else, provided a good view over Thorpe and beyond. Besides the cadets from Benny's, there was the first intake of pre-nursing students, a new concept which sadly hadn't been around when Vale and I had left secondary school, eighteen months before. These lucky creatures could either study for a year before applying to be cadets, or stay on until eighteen when they were ready to start as students. This gave them not only three years of student perks, but the chance to gain a good handful of GCEs in academic surroundings. We agreed they had it very cushy.

I was unable to tempt Vale into the lift: this, along with spiders, was one of her phobias. 'I got stuck in one a few years back,' she confided. 'I was terrified and felt like I was choking. I can't bear the things.' Since we were slightly late, this meant a dash up the stairs; we were both in a state of near collapse at the top, deciding we were not destined for the Olympics. 'Too many hospital rice puddings,' said Vale as we rushed into Room 80, just ahead of the Smallcocks.

I naturally headed for a couple of spare seats on the back row but Vale dragged me to the front, where the first row remained empty. Apart from pop concerts, the first row is invariably avoided, everyone piling towards the back leaving a void, a no-man's land at the front. I was amazed that Vale should want such a forward position.

I didn't think she had intellectual ambitions and I knew her hearing was unimpaired. 'You don't get asked any questions on the front row,' she hissed, adding, 'trust me,' when I looked doubtful.

We'd heard reports of the Smallcocks and they didn't disappoint. Hettie took command as they entered, followed by a scowling Prewitt. Hettie introduced herself and Herbert, nodding towards Prewitt with the words: 'And we are very fortunate to have Sister to start guiding you on your pathway to nursing.' As Herbert sat quietly behind the desk, playing with his fountain pen and looking over our heads to the huddled majority at the rear, Hettie outlined our next two years.

'Has anyone any qualifications?' she asked.

Leslie's hand shot up. 'I have two GCEs, Mrs Smallcock,' she simpered. 'English language and geography.'

'Very good, dear,' Hettie smiled, and I could see that she was about to become a signed-up member of the Nightingale fan club.

'Before you go into PTS training at eighteen, we hope to give you a sound grounding in anatomy, physiology, biology, science, hygiene and some nursing. You will also be able to expand your English education, hopefully to GCE level, develop mathematics to aid you in the future, and learn the basics of special diets and invalid cookery.' I felt quite exhausted listening to her; if we'd expected a couple of nice quiet days each week, our hopes were rapidly being dashed. 'We also trust you will take advantage of the various amenities of the college. As students here you will have access to the library and sports facilities.' At this point she gave Herbert a nod; he was obviously on.

Sadly he missed his cue because he was busy pen-twirling and developing some advanced theory in his head. She gave him a dig and he sprang up like a Jack-in-a-box. 'Well, yes, good morning, gals,' he blustered, dropping the pen. He grovelled round the floor, chasing the escaping instrument which ended up under Vale's shoe. He grappled under the desk ('for a quick glance up my skirt,' Vale assured me later).

'Right,' he said. 'Let's get to know each other. If we could go round the class and introduce ourselves. Just stand up in turn and say your surname, then first name or names afterwards.' This seemed a totally pointless exercise as we all knew each other. There was one fresh face, a new cadet who was starting that day. With a few nervous giggles, we made our speeches. There was something really off-putting about standing up and saying, 'Salt, Susan', but it was soon over.

The new cadet's turn arrived. She was a slender girl with reddish hair and freckles. She stood up, opened her mouth, changed her mind and looked down at the desk. 'Come on, dear, don't be shy,' Herbert urged.

She shuffled her feet and played with the sleeve of her jumper. I wondered whether it was merely nerves or was her name even worse than Smallcock? Herbert was growing impatient. 'Well?'

The poor child took a deep breath and found something fascinating on the desk to stare at. Then in a weak voice she said, 'Strange, Jane.'

The class erupted. As Strange Jane blushed, we screamed with laughter and we continued to laugh until we ached. 'Poor sod,' I thought, 'she's never going to live that one down,' and she didn't: she was Strange Jane from that moment.

Our first science class with Mr Smallcock was nearly our last. I've never been able to understand where science finishes and chemistry begins. The only science we were into at school was domestic science; our teachers were more convinced of the importance of brass and silver cleaning than the inner workings of the atom. I was an expert oven scrubber and could scour a table with the best, I was even capable of making a respectably stiff starch. Only my recent venture into orthopaedic urine could in any way qualify as science.

It was our first Friday college morning when we assembled in the science room. As Herbert wandered in, he had the look of a cocker spaniel that had strayed by mistake into the ladies' toilets; he looked around, wondering if he'd ever seen any of us before. 'Perhaps he thinks he's in the wrong room,' whispered Vale, as Herbert sent the register sliding along the tabletop to splash into the adjoining sink.

He spent the next few minutes fishing it out and drying it, muttering, 'Dear, dear.' He now had difficulty with the smudged, inky remnants of the register. 'Answer to your names,' he announced, rubbing his spectacles before settling to his task. 'Odeby?' Silence, until Jill Hornby realised she'd been renamed. I answered to 'Sat' and Vale to 'Piss', which was an interesting beginning to the day.

Things started to get exciting when we were instructed to get a Bunsen burner and a rack containing glass vials from our cupboards. Being an expert wee cooker, I had a slight edge on some of my fellow yellows. Only the indispensable Nightingale was any better, having received special instructions from Sister Mandrake.

'I see clever pants is sharing her wisdom,' said Vale, nodding in Leslie's direction.

'Let's hope she blows herself up,' I muttered.

'Attach your rubber tubing to the gas tap, girls, but don't switch on yet.' Herbert had an unfortunate habit of lowering his voice at vital moments so his instructions tended to vanish into his moustache. Because of this, a strong smell of gas wafted from most work stations. 'No, no, switch off,' stammered Herbert.

'Be careful when you do light it,' I warned Vale. 'The

first time I encountered a Bunsen, I had it too high and I nearly melted my eyebrows.'

Herbert had assembled an assortment of various-sized glass jars containing a multi-coloured mixture of elements, the use of which he had failed to explain. We weren't even sure what concoction he wanted us to boil. He pushed the jars around his worktop, lovingly caressing a jar of some yellow, powdery stuff.

'Gunpowder,' Vale assured me, as he took a small scoop and added it to his glass holder.

'Watch carefully, girls,' he advised, pouring in a little white fluid. It bubbled happily as it started to heat up over the Bunsen, turning a sickly green colour.

'Whatever's he making? asked Rose Browning, who was at the next table. 'It looks like boiling frogspawn.'

'My baby brother filled his nappy with something like that the other night,' another yellow was heard to say.

'All take a measure,' said Herbert, as the bottle containing the yellow stuff was passed from table to table.

'What did he say?' asked Vale, as most of the others looked puzzled. 'Was it "take pleasure"?'

'A measure. What's it smell like?' I asked.

'Bad eggs,' said Vale.

'What are we making?' asked Browning, looking alarmed as her green liquid started to smoke.

'It's a surprise,' Vale hissed. Quite a few were having Bunsen-burner troubles, and I was delighted to see Leslie leaping back in fear as her flame shot up in the air, narrowly missing her nose.

We all had a good boil going and the air was gradually growing thick with steam and pale green smoke. A few were coughing and most of us had trickles of sweat beading our brows. I noticed that only Hudson remained unaffected and continued looking calm and cool as she fried her green goo. 'It's all that laundry training,' said

Vale. 'She'll most likely need a fur coat in a hothouse after being used to all that heat.'

'Now we add the final ingredient,' said Herbert triumphantly, unscrewing a dark brown bottle, the contents of which I never discovered. It was marked with some obscure formula known only to Herbert. He plunged an eye-dropper into it and, as we waited in growing expectation, he slowly added four drips to the boiling concoction.

We watched as if a genie were about to burst out and grant us three wishes. For a few seconds nothing happened; the only sound in the room was from the jolly bubbling of numerous green mixtures. Then, to Herbert's delight, the solution turned red then orange. 'See,' he said with satisfaction. He was just on the point of passing the final mystery ingredient around, when his bubbling mixture suddenly shot upwards like a volcano and orange smoke began to billow from the gurgling remains.

The smell was appalling, as if twenty skunks had let loose at once. Trying to hold our noses, we made a dash for the door through the thickening orange cloud. 'Leslie's passed out,' someone yelled, as a body slumped at my feet. Eyes streaming, I grovelled around and found her gasping on the floor.

'You take an arm and I'll take the other,' Vale gagged, as we pulled her towards the door. We made slow progress; the Nightingale felt as heavy as a St Bernard as we dragged her across the science lab floor. Through the choking smoke and coughing I could hear Herbert.

'It wasn't supposed to do that,' he kept repeating.

We poured out of the lab pursued by stinking orange smoke, which travelled like marsh mist on our heels. Coughing and choking, we assembled at the far end of the corridor. Faces pouring with perspiration and a slight orange tinge to our wet cheeks, similar to a ward of elderly bronchitics, we hacked and spat into increasingly soggy handkerchiefs.

Hettie came flapping up the corridor as the pre-nursing students emptied from a classroom and made a dash for the stairs. Herbert, the captain abandoning his ship, was last out. He staggered through the laboratory door clutching his throat dramatically, a good splatter of orange coating his jacket front. I couldn't help noticing a new hole in his lapel where the potion had melted the fabric. He fell into Hettie's arms as she cooed, 'Herbert, Herbert, whatever have you done? Are you all right?'

'True love,' whispered Vale, between coughs.

Thankfully Leslie had come round and I noticed she was rallying rapidly, not even coughing – unlike the rest of us. I had a sly suspicion she'd been playing for effect, and could just imagine the tale she would tell Sister Mandrake.

Hettie, having assured herself that Herbert would live, now directed her attention to us. Most of the coughing had subsided and her main aim was to make sure that we were all kept sweet so that no one created any trouble by daring to suggest that Herbert had nearly killed us. 'Well,' she started, choosing her words, 'is everyone all right?' The other students had vanished downstairs, leaving our group like the remnants of the *Titanic*'s passengers hove-to on the landing. 'These things happen,' Hettie added. 'No harm done. You can all take an early luncheon.'

A couple of anxious looking men came rushing out of the nearby lift. They groped for hankies as they drew nearer, screwing up their faces against the prevailing pong. 'Whatever happened, Mrs Smallcock?' asked one of the men. 'Do we need to evacuate the building?'

'Oh, no, no, no, Mr Jones,' said Herbert, before Hettie could open her mouth. 'Faulty Bunsen burner caused my potions to intermingle; be fine when the smoke clears.'

'Are all the students all right?'

At this point Hettie took control. 'They're fine, just slight coughs.'

'But the smell, Mr Smallcock,' complained Mr Jones, as the chap with him heaved.

'It will soon dissipate, never worry,' Herbert assured him.

'Off you go, girls,' cooed Hettie. 'Come along, Herbert,' she ordered. 'We'll go to the staff room, for a nice cup of tea. I hope you're not going to have one of your chests,' she added, as she led him away.

For some strange reason, they called the students' dining room the refectory. 'Must think we're a load of monks and nuns,' Vale had remarked the first day. It was spacious and well appointed. The food was plain and basic but a definite improvement on Benny's cuisine. It was to here that we debunked, some still coughing and Leslie looking an odd shade of orange. Most of us didn't have much appetite and I felt vomity. The obnoxious smell seemed to cling inside my nostrils and I could have done with a bath and change of clothes.

'We still don't know what the daft bat was making,' said Vale. She'd chosen a red jelly and tea, scorning the offered lamb, mint sauce and veg. Everyone from the top floor was there and we swapped survivor stories.

'I thought the whole building was going to blow up,' said one.

'I was terrified we'd be gassed,' said another.

Browning thought the gas might be poisonous and quite a few felt a fleet of ambulances should have ferried us to hospital.

Vale had dredged her mirror from the depths of her bag. 'It's made my mascara run,' she moaned.

Hettie appeared some time later and swept around us like Old Mother Hubbard. Mr Jones, who was the college principal, felt the upper floor should be left empty for the remainder of the day to allow the smell to disperse. The pre-nursing students were to go home and the cadets could go into the library reading room for private study. Hettie came up with 'The Life History of Urine' as our essay assignment. 'Make us all want to pee all afternoon,' Vale advised. 'Make sure we flush the evidence away.'

The reading room was an annexe to the main library set apart for private study. Reference books filled shelves along one wall; the remainder of the room was filled with tables and chairs. We settled in, our minds far removed from urine. Our original intake took up part of the centre table: Pierce, Browning and Laundry Hudson, along with me, Vale and Leslie. The remaining seats were soon filled by three lads who had a free period from their General Studies course.

The combination of men and female nursing cadets, especially when Vale was present, was not to be underestimated. Urine was soon pushed into second place as the boys made jokes, the girls flirted and adolescent hormones started to go into hyperdrive. Vale wasn't really interested but if the options were between male company and investigating urine, the choice was easy.

Leslie was having none of it and, ignoring the proceedings, buried her head in a book. She was very into pee. 'Did you know that they drink their urine over and over again in London?' she said, looking very knowledgeable.

Vale gave me a wink. 'Well, that's one place I'll leave off my round Britain tour.'

'Is it true what they say about nurses?' asked one of the lads.

'What's that then?' Vale asked in all innocence.

The boy sniggered. 'You can practise nursing on me anytime, sweetheart.'

'I'm particular who I practise on,' said Vale.

'It's a miracle we're here to practise on anyone,' put in Hudson. 'We were all nearly killed earlier today.'

'What happened?' asked the lads and Chris Hudson, who we were to discover was not as quiet as she made out, plunged into the story, happily embellishing all the gory details.

'Wish I'd been on hand to do mouth to mouth on you,' said one of the lads.

'I'm an expert in mouth to mouth,' said Hudson, slipping from her chair to sit on the table.

'Fancy doing mouth to mouth on me, sweetheart?' It was the lad in the centre, Bad Taste might have been his middle name. He was all leather and badges; I wondered how they ever allowed him into college. 'What part of the hospital do you work in?'

'The operating theatre,' declared Hudson. 'You have to have a strong stomach to work in there.'

'I bet you've seen some sights,' cooed Bad Taste.

'There's nothing I haven't seen,' said Hudson, shuffling up the table and running a finger through Bad Taste's hair. 'Mind you, once you've seen one, the rest are very much the same.'

The conversation was heading into troubled waters and, with a cough, Leslie changed tables and started to hunt through a shelf of reference books.

'Oh, I don't know sweetheart,' said Bad Taste, his hand wandering to Hudson's leg, 'I bet you got something worth seeing.'

'Cheeky,' said Hudson. 'Mind you, it's that hot in the theatre, we hardly wear anything under the gowns.'

'It's all that heat in the laundry, it must have made her randy,' muttered Vale into my ear.

'You've missed yer way, love,' said Bad Taste. 'Yer should have been a model or a dancer. I'd have loved to see you do the dance of the seven veils.'

'I've always fancied being a dancer but me mum wanted me to be a nurse. Pity you don't need your appendix removing, you could drift off under the anaesthetic with me holding your hand.'

'Can't you put on a show and I'll hold on to me appendix, nurse?'

'Ooo, I wouldn't dare give you a show here,' sighed Hudson.

'Thank God for that,' I muttered.

'Come on, Hudson, we better make a start on urine. I haven't got any further than drinking water yet,' said Vale, trying to edge the conversation away from danger.

'Nurse, Nurse, get 'em off, pretend it's the operating theatre,' shouted Bad Taste.

'Off! Off! Off!' chorused the boys in unison. I saw Leslie, slipping out through the door.

Vale nodded in her direction. 'Off to the loo, no doubt.'

Hudson, in the meantime, had climbed up on the tabletop and was busy playing the crowd, refusing to remove anything apart from a pocket handkerchief. She twirled it around her finger in a tantalising way then sent it drifting down onto Bad Taste's head.

'Most likely packed with germs, he'll have flu next,' observed Vale.

'Or even worse,' I said, starting to get slightly alarmed as Hudson slowly, but in a very alluring manner, started to unfasten cardigan buttons one by one. She slid demurely out of her cardy, swung it around a finger then sent it down with a woolly flop over Bad Taste's friend, who quickly struggled free so as not to miss an eye-full.

Hudson was now down to skirt and blouse and I think we all expected her to call it a day and regain her seat. Unfortunately Hudson had different ideas as she gracefully removed both shoes then, running a well-manicured finger up a trim leg, she arrived at a suspender. Tights were in their infancy and we all wore suspender belts and stockings, which were much sexier for the enthusiastic amateur stripper.

She twanged each suspender and then slid each stocking down her leg in turn before drawing it over her wriggling toes. The lads hooted in delight as she used the stockings like scarves, curling them round her neck before draping them one by one over Bad Taste's shoulder.

'I could never do that,' I whispered to Vale. 'My feet are much too sweaty, most likely knock the poor chap out.' Bare footed, Hudson trod the table, twirling ever so often. Surely this had to be the limit of her theatricals.

'Off! Off! Off!' chanted the lads, drumming their hands up and down on the table. It was Pierce and Browning's turn to chicken out. Grabbing their books, they did a bunk to the far end of the room. I had a feeling Vale and I should go as well but I felt some sort of responsibility for the crazed Hudson.

'Come on, Chris, get down,' I urged.

'You've proved your point, Chris,' said Vale. 'Don't let these idiots egg you on.'

'Off! Off! Off!' yelled the lads, gaining volume.

'She's not got the nerve,' put in Bad Taste. 'She's all mouth and knickers.' The mention of knickers seemed to have a bad effect on Hudson, who started on the top button of her blouse and slowly worked her way down to reveal a pink underslip.

'I hope she's wearing a vest,' I said to Vale.

'At this rate, she soon won't be wearing anything. Do you think she's on something?'

I shook my head in disbelief as Hudson's blouse went sailing across the room in the wake of her cardigan. This was followed rapidly by her skirt which, as she freed button and zip, slid down onto the table where she stepped out of it and paraded up and down the table in her pink slip. I was getting desperate. I stood up and tugged at her undies. 'Do get down, Chris, there'll be hell on if anyone comes in. You're just making a fool of yourself.'

'Oh leave her alone, Salt, if she's got no more sense,' said Vale.

'But what if someone comes? Oh, do get your clothes back on!' I pleaded.

'Spoilsport,' said Bad Taste.

'She won't take anything else off, she hasn't got the bottle,' said his mate. He got up as he spoke and I detected a slight paleness around his gills. I wasn't the only one worried that someone would walk in. 'Come on, Jeff, let's go and grab a coffee.' I realised I had an ally as he tried to dislodge his pal from the performance. But the main participants had other ideas.

'Five pounds says she won't peel the rest,' said Bad Taste, pulling a fiver out of his wallet. A fiver was rarely seen in our circle and Bad Taste slipped up a notch into the 'well-heeled, but foul and scruffy' category.

His pal hesitated, torn between winning a fiver and the horror that she might actually 'do it'. Common sense prevailed. 'No bet, she's daft enough for anything. Get yer kit back on, darling, or we'll all be in the shit!'

I noticed that our half of the room had emptied. Some of the cadets had followed Leslie and debunked, most likely for urgent bladder emptying. The remainder had found the far end of the room safer and were poring over books and scribbling intently in the pursuit of urine.

'Five pound for you then, darling,' said Bad Taste Jeff, wafting the fiver. 'Five pounds says you haven't the nerve to take the rest off.'

'You're on!' she cried, slithering out of her underslip to reveal white bra and knickers.

'Good job she turns out respectable, with everything freshly laundered,' said Vale, who had abandoned all thoughts of urine.

'That's it, we're off,' I said, grabbing Vale by the arm. 'If anyone comes in, we're not going to be caught leering up her bum.'

'I was enjoying the show,' moaned Vale, bundling up her books. We retreated to where the alarmed, huddled masses were whispering and exchanging worried expressions.

'She's a right one!' said Browning. 'I always thought she was really quiet.'

'It's all that heat in the laundry, addled her brain,' said Vale. 'Oh God, she's unhooking her bra.'

'She's crackers. Here grab this book, look busy,' I urged, thrusting a book into Vale's hands. My unfortunate choice from the shelves was *The Naked Ape*.

Hudson was prancing around the table in nothing but a wispy pair of knickers, twirling her bra around an extended index finger. The bra did a number of cartwheels before she let it fly. There was a distinct intake of horrified breath as the bra spun from her fingers to plaster itself in a delicate swirl of lace across the open mouth of Hettie Smallcock.

We didn't see Hudson again after she was bundled out of the library wrapped in Hettie's copious pink cardigan. It was decided that she was an unsuitable candidate for a future nursing career and that the hospital laundry would have to rub along without her. I never discovered what path she took, but she certainly had both the nerve and the attributes to follow in the bare toes of Gipsy Rose Lee.

I did hear that Bad Taste was suspended for a week. I dare say he returned to his studies with an enhanced reputation and not a stain on his character, but such is life.

We were sent from Hettie's presence with a lecture on decorum and homework comprising not only an essay on the dreaded urine, but for some reason a chapter to read and questions to answer about the structure of the

Victorian sewer system.

'That woman is obsessed with bodily waste,' said Vale.

Chapter 11

Wendy

I was sitting in the laundry room a few Saturdays later. By now the hullabaloo over 'the great college striptease' had died down. We had received a long lecture at Miss Pettigrew's weekly gathering, and even Miss Patton had made an appearance. She stood in stern rebuke before our assembled ranks and assured us that, in all her years in charge of junior staff, she had never heard of such a disgraceful incident. She hoped that nothing like this would ever happen again and said that Matron had been obliged to write personally to the college authorities to apologise. The senior cadets treated the event as hilarious, only wishing they'd been present when the bra found its target. As a group we felt the lecture unjust; Miss Pettigrew behaved as if we'd been indulging in a naked orgy.

I'd rapidly got the hang of the workings of the laundry, enjoying my peaceful Wednesday afternoons when the large tin boxes arrived. These had to be opened and the contents sorted onto the relevant shelves in alphabetical order. This took a couple of hours but I made sure I stretched the task out by spending time neatly arranging the bags. I also locked the door so no inquisitive person of importance could wander in; this allowed me to curl up with my latest novel before official home time. Yes, Salt, I thought, you finally have got lucky.

I now had Saturday mornings under control. I arrived promptly to open up and, because of my careful sorting, I could lay my hand easily on the required item, no matter how irritated or rushed the intended recipient. There was the awkward customer, of course. Some bitchy staff nurse would arrive demanding clean linen. With increasing impatience and purposeful looks at a fob watch, the nurse would wait as I hunted. She could be called anything from Ainsworth to Zabbin, but if her linen wasn't on the right shelf, I didn't have it; trying to convince her was another matter.

'It doesn't seem to be here,' I would say.

'Look again, it must be,' she would demand. After a second search, I would still be empty-handed.

'It must have been put on the wrong shelf,' Irate would declare. 'Check the ones around it.'

I obeyed orders even though I was certain nothing would be found. My search complete, I still had no linen bag for her. She would now take matters into her own hands since she was dealing with a brainless cadet. She would plunge in like a tomb robber pillaging an Egyptian treasure house and everything would be dragged out and tossed around, resulting in a general mess. Empty handed, she would stand amid the debris without a word of apology.

Linenless, Irate would now be blowing fire and the third degree would begin. 'Why isn't my clean linen here?' she would demand.

'It mustn't have come from the laundry,' I'd say, stating the obvious.

'Why?' she'd yell, as if I were personally responsible not just for the cleaning of her mucky uniforms but also for pressing, sorting, packing and delivering every item. I would try to explain my minute part in the many stages from her sending her blood or vomit-stained pinnies to the wash until they eventually arrived back into my care. It was wasted breath; as far as she was concerned I was the villain.

This particular Saturday, all had gone well and the initial rush was over. I could now expect an intermittent trickle for the remainder of the morning. My role as laundry cadet meant I was unable to take a morning break but I did have the compensation of being able to lock up at one and get off duty a little early.

I'd just unpeeled a chocolate bar when a voice interrupted. 'Oh Sue, I've had the most awful two days.' It was Wendy. I sat her down on an empty linen tin and shared the chocolate. The poor girl was really in need of a stiff drink and it wasn't long before the tears gushed out, and both of our hankies were needed to mop up the flood. She bubbled on about Sister Mandrake and her cruel tongue. 'She said-d-d,' Wendy stuttered between sobs, 'that I was completely useless, and – and that if I don't improve, she'll, she'll report me to Miss Patton. The only thing that's keeping me going is Charlie,' she added.

I edged around the subject. 'Do you see much of him?'

'It's difficult, we don't dare let anyone know.'

I tried to look puzzled. 'Why don't you want anyone to know?'

'Well, I told you he works here.' I nodded. 'He's quite a bit older than me but I'll be eighteen in December,' she added defensively.

I was never very good at deceit, even after Vale's lessons. 'It's Charge Nurse Bree, isn't it?'

Wendy leapt up in horror. 'How do you know? No one knows. Does everyone know? Oh God! I'll get Charlie sacked!' and she dissolved into further tears.

'It's all right,' I said, putting an arm around her shoulders and patting her hand in what I hoped was a consoling manner. 'Only Vale and I know and we won't tell anyone. Honest.'

'But – how?' she blubbed.

'Vale saw you and Charlie together on her way to X-ray. You were down that side corridor,' I coughed, 'and you were kissing. If you don't want to get found out, you'll have to be more careful. Anyone could have seen you.'

More tears. 'I love him so much, Sue. He's a lovely man.'

'He is a lot older than you, isn't he?' I ventured.

'Not really, he's thirty-six but it's with him being a charge nurse and me just a cadet, there'd be hell on if anyone knew.'

'You'll have to keep your distance while you're on duty. If anyone else gets wind of it, the story will be round the hospital in minutes. The grapevine works like jungle drums.'

'If I could just see him during lunch breaks, I think I could put up with Sister Mandrake. He can't even give me a lift in case anyone sees.'

'Why ever did you come to work here?'

'I wanted to be near him,' and she dissolved into tears once more.

'Why don't you give in your notice? There's other hospitals, and if you didn't work here it wouldn't matter who knew.'

'I must have a job Sue; we're saving up.'

'Well, you could earn a lot more in a shop or factory.'

'But I've always wanted to be a nurse.'

'Be honest, Wendy. As cadets, we're treated more like domestics than nurses. Why not earn a bit of money somewhere for a few months then come back as a student?'

'But then I'll see even less of Charlie. We do manage to see each other occasionally during the day. If only we had somewhere safe we could meet for lunch now and again.'

'That's almost impossible in this place, everywhere's like a railway junction. The only spot I ever find any peace is down in the orthopaedic basement.' The moment the words were out of my mouth, I knew I'd put my foot in it.

'That's it!' Wendy exclaimed, mopping at the remaining tears as her face suddenly brightened. 'We could meet there for lunch.'

'But Wendy, it's full of spiders and even though I've cleaned it up a bit it's really gloomy.'

'Oh, I'm not frightened of spiders and I'm sure they won't bother Charlie. Just so we can be alone for a little while and if Sister Mandrake's been a bitch, I can tell Charlie all about it.'

'But we're only together on the department Monday and Tuesday, surely it's not worth all the hassle?'

'Two days would be better than nothing. Oh please, Sue!'

'But what if someone wants to go down there while you're' – I hesitated, unsure of what actually would be going on in the dark recesses of the basement – 'together.'

'You can keep the key. Charlie could slip in through the side door, you could let us into the basement then lock it behind us.' Wendy was warming to the idea. 'Then at the time we fix, you could come and open up and Charlie could nip back out through the side door. It's perfect.'

Perfect, wasn't quite the word I had in mind. I still looked doubtful as Wendy went on, 'I've been going to first lunch and she's bound to keep you and Leslie back for second lunch. So you'll be around to keep an eye out and stop anyone going down into the basement.'

'What if I have to go to the same lunch as you?'

'Well, just take the key with you and let us out when you get back.'

'But Wendy, it's a dismal spot to have lunch and what

if anyone sees Charlie sneaking into orthopaedic?' I was rapidly being drawn into more trouble and I could just imagine what Vale would say.

'You could give him a wave to come in when the coast is clear.' Wendy had obviously been reading too many spy novels.

'I'm sure Charlie will think it's much too risky.'

'Oh no, he'll be thrilled to bits. He told me to try and find somewhere safe for us to meet. Oh Sue, you are a pal.' That was me, pal extraordinary, or as Vale would put it, daft.

Wendy was busy planning. 'I'll get some cushions and perhaps a blanket. If I wrap them in a black bag, they could stay down there under one of the shelves.'

I had visions of the basement turning into a boudoir, with Wendy gradually squirreling away items to make her secret trysts with Charlie more comfortable. Perhaps a coffee table with lace doilies and the best china would appear, a candlestick, a couple of stools might follow, with a small Persian rug. I had visions of a mattress being lugged in while I kept watch to make sure Sister Mandrake wasn't on the prowl. At the thought of Sister Mandrake I went cold; what if she went down there for any reason? What if she suddenly took it upon herself to inspect the basement while I was on guard, and they were 'at it'?

God forbid!

'I'll tell Charlie tonight and we'll start on Monday. Oh Sue, you've saved my life,' she said dramatically, giving me a hug. Before I could outline my doubts, Wendy was off with a new spring in her step. It was the elephant all over again: I was lumbered.

'You want your head examining,' said Vale. 'Talk about asking for trouble. Why can't they sort out their own romance? Fancy dragging you into it.'

'I felt so sorry for her.' It was Monday morning and

I'd just met Vale off the bus. I'd been worrying about the assignations in the basement all weekend. I was hoping that Charlie would refuse to have anything to do with it. I poured out the story to Vale as we made our way to sign in, huddled under umbrellas against the October downpour.

'You're a romantic, it'll be your downfall, Salt. If I were you and they decide to go ahead with it, just give them the key and let them fend for themselves.'

'The door won't lock from the inside.'

'Well, can't they jam a chair behind it? If the Dragon finds out, it's not just them that'll be for the chop. She's just waiting for an excuse to get rid of you and if you're not slung out, you'll be off to the laundry before you can say soap.' This threat of 'being sent to the laundry' was a running joke amongst the cadet community. It was akin to being relegated to the lowest football division, or made to sit with the babies in primary school. 'Anyway what happened to your "he's a dirty old man" stance? I'm shocked at you, aiding and abetting naughty nooky,' she went on with mock disapproval.

'It's just somewhere private for them to meet and have lunch.'

Vale gave one of her dirty laughs. 'You don't really think they're going to gather on their cushions and blanket and nibble sandwiches. Come off it, Salt!'

'I did wonder what they could eat down there. I hope they don't leave any crumbs.'

'You're priceless. The only thing they'll be eating is each other. I hope you cough before you walk in on them.'

'Well she is eighteen in December, and he's only thirty-six.'

'Thirty-six!' said Vale. 'He's ancient, twice her age. I think she's looking for a father figure.'

I considered the father-figure idea, unconvinced.

'He's her sugar daddy,' said Vale nodding sagely

I was starting to get more worried; perhaps the dastardly Charlie Bree was trifling with Wendy's affections and once he'd finished having his wicked way with her, he'd leave her with a broken heart. 'It's just like a novel,' I murmured.

'It could end up as a horror story.'

'Perhaps I should have a word with him and find out what his intentions are.'

At this comment Vale laughed so much she choked, the tears running down her cheeks. 'Salt, you're a caution,' she managed at last. 'You'll be taking up marriage guidance next. I can tell you what his intentions are in one word: sex.'

***

Wendy arrived in a last minute dash as Leslie and I were about to report on duty. 'Just give me a sec,' she gasped, as she threw her cloak onto a hook and dragged a comb through her hair. She was still breathing heavily when we reported to Sister Mandrake.

As usual, Leslie was to work in the day ward with the operation cases, and Wendy and I were to look after the clinic, receptionists' needs and all the necessary cleaning. I'd got over my 'senior cadet complex', and consoled myself with the relief of being able to keep out of Sister Mandrake's way. I was far happier dashing around the hospital after lost notes and X-rays or even scrubbing sinks than having to work cheek by jowl with that woman for a whole morning. I still was called upon to test wee if Leslie was too busy in the ward but apart from that I was kept strictly in my place as a down-trodden work horse.

The moment Wendy and I were alone, she gave me a hug and whispered, 'We're on! Charlie will be here at twelve, ready for me to go to first lunch. Oh Sue,' she bubbled, 'it doesn't matter what happens this morning, I'll be fine knowing I'm going to see Charlie at lunchtime.'

Before I could say a word, she rushed off with a contented grin to take a patient to X-ray.

Wendy lived on a wave of expectation all morning. I just worried. The 'what ifs' were growing longer as the appointed hour grew near and, as I surreptitiously slid the basement key off the hook where it was kept behind the reception desk, my heart was thumping. I hid the key in one of my hefty pockets and checked the time, ten minutes to twelve, as I slipped into the day ward to ask about cadet lunches. The last patient from the morning operation list had just returned and was in the final stages of regaining full consciousness. Leslie, looking efficient, was helping another patient to dress. I found Sister Mandrake checking blood pressures and pulses; she gave me her usual glare.

'Send Broadbent to first lunch. Cadet Nightingale will finish off in here and you and she will go to second lunch. Has Sister Phipps almost finished in the clinic?'

'There's about six left to see, sister.'

She nodded. I was dismissed.

I found Wendy hovering outside the plaster room. 'Well?' she asked.

'You're to go to first lunch.'

'Yes!' she burst out, thumping the air in triumph as I passed her the key. She grabbed her cloak and walked along the corridor past Sister's office to the glass swing door, at the far side of the waiting room. As I watched, she slipped into the short hallway leading to the back entrance. Passing the basement door, she paused briefly to slot the key into the lock.

We'd made our plans carefully. Wendy would stay by the side exit where she could keep an eye out for Charlie and see me through the glass door. I would remain in the waiting room and keep watch. When the coast was clear, I would take out a handkerchief and blow my nose (that had been Wendy's idea – I thought it was a bit dramatic). After I gave the signal, Wendy would wave Charlie in and they'd make a quick dash for the basement. Then I would wander along and lock them in. At twelve forty they'd be waiting on the stairs behind the door. I'd unlock it and Charlie would make a quick getaway, while Wendy strolled back into the department as if she were coming back as normal from lunch.

I tried to look casual, wandering around the clinic. Val was busy behind the reception desk and Sister Phipps was ensconced in the clinic with the last dregs of the fracture clinic. Of Sister Mandrake there was no sign; she was still with the day cases at the other end of the building.

I glanced through the glass door and saw Wendy waving; Charlie had arrived. I took a quick glance around, had a final peep up towards the plaster room then, trying to look relaxed, I withdrew my hanky and took a delicate blow. From the corner of my eye I saw a quick rush of yellow and trouser legs then the basement door closed. They were in! As I turned the basement key in the lock, I wondered how often this complex operation would take place.

Throughout the next forty minutes, as I finished off the clinic work, dashed over to X-ray and busied myself with a multitude of tasks, part of my mind was in the basement. The waiting room was deserted as I made my way to unlock the basement door where Wendy and Charlie were waiting. It was the first time I'd seen Charge Nurse Bree close up. He looked older than thirty-six and reminded me of a pair of comfy shoes, worn but reliable. He had a good head of brown hair with slight tints of grey and a swarthy complexion which seemed more fitted to a seafarer than a nurse.

'Thanks, Sue,' he whispered. 'See you tonight, darling,' he said to Wendy, giving her a final peck before he rushed off out through the side door.

'Oh, we are grateful,' said Wendy. 'I've had a lovely lunch break.'

We were to repeat this hazardous scheme every Monday and Tuesday for the next few weeks. Luckily Wendy nearly always went to first lunch and occasionally I went with her. Then, having let the lovers into the basement, I took the key with me, figuring the worse that could happen was a telling off from the Dragon for being foolish enough to keep the key in my pocket. This was far preferable than leaving it lying around.

I appeared to have a constant runny nose as I was always flourishing a hanky in the waiting room. I also looked as if I were developing a nervous tic as I was forever flicking my neck round to watch for Wendy's wave before delving into the hanky. One Tuesday I'd seen Wendy give the sign and I was just bringing out my 'all-clear-signal' when Digby suddenly slipped out of the main clinic. I was caught, hanky halfway to my nose. 'You got a bad cold, Sue?' Digby asked, as he sailed past. I saw a flurry as Wendy and Charlie rushed through the outer door then out again; luckily Digby was too concerned with my germs to notice.

I stuffed the hanky out of sight. 'Oh, just a sniffle,' I said. Digby vanished back into the clinic as Wendy waved again. I had another look around and pulled out the hanky just as Digby popped back out of the clinic. Out of the corner of my eye I saw another dash back and forward. 'You look feverish, love,' said Digby, dabbing a hand onto my forehead. 'You better take an aspirin.'

As the weeks advanced and the lunchtime canoodling sessions continued, Vale persisted in her warning that I was dicing with disaster. 'Hope you've got some plans for alternative employment,' she said. It was the end of November when my luck ran out.

It was a typical Tuesday morning, a busy clinic and

preparations being made for the afternoon. Most of the notes and X-rays had been assembled, with one important omission. Dr Godfrey Leighton was on the afternoon list; he was a well-known local GP. He'd got back trouble and a special appointment had been made for him to see Mr Caldew, the senior orthopaedic consultant. Dr Leighton was first on the afternoon list and it was crucial that his appointment went without a hitch, as any delay caused by missing details would reflect badly on Sister Mandrake.

I spent a good proportion of the morning seeking his notes, which thankfully were located at the bottom of a pile of files in a remote corner of the medical records department. I returned in triumph with my booty, only to start on an old X-ray hunt. Dr Leighton's recent plates were available but Mr Caldew wanted his old X-rays for comparison. The hunt took me to every corner of the X-ray department, around outpatients, until eventually I ended up in the orthopaedic basement.

I hadn't been down there for a while and couldn't help having a quick nosey at Wendy's secret store. I noticed a large black plastic bag tucked under the far corner shelf unit. A quick inspection showed it contained a white hospital blanket and a couple of pillows. There were also two cups, a small tub of sugar and a packet of custard creams. It was a bit like the teddy bears' picnic.

Like a hound on a blood trail I leafed through the elderly X-rays. The designated number was missing and a misfile search on either side revealed nothing. Up and down I went with growing desperation. This was my last chance; if the X-rays weren't here, I was out of ideas. Fran was understanding. If they couldn't be found, that was that, they'd just have to manage without them. Relieved, I moved onto the next task and it was soon time for lunches to be decided.

Leslie was busy finishing off with Sister Phipps in

the main clinic and Digby was well on with the plaster room cleaning. 'You and Broadbent can go to first lunch,' ordered the Dragon.

This meant we were into plan B. I took up position in the waiting room, blew my nose for the all clear and saw the flurry of legs sprint through the basement door. Afterwards I turned the key and pocketed it then, throwing my cloak over my shoulders, slipped out through the side door and went off to lunch.

Vale was telling me about Brian and his new motorbike as we finished the Tuesday mutton stew with cabbage. Hospital food turned us into human dustbins over the years, giving us stomachs like wild boars. We were generally hungry as we expended so much sweat and energy; I never knew an anorexic cadet. We would grudgingly shovel in almost anything, with little thought for taste or presentation; we could also eat at top speed. Meal times were short and even if we were sent off duty ten minutes late, we still had to be back on time. Add on the time spent walking from outlying areas of the hospital to the dining room and the available eating time became very limited. I could guzzle down a laden plate in minutes, no matter how hot. This was a difficult habit to break when I was away from work and it was not unknown for me to bolt down my Sunday lunch like a hog at the trough.

'Brian's taking me to a new nightclub in Manchester on Saturday,' Vale confided.

'How'd you get in, you're under age?'

'Oh, I can easily pass for twenty with me slap on.'

We were just off for a helping of rice and ice when one of the serving ladies shouted, 'Nursing Cadet Salt!' The whole dining room stared in my direction, especially the cadets. To be summoned from a meal meant trouble. 'You're wanted back on orthopaedic by Sister Mandrake,' she continued.

'It's most likely nothing much,' Vale reassured me. Grabbing my cloak from the coat-hooks, I bolted.

My whole cadet career from day one to that moment flashed before my eyes on that short journey, and I was expecting the worse when I arrived at orthopaedic. The morning clinic had finished and an ambulance was rolling away with the last stretcher case. Sister was not in her office but was standing behind the reception desk with an irritated Fran beside her. 'Why didn't you tell me that you had been unable to find Dr Leighton's old X-rays?' she demanded the moment she spied me.

'I didn't think, sister,' I bleated. X-rays were always going missing and I had discovered, with a small sense of pride, that if I couldn't find them no one else could.

'That's your trouble, Salt, you just don't think,' she snarled.

'I looked everywhere I could.'

'Cadet Salt is really good at hunting out lost notes and X-rays,' Fran put in. I could have hugged her.

'Not on this occasion. Where have you looked?'

I repeated the list of possible hiding places that I had exhausted. I tried to put the basement into the list in a non-committal, 'it couldn't possibly be there' sort of tone. Acting was obviously not my forte as she replied, 'It's bound to be in the basement, you can't have looked properly.'

'I'll go and have another search,' I said, hoping my eagerness would put her off the scent.

'Where's the key?' she demanded, looking at the empty hook.

'Oh! I think it's still in my pocket.' I tried to look both surprised and penitent.

'You should know better than to go to lunch with a key in your pocket.'

'I'm sorry, sister, I must have forgotten. I'll put it back

197

as soon as I've finished.' I turned to go, desperate that I should go down the steps alone, but doom stalked me.

'I'll come with you. I must have those X-rays before the clinic starts.'

Like Mary Queen of Scots on her way to the axe, I trod my path to disaster. There should have been a roll of drums: such calamities in life should always be played out to the steady beat of the death drum. I set the key into the lock. Her hot breath blew across my neck. I turned the key, managing to bang the door as it opened. Her shadow blocked the top stair. How slowly could I take the steps? Would the lovers have heard? Was there anywhere they could hide? I was half way down the steps. She trod behind.

As I descended the stairway to hell, I decided a broken leg was better than discovery. Four steps from the bottom, my foot slid off the edge. With a scream, I flailed at the wall and toppled like a drunk down two more steps. The tears of pain were real as one knee scraped the rough stone step, ripping my black stockings. An elbow dragged along the rough casting of the wall, tearing a deep gash. The blood welled dramatically from my wound and I felt light-headed with the shock. Since she was following close on my heels like a lion stalking game, Sister Mandrake nearly came to grief as well. I felt her bump into me. She let out, a very unladylike curse and just saved herself from toppling headlong into me. Instead she wobbled backwards onto her bony bottom with a flap of navy-blue and white. For a second, her legs shot up into the air while I was sprawled in an ungainly heap near the foot of the steps, peering up Sister Mandrake's skirt to her stocking tops and plain white knickers.

She rapidly regained both her feet and composure as I waited for the outpouring of venom about my clumsiness. But in that brief second, without realising, I had been transformed from 'despised cadet' to 'injured patient'. During my time in orthopaedic I had always noticed the kind tolerance that our hard-natured sister, reserved for the milling herd that daily clogged up her domain. No matter how demanding they became, she always treated them with consideration, often apologising to them for their prolonged wait. 'Have you hurt yourself, Cadet Salt?' she enquired gently, edging past me to examine my knee.

'I think I'm alright, I've just cut my arm, sister.' She brought out a clean white hanky from her pocket and wrapped it professionally around my wound.

'Can you stand?' With difficulty I struggled up, the blood trickling underneath the temporary dressing. Thankfully only silence came from behind the closed basement door. 'Let's get you back up the stairs and into the treatment room,' said Sister, all care and concern. With her help, I managed to get back up the stairs. 'Are you feeling dizzy?' I nodded. 'It's the shock. Put your arm over my shoulder and let me take your weight,' she said in the most tender tone of voice she had ever used to me.

We made our way back into the waiting room. Fran came from behind reception and Digby was summoned with a wheelchair. I was pushed into the treatment room where Sister Mandrake bathed my elbow and applied a dressing, while a doctor was summoned. As I explained to Vale later, it was like being the heroine in a melodrama.

At this point Wendy made a quiet entrance, running a finger through her ruffled hair. She looked distressed for my plight and mouthed 'thank you' behind Sister Mandrake's back. One of the doctors appeared, assured Sister no stitches were required but ordered a non-stick dressing, tetanus injection and precautionary X-ray. 'Take Cadet Salt to X-ray, Broadbent. And do tidy your hair with a comb, not a fingernail, before coming back on duty.'

Wendy bubbled the moment we were clear of the

building. 'I nearly died when someone started coming down the steps, then we heard Sister Mandrake's voice. Oh Sue, it was awful. We were scrambling round, trying to gather everything up and expecting the door to burst open any second.' I grimaced with pain as we bumped across the hospital yard. 'Oh, your poor arm, and you've ripped your stockings. You must let me pay for a new pair. I feel terrible.' She gave a small gasp as realisation dawned. 'You did it on purpose'

'Well, I couldn't let her come in and find you.'

She stopped the wheelchair and hugged me. 'Sue, you're the best friend I've ever had.'

I blushed as she conferred purple-heart status on me. 'Oh, it was nothing. I panicked and it was all I could think of.'

We were heading through casualty, on our way to X-ray. Between Vale and me, our accidents were starting to have an expensive impact on the NHS budget. 'I've got something to tell you,' Wendy whispered bending over the back of the wheelchair. I should have seen it coming but I hadn't. 'Me and Charlie are going to have a baby.'

The thought made me go cold. It was the dread that kept most of us on the straight and narrow. 'Getting into trouble', 'being up the duff'. Fear was the most efficient form of birth control. The pill was still a few years off and abortion on demand had yet to come. There were septic abortions carried out on the desperate in seedy back-street houses. Marriage was the usual solution, the man being expected to do the honourable thing.

Wendy appeared to have no worries. 'Isn't it marvellous? Charlie's really made up,' she gushed, as I pondered on whether the little sprat had been conceived on the basement floor.

'What's your parents say?'

'Oh, they don't know yet, but they won't mind. We're

getting married, of course, the Saturday before Christmas, on my eighteenth birthday. It's all arranged.'

Well, that was a relief. Charlie was going to make a decent woman of her. The well-worn clichés ran around my mind as she added, 'We're having a small church do with a reception afterwards, and I want you and Vale to be bridesmaids. You will do it, won't you?'

'I've never been a bridesmaid,' I said, picturing myself in flowing pink or lemon, following Wendy down the aisle with her emerging bump showing through her virgin white dress. 'I'd love to and I'm sure Vale will. Ask her as soon as you see her.'

'We owe you so much for keeping our secret and guarding the basement.'

'You won't be needing to meet up at lunch time again, will you?' I asked.

'Oh I don't think we dare chance it again.'

I signed with relief.

By the time I was wheeled back to orthopaedic, Miss Pettigrew had arrived and the junior doctor had been replaced by the consultant, who examined my elbow and the remainder of the arm and shoulder, holding up the wet plates to the light. 'Nothing broken, my dear,' he assured me.

'Luckily you didn't hurt your legs, you could have so easily broken one or even both.' Miss Pettigrew shuddered, most likely thinking about the narrow escape she'd had from all that paperwork. 'And the cut is messy but superficial. Sister's ordered an ambulance to take you home but hopefully you'll be back on duty tomorrow. With it being Wednesday, you can stay at home in the morning and come in after lunch to sort the laundry so you won't have to do too much. Both you and Cadet Pepper have had nasty accidents in that basement; I'm going to make sure the maintenance men improve the lighting and perhaps a handrail needs fitting to the stairs. Until then, take care if you venture down there.' I could almost hear her formulating her next cadet lecture.

'I'll get Digby to make you a cup of tea while you wait,' Sister Mandrake said sweetly, reducing me to an advanced state of amazement.

Wendy was dispatched to the locker room to retrieve my things and, like a victim rescued from a train crash, I was cosseted until the ambulance came. Sadly I didn't warrant a siren and I discovered the rear seat of an ambulance was distinctly uncomfortable. Suffering from a bout of travel nausea, I was glad to reach home.

I created a minor sensation amongst the neighbours when the ambulance pulled up at our door. Quite a few heads appeared and my worried mother dashed out, tea cloth still over one arm. Since neither we nor anyone on our street had a telephone, there had been no way to warn her of my impending arrival. The appearance of an ambulance usually meant disaster and she was relieved when she discovered it was only my elbow. I was unloaded with much fuss and settled in the armchair before the fire, feet propped on the pouffe with my injured arm swathed in bandages resting on a cushion. As I sipped yet another cup of tea and watched the dancing flames, the wedding march was playing in my head.

Chapter 12

The Party

The elbow was sore for a few days but I managed to work. Vale thought the whole event was a hoot and said she wished she'd been a spider on the wall when I'd gone crashing down the steps. She demanded a detailed description of Sister Mandrake's knickers. She agreed to be a bridesmaid, not because of any fond regard for Wendy who she condemned as an idiot, but because she said she looked good in blue which Wendy fancied for our gowns. Vale had been a bridesmaid once before but since she was five at the time, the only thing she remembered was sicking jelly all over the bride.

It was the following Monday before my next appearance in orthopaedic. By then the bandage had been replaced by a large sticking plaster. Fran was all concern. 'Does it still hurt?'

'You were reet lucky not t'break yer neck,' said Digby. 'You go carefully on them steps, they're a death trap.'

Trump had made me some fondant fancies, coated in pink royal icing. 'It's the least I could do, you could have been killed, my dear, or paralysed.' Trump was always the optimist. I thought it wise not to confide the true reason for my near-death accident; sweet she might be but I had a feeling Trump was of the old school and would find the goings-on in the basement disgraceful.

Sister Mandrake's kind 'Digby-make-Salt-a-cup-of-tea' attitude had vanished back up her knicker leg, leaving the Dragon in full fire-blowing mode and, if anything, more nasty than normal. 'You really will have to stop being so clumsy, Salt,' she reprimanded. 'And we never did find Dr Leighton's old X-rays. Mr Caldew was really angry.'

November advanced rapidly and, apart from feeling a bit tired and gaining a little weight, Wendy's secret remained under her yellow overall. 'Good job they fit like sacks,' had been Vale's caustic comment. One Saturday afternoon the three of us went on the trolley-bus into Manchester and bought three off-the-peg dresses. Wendy's was traditional white with a flowing train and net veil. We were careful to choose something with room for expansion and hoped the layers would conceal her bump. Her mum and dad had reluctantly agreed to the nuptials, mainly because of the forthcoming little stranger, but not with the enthusiasm Wendy had hoped for. 'Mum didn't say much, just looked disappointed, but dad said he'd storm up to Matron's office if Charlie didn't do what was expected.'

As December dawned, the impending secret wedding, the hospital party season and our Christmas holidays started to grow in importance.

The nursing cadets finished college three weeks before Christmas, which meant that we returned to work full time at the hospital. We had grown accustomed to the Smallcocks who, though unfortunate in both name and behaviour, were quite good teachers, and the two days respite from orthopaedic had been a relaxing relief. Vale had treasured the break from a continuous diet of Tizzy and said that without the respite she couldn't have managed to make it until Christmas. 'Three and a half days in that mad house is my limit,' she moaned. 'Any longer and I really would have packed in.'

We were to go on holiday a week before Christmas, and our final Saturday before the break was also Wendy's wedding day. It seemed a long time since July. 'I've given in my notice to Matron. She thinks I'm leaving as the Christmas holidays begin but I'm not coming near the place that last week,' said Wendy.

'You didn't tell Matron you were getting married?' I asked. Wendy was the first yellow to quit, which was quite amazing considering the way we were treated.

'Goodness, no. She asked me why I wanted to leave and I just said I didn't think I was ready to take up nursing yet and would try again when I was older.'

'Will you? I mean with the baby, it's going to be quite a while before you have another chance. And you did say you always wanted to be a nurse.'

'Perhaps one nurse in the family is enough but who knows? When the baby's older, perhaps we can work something out.'

'You must stay until after the orthopaedic party, you can't miss that. We deserve to enjoy the party after all the suffering.' Orthopaedic closed down over Christmas and New Year, so the party was held on Tuesday the week before Christmas.

She looked doubtful. 'Well, I suppose I could make the final arrangements in three days. Do we get to wear party dresses or do we have to wear our overalls?'

'Haven't a clue,' I said, 'but I heard some of the cadets talking and they said it's the best of the department parties. Lots of food, music, dancing and even sherry.'

'Where's it held?'

'It seems the beds are taken out of the day ward and it's decorated and there's a tree and presents for everyone. It'll be great. Then only a few more days before the wedding.

In the new year there's a change list due, so no more Sister Mandrake. I might be sent somewhere nice like X-ray or physio. Even outpatients is supposed to be quite good.'

'I hope you don't end up on Cas.'

My face fell. 'Good God, I hope not.'

Vale was also looking forward to the holiday but mainly the change list and getting off casualty. 'I'm marking off the days on the calendar.'

'Do you have a party on Cas?'

'Oh, they have a real shindig on the Wednesday evening before Christmas. I'll be off by then but the cadets and any staff who've recently left the department get invited back. Wednesday is usually the quietest night, but knowing my luck they'll have a bus load in.'

'Can you go dressed up?'

'Oh yes, I've got a new black dress specially and Staff Nurse said I can take Brian.'

The days ticked away and Christmas drew nearer. A large tree, lit from base to peak and with a huge star on the top, turned up on the lawn in front of the main hospital building. All over Benny's, plans were well advanced for the decorations. Each ward and department vied for the best display and there was much competition between the sisters. Some were renowned for their creations and, even amongst all the routine work, time was found to make large tinsel balls, bundles of silver bells and even a lifelike model of Bethlehem.

A large sleigh with a very authentic Santa and reindeers appeared in the entrance hall of casualty, X-ray was transformed with gold hangings, and even outpatients and medical records were bright with paper chains and tinsel. A tree arrived in the dining room and bright green and red garlands brought colour to the lacklustre room. The cadets gushed on about helping to trim the trees, making decorations and the impending parties.

Thompson was working on men's medical. 'Sister's put me in charge of all the decorations. We're having angels with big fluffy wings and trumpets up the hall, and a large Angel Gabriel in the centre of the ward,' she said. 'And Sister's invited me to the ward on Christmas Day for lunch.'

Christmas preparations seemed to be a low-key affair on orthopaedic and we hoped things would buck up nearer to the party. I asked Trump about it one morning. 'I never get an invitation, my dear. Not that I'd go if I was invited. The idea of sharing a social engagement with that woman is intolerable. She either ignores me or goes out of her way to be objectionable all year, so it would be more than I could manage to smile at her across a mince pie.'

Fran was slightly less scathing. 'I keep as far away from her as possible but it is a good do. You'll enjoy it.'

Leslie did little but gush about how she'd been asked to help. 'Help?' I asked puzzled.

'Hand round drinks and food and keep the used plates and cups cleared away.'

'Poor Leslie,' I confided to Wendy. 'She's expected to work at the party.'

'She most likely offered,' said Wendy. 'You know what's she's like. Anything to make us look bad.'

'I suppose we'll have to help her with the washing up.'

Wendy scoffed. 'I wouldn't dream of sharing Leslie's glory. Think of all those brownie points she'll get from Sister Mandrake.'

Vale was surprised when I told her. 'I thought she was Sister's blue-eyed girl. Strange her having to get her hands wet. You sure she's not up to something?'

'Well, I can't see what.'

On the Thursday before the party, Digby was busy taking all the beds out of the day care ward. I went in and helped wrap up the bedding. 'I'll put it back in the linen room,' I offered.

'Grand,' he answered, 'then you can help me get the old decorations out of the top of the linen cupboard. Her nibs is bringing some new ones and the tree should be here any time.'

'Do we get to dress the tree? And what about the decorations?' I asked, starting to get excited about doing something in orthopaedic that I might really enjoy.

'I don't know, Sue. I suppose it depends on Sister.'

My linen cupboard was immaculate. It tended to be Wendy that spent time hiding in there these days; I'd found more reliable bolt holes. Digby got the steps and hauled down the box. We were busy sorting through the tinsel and multicoloured tree balls when Sister Mandrake stalked in.

'What are you doing here, Cadet Salt?' she demanded.

'I was just helping Mr Digby, Sister.'

'Digby is quite capable of managing without you. The sluice sinks need cleaning and the chairs are untidy in the waiting room. When you've finished, Mrs Hughes will have some filing for you to do.' I was dismissed and returned to the Gumption without a further word.

I noticed the tree being carried in half an hour later. Wendy was busy hunting over in X-ray and I was on my way to medical records with a pile of notes. I gave it a wistful look but it was obvious that my tree-trimming or party-room decorating skills were to be left untapped. Having grown used to disappointment during my months on orthopaedic, I could live with it but the news, passed on by a resentful Wendy (who by now was scrubbing mackintoshes in the plaster room), that Leslie was helping decorate the Christmas tree left a very bitter taste.

I searched through my new vocabulary of invectives, mainly learnt from Vale, and muttered all of them under my breath as I polished the wheelchairs and emptied the treatment room bin. 'Never mind,' said Wendy, trying to cheer me up. 'We've got the party to look forward to and not even Sister Mandrake's going to spoil it for us. It'll be my last day at Benny's and we're going to have a good time.'

I curtsied. 'I hope my lady will reserve the first dance for me.'

'Charmed,' said Wendy.

Tuesday, the day of the party, arrived and I could hardly restrain my excitement as I walked with Vale to sign in. She'd had a few ripe words to say about Leslie and the tree when I told her what had happened.

'Pity you and Wendy didn't stick her on the top with a fir-twig up her bum,' she said.

Wendy and I had decided to bring dresses in case we were allowed to change out of our overalls. We also came armed with combs and makeup, ready to transform ourselves from rag-bag yellow lumps into presentable teenagers.

There were just a few patients booked in that morning but the clinic was due to finish early and the department was officially closed for the afternoon.

I sneaked into the day ward just before lunch. The tree was a mass of lights and filled with gold and silver trimmings. Paper chains and balloons swung across the ceiling and a long table had been prepared at one end. I peeped under the white cloth which hid a selection of sandwiches, sausage rolls, canapés, mince pies, chocolate biscuits, trifle and a frosted Christmas cake; there was even a large glass bowl of punch with a very inviting ladle. On another table, trimmed with green and white Christmas crackers, were plates, cups, saucers, cutlery and wine glasses. Every windowsill had been decorated with holly and flowers and there was a bunch of mistletoe over the doorway. Chairs and tables were dotted around and a record player had been installed with a good selection of the latest hits. The centre of the room had been left clear, obviously for dancing.

'Isn't it pretty?' said Wendy, who'd followed me and was peering over my shoulder. 'I'd have never thought this room could be done up so well.'

'Pity it's all got to come down tomorrow. I wonder what's in the presents?' I asked, pointing to the small pile under the tree.

'Well, we'll soon find out, everyone's supposed to get one.'

We shot off before anyone found us and rushed about getting the morning's work finished, not wanting anything to delay our enjoyment of the party.

Leslie had been helping Sister Phipps in the clinic. She popped into the plaster room where Wendy and I were just finishing. 'You're both to go to first lunch,' she said. Recently it had become her task to inform us about luncheon arrangements, but it saved me having to search for Sister Mandrake.

'I wonder if we'll be able to change into our dresses when we get back?' Wendy asked as we bustled off to the dining room.

'Don't know. That's the trouble with this place, no one tells you anything and it's a major crime to ask.'

We both decided just to have a bit of bread and jam for lunch and sat there nibbling while Vale and the others tucked into great bowls of hospital stew and beetroot.

'Hope you have a good time,' were Vale's parting words.

We hurried back to orthopaedic and reported on duty. There was no sign of Sister Mandrake; we assumed she was busy making the final preparations in the party room. Sister Phipps was sitting in the office, completing some forms.

'Reporting back on duty, Sister,' I said. I was wondering if I dare ask about changing out of our overalls. I was just building up to my speech when she laid down her pen and, picking up a piece of paper, turned towards us.

It was the one and only time Sister Phipps ever spoke to me, apart from a whisper, as she passed a piece of paper filled with Sister Mandrake's neat writing.

'This is the list of cleaning Sister wants you to do this afternoon,' she said, either not seeing or ignoring our startled expressions. 'If you finish the list before you're due to go off duty, you are to report to Sister Tissleton and work on accident and emergency.'

My hand trembled as I took the cleaning list, realising that Wendy and I were not invited to the orthopaedic Christmas party. We headed to the plaster room, stunned into silence. With each step the need to cry grew stronger then a terrible rage gripped my soul. If this was the truth about nursing, they could keep it, I'd had enough. My young, long-suffering shoulders had stood so much since my arrival in July. I wasn't perfect but I had tried. I'd worked hard under difficult conditions with little help; I'd overcome my fears, learned a great deal and made the best efforts I could to contribute to the smooth running of the department.

I felt like Cinderella who'd taken the wrong turning out of the pantomime. My fairy godmother had gone on strike and, 'You shall not go to the ball, and that's that!' were the words that tumbled around in my head.

We stood in the plaster room, seething with resentment, the two ugly sisters in yellow. 'Well, you won't be needing your party dress,' I said. 'If we'd have known, we could have at least have had a decent lunch.'

'It stinks! I wonder if the cadets normally go to the party?' said Wendy. I think she was more upset for me than herself; after all she was only three days away from her wedding.

'Fran and Digby didn't say anything and I'm sure they would have if they knew we wouldn't be invited.'

'And that bitch Leslie's there.'

'Helping.'

Wendy snorted. 'Helping herself to a plate full of goodies.' She threw a tin of Gumption in the sink. 'I am so glad I'm leaving, I feel like walking out this minute.'

'Well, it's done for me, I'm not coming back after Christmas.'

Wendy looked shocked. 'But it's different for you. I'm only leaving because of the baby and Charlie. You've never thought of doing anything but nursing.'

'No, when I was six I wanted to be a ballerina and I went through a short holy spell when I fancied being a nun.'

'I don't think you could manage the "bally", you'd never get up on your toes. But there's still time to take holy orders,' said Wendy, and we started to laugh. It was laugh or cry, and we'd both dripped too many tears over orthopaedic since we'd crossed its threshold. I looked down the list of cleaning and screwed it up in a tight ball. 'If she thinks we're going to clean this lot, she's wrong. All these damn cupboards are spotless, she won't have a clue whether we've done them or not.'

'What if she comes checking?'

'She'll be too busy stuffing her face and chatting.'

'I hope she chokes on a sausage roll,' said Wendy. 'Are you really going to leave? You might be sent somewhere nice after Christmas.'

'Knowing my luck I'll end up on Cas with crazy Tizz. No, I'm off.'

We decided to take a few things out of the treatment room cupboard just for show, in case anyone came in. Not that I really cared. I was tempted to throw on my cloak, head for the locker room and then dump my wretched yellow overalls outside Sister Mandrake's office.

The sound of Beatles' music throbbed through to us from the day ward, where the party was in full swing. Since the ward was up a short corridor from where we were supposed to be working, we couldn't fail to hear the hum of voices, laughter and the clink of glasses. We tried to ignore it and spent time discussing the wedding, babies and my future employment plans.

I was wondering if my six months training in advanced cleaning would be of use when applying for another job when the door opened and Fran popped her head in. 'This is where you are,' she said. She held two laden plates. 'I've brought you something to eat. Me and Digby feel so awful that you've been left out, I've sneaked off with these.'

One plate held sandwiches, a pile of cheese straws, a dinky pie each, crisps and pickles on sticks. The other plate held mince pies and Christmas cake. 'I couldn't manage any trifle or punch, but' – and she laid the plates down, groping in her skirt pocket she pulled out a box of chocolates – 'I got you these.'

'You're great, Fran, we're starving. We didn't have any lunch thinking we were going to have a big feed.'

'She's a nasty sod,' said Fran. 'I'm not stopping much longer, she can stuff her party. Digby's already left, he was that cross.'

'Who's there?' Wendy asked.

'Oh, the place is heaving with her cronies and Leslie's having a whale of a time, she's doing more eating and dancing than helping.'

Wendy and I exchanged looks at Leslie's name. 'Typical.'

We popped the things back in the cupboard and stole away to the basement with our feast. We decided that should the Dragon come looking for us; she'd think we'd gone over to Cas. We stayed down there chatting for the rest of the afternoon.

We knocked off early and, with party music still ringing in our ears, we threw on our cloaks and headed out. Wendy breathed a sigh of relief as the door closed behind her. 'Free,' she said. It was dark as we walked along the short pathway leading from the main door. We could see into the day ward where the party was going strong. Everyone seemed to be having a great time, oblivious to the two little maidens in yellow who had been excluded from the festivities.

My announcement at home that evening that I was going to quit came as no surprise. Dad had been telling me to walk out from day one; Mum had hoped I'd 'give it a good go' but was amazed I'd stayed as long as I had. 'You could always go back when you're eighteen,' she said.

'You find yourself something that pays well and where you'll be better thought of, our Sue,' said Dad. 'A good union, that's what them cadets need, a good union, then they wouldn't dare treat willing lasses so badly.'

I wrote the letter giving in my notice that evening. I found a piece of posh stationery (an unused birthday gift) and a matching envelope, and used my best handwriting. I truly wished I had a lump of Gumption to enclose in the envelope, it somehow felt like a fitting end. I licked the envelope; once I'd made the decision, I slept well knowing that my final few days at Benny's would soon tick away.

With the letter in my bag, I jumped on the bus to work. It felt like I was carrying a time bomb. I really wanted to wave it around and tell the anonymous travellers that I was resigning. Vale was appalled when I told her. 'You can't leave me alone,' she cried. 'You're the only person I like in the whole hospital. Most of the cadets are either stuck-up pigs or idiots. You just can't leave, Salt, I won't let you.'

'Yesterday finished me. It's just not worth all the upset.'

'You've nearly done on orthopaedic. You need never set eyes on Mandrake after you leave the department.'

'But there's Sister Mandrakes all over the hospital. They run most of the wards. They dress up as secretaries or receptionists but they're just like her. From Matron down, they're a bunch of bitches, ruling their little empires, guarding their X-rays or records. If I leave one behind, I'll meet another. I just don't think I can cope. I'm not like you.'

'Come off it, Salt, you're as tough as hospital beef. Think of how you battled the spiders, how you coped with Ethel and nearly broke your neck to save the lovers. We're a team, Salt, you keep me going. You can't quit.'

I shook my head. 'I've had enough. You'll get along alright without me.' I showed her my letter of resignation. 'I'm going to ask for an appointment to see Matron and put it in before the holidays.'

'Oh Sue, please think about it. Wait until after Christmas and if you still feel the same after a bit of a break, post it then. That way you won't need to see any of them again.'

'I might as well get it over with. I'm not going to change my mind.'

'You might. For my sake, give it until after Christmas.'

We signed in while her words ran round my mind. Wednesday morning: that meant after today I only had three more mornings to sign in. Only two and a half days left on orthopaedic and two laundry sessions. The wedding was on Saturday, Christmas was only a few days away. Did it matter that much if I waited?

She kept on at me as we walked up to the locker room and while we changed into our overalls. It was inspection morning; only Vale and me knew that Wendy wouldn't be there. Leslie was wittering on about the orthopaedic party and what a wonderful time she'd had and how she'd got to dance with one of the doctors. I bit my tongue and vanished into the locker; if I said anything, it would be too much. Vale was fuming about my impending departure. I saw her face and knew she was about to blow.

'Well, I'm really glad you had a good time, Leslie. It's a shame you didn't give any thought to the other two cadets on orthopaedic who didn't get invited and were ignored all afternoon, but you were too busy sucking up to Sister Mandrake to think of anyone but yourself.'

Silence fell in the locker room. 'Leave it, Vale,' I said, 'it's all over and done with now.'

'You mean that Sue and Wendy didn't get to go?' asked Thompson.

'Ask her,' said Vale. 'Little Miss Creeper here.'

'I was only asked to go and help.'

'I suppose dancing with the doctors and feeding your face all afternoon was part of the helping, was it?' Vale snarled.

'What happened to you and Wendy?' said Thompson, as all the cadets listened.

'We got a cleaning list.'

'You didn't even get anything to eat?'

'Fran managed to sneak a plate out to us,' I said. 'Oh, let it drop, it doesn't matter.'

'She's that fed up, she's leaving,' said Vale. 'And Wendy's already gone.' There was a shocked silence in the locker room as the cadets took in the unfairness.

Leslie looked hurt. 'Anyone would think it was my fault. I couldn't say no when Sister asked me to help, and I didn't know the others wouldn't be there.'

'Nothing's ever your fault, is it, Leslie?' said Vale, as she bundled her blonde curls up in a bun.

It was the main topic of conversation as we all made our way, crocodile fashion, down to the administration block for the inspection. I was surprised that so many of the cadets were angry on our behalf and I heard a few muttering how they didn't blame me for leaving, and that they would have walked out there and then. It was as if the treatment we'd received affected them all, a communal affront. As cadets, we knew we were bottom of the heap and we put up with a lot but expected these sacrifices to be appreciated.

We formed our neat semi-circle as Miss Pettigrew walked in. Wendy was the only cadet missing. 'Where is Cadet Broadbent this morning?' Miss Pettigrew stared at me as if her absence were my fault.

'No idea, Miss Pettigrew,' I lied.

'I know she was due to leave at the end of the week but I expected she'd have the grace to work out her notice. Was she feeling ill yesterday?'

She did have a bit of morning sickness, I thought. 'She seemed alright,' I said.

'Perhaps she's been sitting on something damp,' Pettigrew mused. Vale and I exchanged looks and I longed to add, 'Well, the basement floor was quite dry really, only a bit dusty.'

'The change list will be left by the side of the signing-in book on the Monday of your return from the holidays,' said Miss Pettigrew, passing on from Wendy's health. She carried out her usual inspection then managed a thin smile as she wished us 'a happy Christmas'. My last cadet inspection was over.

Leslie was quiet as we hung up our cloaks. 'Has Wendy really left early?' she asked sheepishly.

'Yes.' I found it was an effort to speak. I was still feeling emotional and coming back into orthopaedic the morning after made me feel worse.

'And are you going as well?'

'I've written out my notice but I haven't given it in yet.'

'It's not because of me, is it?' She looked appalled; I think she was genuinely upset.

'No, it's lots of things all added together.'

'Perhaps you'll change your mind.'

'I don't think so.'

I let Leslie knock on Sister's door and report us on duty. If I never spoke to Sister Mandrake again that would be fine – but she had one last knife to dig into me. She was alone in the office; Phipps was off until after Christmas. 'Where's Broadbent?'

'She's not come on duty,' said Leslie.

Sister Mandrake gave one of her, bad-smell-beneath-her-nose looks. 'Luckily the department's fairly quiet and there's only one clinic today. I don't expect Cadet Broadbent will be missed; she's not much use when she is here. Cadet Nightingale you can see what Mrs Hughes needs and then assist in the clinic. Salt, you can help Digby take down the Christmas tree and tidy the day ward.'

The anger rose in me like a pipe about to burst. I had been denied the pleasure of decorating the tree and purposely not invited to the party but it quite acceptable that I should now do all the cleaning. As Vale would have said, 'I could have spit in her eye!'

***

I spent the remainder of the week saying goodbye to things in my own mind. I kept thinking, well I won't be doing this again, and that's the last time I'll have to clean that cupboard. I said farewell to the famous basement, I hunted out my last pile of X-rays and delved into the recesses of medical records for a final time.

I choked down my last plate of hospital stew with no regrets, and sat round listening to the gossip, knowing I would soon be forgotten. I'd been a tiny, unimportant cog in a large, busy wheel; I would slip out as ignominiously as I'd come in. I was only a cadet, after all.

Vale was still working on me and I hadn't sent in the

resignation letter, which remained in my bag. Dad couldn't understand why I was hesitating. Mum kept saying, 'She must make her own mind up in her own time. It's a big decision.'

I'd confided in the Trump that I was leaving. She'd been disgusted about the party but not surprised. 'That woman is capable of anything. The way she's treated me over the years is beyond belief. She's evil, my dear, evil. It's a wonder I'm still here. It's had a terrible effect on my health. She'll see me in my grave, she will, but I'm not having her come to my funeral, she'd enjoy it too much. I'll miss you and our little chats.'

I gave her a hug that last day as she pressed a small gift into my hand. 'It's not much,' she whispered, dabbing her eyes, 'but it's been so nice to have someone to talk to for a change.'

'I'll come and see you,' I promised as I thanked her and said goodbye. I closed the door and walked out of her life and, such is the capriciousness of youth, I never saw her again.

I didn't expect a word of goodbye from Sister Mandrake and I didn't get one. She went off duty early that last Friday; the department was closing down for two weeks and she was going on holiday. I presumed Leslie would be coming back to orthopaedic after Christmas, but I was certainly going and Sister Mandrake knew it. As far as she was concerned I'd be off to some other department, with a poor report following me. I was tidying the clinic when she slipped in. Leslie was off somewhere; it was four o'clock, an hour before we were due to finish. She glanced round, her face expressionless. 'Haven't you finished in here yet?'

'Nearly, Sister.'

'I've left some bowls out in the treatment room that need an extra scrub. And make sure all the refuse bins are empty before you go off duty.' With that she was gone, not even a 'Merry Christmas'. Our parting served to stiffen my resolve.

I locked the laundry room on Saturday with a flourish. This had been my final job as a cadet. It was over. No more sloppy yellow overalls; no more being treated like an idiot; no more bad-tempered sisters or secretaries; no more fingernail inspections. I was free. I would enjoy Christmas and, true to my promise (which Vale had managed to tear out of me), I would not post my resignation until Boxing Day.

We met up in the locker room. It was a rush to get to Wendy's, have our hair done and then into the dresses and off to the church ready for three.

'Are you still leaving?' asked Thompson.

'Yes, I think so. I've had a real sickener.'

'I know how you feel. I nearly packed in after the first week,' she said. That statement amazed me: the confident, efficient Thompson, a model cadet, nearly left after only a week. 'I was so miserable,' she continued, 'I used to cry every morning.'

'I could never imagine you like that.'

'It's true. It's a pity you're going, you've come through the worst. It can only get better from now on. Six months and you'll be on the wards and it's different once you're working with in-patients.'

'See,' said Vale, 'it's going to get better.'

'It couldn't get much bloody worse.'

'Think about it,' said Thompson. 'You're done with orthopaedic. It's quite exciting waiting for the change list and wondering where you'll be going next.'

'The laundry, knowing my luck.'

'Who knows? I hear they get cream cakes once a week for all the staff, including the cadets, and ice cream in summer.' She picked up her bag and headed out. 'Have a nice Christmas. Hope to see you back in the New Year,' she said as she closed the door.

I took a long, final look around the locker room, another goodbye. It was a grotty little room, only fit for cadets, stuck away in a neglected underpass. The majority of people who worked at Benny's wouldn't even know it existed and yet it was a tiny piece of space just for us. I followed Vale out with watering eyes.

Chapter 13

Here comes the bride

It was chaos when we arrived at Wendy's. She lived at the better end of Thorpe on a road with trees, gates and front gardens. The neat red-brick dwelling boasted a garage, front bow-windows and an attic. Unseen at the rear was a long lawn and small fish pond, bordered by bushes and a few fruit trees. Her father was a warehouse manager, quite upmarket in those days, and from the sour frown he deposited upon her two eager bridesmaids, obviously believed we were responsible for her fall from grace.

Wendy was blessed – or perhaps burdened would have been a better description – by a clutch of female relations. Her mother was the youngest of six girls, all having produced a welter of female offspring. Wendy was therefore bottom of the pile and had confided that they were a real bunch of stuck-up madams. She had an older brother, Chris, whom she adored but since he was in the navy she saw little of him. Mrs Broadbent had 'come from money', her grandfather having been an obscure member of the landed gentry. Wendy was still taken occasionally to some big hall in the country to visit elderly aunts. Sadly, little of the money had trickled down to Mrs Broadbent, whose comfortable circumstances came with her marriage.

We were ushered in by Celia, one of the cousins, a plain girl in her twenties who looked anaemic. She extended a limp, cold hand. 'You'll be Susan and Val,' she said.

'Vale,' said my companion, immediately relegating Celia to her long list of people never to be seen dead with.

'Wendy's upstairs, she's been vomiting on and off all morning. She must have eaten something that's disagreed with her.'

We exchanged looks as we headed for the stairs. We passed Mr Broadbent and retreated to the front room, where a variety of the female clan were assembled. 'Perhaps it's a bug,' added Celia. 'There's a lot going round. I felt a bit queasy myself the other day.'

It was nudging two o'clock and the wedding was at three. The bride-to-be was throwing up in a plastic bowl as we entered her bedroom. She looked awful, wrapped in a large bath towel, her damp hair plastered around her white face. Mrs Broadbent was in her underskirt, hair in rollers, clutching a crumpled hanky. 'We'll never be ready in time and poor Wendy's ever so sick.'

We'd met Mrs Broadbent a few weeks before when she'd entertained us to afternoon tea. She was a quiet, gentle creature with few attributes. She reminded me of a pedigree poodle who always received second prize but never the cup. Mr Broadbent was obviously the boss, a situation that seemed to satisfy them both. He'd not been present at our first meeting and, having now briefly made his acquaintance, I was sure his absence was planned and not accidental. Our parents had also been invited. Vale's mum had refused; Mrs Pepper was not into social gatherings but preferred her small circle from the bingo. I'd only met her a couple of times and found her distant, with a faint air of sadness. My dad had been working, so only Mum had come. Very impressed, she was, especially by the mock chandelier and glassware. It had been during this gathering, as the two older women hit it off, that my mother had become involved in the forthcoming nuptials and had been booked for the reception as 'the turn'. My mother played the piano and sang and was quite often in demand for similar occasions.

'You go and get your gladrags on and we'll get Wendy sorted,' said Vale, taking control.

Mrs Broadbent nodded and headed out. We could hear a commotion downstairs, laughter and male voices. Wendy lifted her head from the bowl and managed a smile. 'That'll be Chris with his mate. It was just chance him being on leave. He said he'd be here for the wedding.'

'Well, you don't want him to see you like this. Come on into the bathroom for a wash then I'll do your hair and we'll all get dressed,' said Vale.

I grabbed the plastic bowl, which was threatening to tip up all over the carpet. 'Happy birthday,' I said, trying not to look at the yellowy stomach contents, which floated just below my nostrils.

Wendy muttered 'Thanks', then sicked some more. I nearly joined her. I'd never been that good with vomit which helped to reinforce my decision that I really was not destined for nursing.

'Try a glass of water.'

'Take deep breaths,' advised Vale.

We mopped her up as Wendy and I took in lungfuls of air. Vale rushed away to empty the vomit and I shot a tissue back under Wendy's chin as she threatened to shoot out some more. I offered the water, glancing anxiously at the clock which was edging towards quarter past two. Her dress was hanging up alongside the two bridesmaids dresses, but we still had a lot to do before we were ready for the off. Vale came back in minus the sick. 'Right, stop all this daft vomiting. Bathroom,' she ordered.

While Wendy freshened up, Vale attacked my hair. 'Perhaps she won't be able to stop,' I said, as Vale got busy backcombing.

'Well, she'll just have to try. She can't go up the aisle heaving her guts up. She'll have all the congregation at it before she's finished.' The thought made me heave again, bringing an immediate reprimand: 'And don't you start.'

'I think it's the smell,' I said.

'Good grief, what a subject for a wedding day. I wonder what the brother's like?'

'I've never met a sailor.'

'Got bad reputations have sailors, girl in every port. You keep clear, Sue, you've enough problems.'

The bride looked a bit green round the gills when she returned from the bathroom. 'How are you?' I asked.

'A bit better.'

'Come on, Wendy, your turn,' said Vale, popping her down in front of the dressing-table mirror. 'Sue, you be getting your dress on and don't muss your hair,' she ordered. Vale was a great one for taking command. 'She'll be a right bossy sister, one day,' I thought.

It was ten to three and everyone apart from Wendy's parents and us had left for the church. The two hire cars had been waiting fifteen minutes and Mrs Broadbent was hovering in the bedroom doorway. She'd scrubbed up well and, arrayed in a green two-piece with matching hat, looked the perfect 'mother of the bride'.

We'd managed to get the bride and ourselves into our finery. Wendy's silk and net gown billowed down to the carpet, thankfully concealing her bump. Her veil sat in place topped with a tiny replica tiara, and she clutched a flowing bouquet of flowers in one hand and a big handkerchief in the other. The 'bride-trimming' had taken time, with two false starts for minor bouts of vomiting. We'd tried more water and smelling salts provided by her aunty Joan, who'd taken a suspicious glance at Wendy's belly before departing without comment. Looking in the long bedroom mirror, I had to admit that the bridesmaids looked pretty in blue, especially Vale who would have looked gorgeous in a tramp's cast-offs. Taking care of her train, we helped the bride down the stairs. Wendy's mum waited in the front hall, crying. Where did that woman find all that water?

'What a beautiful bride you are,' she wailed.

We were to go in the first limousine with Mrs B and Wendy was following behind with her father. It was just striking three when we climbed into our transport. The church was half a mile away on the far side of town. Our route lay through the busy Saturday afternoon traffic of Thorpe's town centre; we were all going to be late.

'Do you think she'll be okay?' I whispered to Vale.

'Let's hope so.'

Carefully holding her train, we helped Wendy down the short path to the car. Neighbours who were not going to church were out on the street; everyone loved a wedding. There was lots of clapping and 'good luck, girl' being shouted as we settled Wendy into the car. Mr Broadbent still looking stern and said little, but I thought I detected a smile of pride as he saw his daughter looking so radiant.

We slipped into the first car and waved to the crowd. Mrs Broadbent seemed to have controlled herself at last and, giving her eyes a last pat, she slid her hanky away. 'Well, she's made her bed, she must lie on it,' she said. I'd heard this cynical statement before but it seemed out of place coming from such timid lips. I wondered if Mrs B had been in the same position and whether the bed she'd had to lie on had lived up to expectations.

We lost Wendy's car at the cross-road traffic lights. The sky was growing darker by the minute and it was starting to snow as we reached the church. It had been threatening all day and at last the forecast blizzard descended in full fury. Sheltering under umbrellas, we clambered out of the car and made a dash for the church porch. It was twenty past three.

'Tell Charlie not to worry,' I said, as Mrs Broadbent walked into church.

'I don't know about Wendy, we'll have pneumonia,' said Vale, her teeth chattering. 'Why couldn't she have got married in spring?'

'It would have been a bit obvious by then.'

As the minutes ticked away, various anxious relatives popped out of the church, asking for a progress report. It was decided the weather must be to blame as the blizzard was settling into a whiteout. I took a glance up the church where the poor groom was pacing.

Charlie had little family: an unmarried uncle and a few distant cousins. He did have a small circle of friends and one of them, Clive, an old school chum, was his best man. As the time edged towards three thirty, he came down the church. 'Any sign?' he asked hopefully.

I shook my head. 'Don't worry, she coming.'

'If she doesn't come soon, I'm going to need a brandy to ward off hypothermia,' muttered Vale as, through the swirling curtain of snow, I saw the bridal car drawing up. I could just make out the outline of the bride scrambling out of the car, trying to huddle under a small umbrella. Mr Broadbent was looking put-out as he escorted her up the steps into the church. 'We had to stop a few times for Wendy to be sick and the driver couldn't see a thing in this snow.'

Wendy gave us a smile as we sorted her dress. She actually looked relaxed. 'Deep breaths,' I whispered.

We stood like four pigeons on a pole near the font at the bottom of the church, Wendy on father's arm, Vale and me in attendance. The aisle waited ahead and numerous faces turned around, relieved that the bride had arrived. The organ struck up the wedding march and we were off on our stately walk.

Thorpe Parish Church was like the inside of an ocean liner with all the bits removed. It echoed and felt like a vacant car lot, dwarfing the tiny pocket of wedding guests. Wendy's mum stood next to her son and his mate, who both looked very handsome in their uniforms. Her aunties, with their husbands and daughters and a few neighbours, were on the bride's side, plus various family friends and business associates of Mr Broadbent. My mother, who'd been determined to see me in 'me posh frock', sat towards the back, giving me a surreptitious wave as I glided serenely onwards. The groom's family, with the addition of a few friends, only filled three rows on his side. There could have been a better turn-out but since the wedding was still top secret at Benny's, only a few trusted confidants had been invited.

As we neared the groom and best man, I saw Wendy shudder and realised in horror that she was heaving again. 'Who gives this woman to be married?' intoned the vicar, as Mr Broadbent did his bit. As I stepped forward to take the bouquet, Vale slipped me a paper bag she'd been hiding up her sleeve.

'Do you need this?' Wendy shook her head and gazed lovingly at Charlie. He stood holding her hand; his face seeming to shine from happiness within. In his grey dress-suit, silk cravat and carnation, he looked quite marriageable for an old chap and I realised, with relief, that everything was going to be alright.

It had stopped snowing as we left the church and one of those late winter suns was coating the new snow in silver. The old gravestones had taken on a mantle of ermine and the wrought-iron fence around the church was picked out in fine detail. We didn't linger long for the photographs but made a dive for the cars which took us to a small but elegant hotel where the reception was being held.

'It went off quite well in the end,' said Vale, as we hurried out of the cold.

'I hope there's a good feed on, I'm starving. Have you been here before?'

Vale shook her head. 'Could you see Brian bringing me somewhere like this?' We walked past the large log fire set between oak panelling. Horse brasses glinted from the walls alongside assorted stags' heads, and the smell of warm food drew us into the dining room.

The remainder of the afternoon was taken up with food and speeches, those traditional after-the-wedding festivities where the upsets become jokes, and the chat and laughter flow over the refreshments. The dramas of the last few weeks were cast away in the joy of their wedding day and, as it was also Wendy's eighteenth birthday, it was a double celebration.

Later, as evening crept into night and Mother got into her stride on the piano, banging out hits of the day and old favourites, a few more of their friends turned up. Most thought they were coming to Wendy's eighteenth and there was a lot of excitement as they found they were congratulating the bride and groom. Vale and I had pooled our resources and bought them a rose-trimmed tea-set, with a small bottle of perfume as a birthday present. Vale noted there was a shortage of men but we girls danced round our handbags, as was the tradition in the sixties, and they had laid on a good buffet.

I was just helping myself to an extra sausage roll and a few cheese straws when I noticed Mr Broadbent's younger brother, Jack, standing beside me. He'd been introduced earlier and, as so often happened in families, he bore no resemblance either in stature or character to his older sibling. 'Well, it went off alright,' he said. 'You and the other lass did a grand job.'

'Wendy was the star. She was fine once she stopped feeling queasy.'

'She's a silly wee thing but Charlie'll be good for her. Did she tell you he's got a job down south? Better pay and a nice little house. Good for them getting away, new start and all that, especially with the baby.' I started with surprise; I didn't realise he was in on the secret but he just laughed. 'Don't worry, not many of the others know. I think a few guess, but since they've wed before much is showing, it'll soon fade into the ether. She's not the first and she certainly won't be the last.'

'She did mention something about moving away but I thought it was just an idea.'

'Charlie only got the new job confirmed yesterday. She won't have had time to tell you with all the hoo-ha.' He helped himself to a pile of crackers and pate. 'Wendy was saying you've had enough of this nursing lark.'

'Yes, I think so. It's not much like I expected.'

'If what she's told me is anything to go by, you're better away. Have you got something else lined up?'

'No, that's one of the reasons I'm not sure. There's not much else I fancy. I've always had my heart stuck on nursing.'

'Ever thought about antiques?' he asked.

I laughed. 'No, it's never sprung to mind, though mum's dad was an antique dealer. He left us a couple of pieces of silver and a clock but he died when I was quite small.'

'I don't know if Wendy told you, but I have a few antique shops. Two down in the city and another up in Moresbry.'

Vale was waving from across the room for me to come and dance. I didn't want to be rude so muttered something like 'fancy' and started to edge away but Jack Broadbent hadn't finished with me. 'I'm opening a new shop in Thorpe in the New Year. I was wondering if you'd like to come and work for me.'

I stopped in my tracks. 'In an antique shop?'

'There's money in antiques lass. Your granddad would have told you that if he'd still been around.'

'But I don't know anything about antiques.'

'Oh that doesn't matter as long as you're willing to learn. I'm putting my nephew, Harry, in as manager and he'll teach you the business. You'll get to go to house clearances and auctions, and you'll soon catch on what to look for. The pay's not wonderful, well not at first, but I think you'll find it's four times what you're getting now. And the shop's only just round the corner from where you live, so it's nice and handy. If you stick at it, you could be managing one of my shops in a few years.'

For a second or two I didn't know what to say. I'd been considering going to college, wondering if I could manage to pass as a teacher or a secretary, though my spelling was appalling; perhaps it would improve. I liked books; could I get a job in the library? If all else failed, I'd seen myself in a factory or perhaps struggling with obstinate curls in a hairdresser's, even behind the counter of a cake shop sampling the produce – but an antique shop?

'You needn't make your mind up now. This is my telephone number,' and he passed me a card with his name, address and phone number. 'Give me a ring when you've decided what you want to do.'

I took the card, thanked him and slipped away to Vale, my mind busy on elderly chairs, china and chintz. I tried to picture myself rummaging through old brass, blowing dust off ancient pictures or parading my new-found knowledge of the history of Wedgwood. Was this really me? Grandfather, I knew, had grown wealthy on aged pieces of furniture and crockery, not that he'd maintained his fortune, dying almost penniless. Did this interest in antiquated bits and bats run in the blood? Was I destined to be an antiques millionaire, living in a mansion, and not a poverty-stricken nurse making my fortune in heaven, not on earth?

As we circled the handbags to a Rolling Stones hit I drifted away, pulled one way then the other as this new proposition worked its way into my thoughts. The few antique shops I'd entered had been dark, silent and smelled of old man, cigarettes and damp, but did they have to be like that? I wondered what Jack's nephew was like. Certainly not old, and the shop would be newly refurbished, but did I want to dwell in the world of the past and learn more about the dead than the living? My unknown future had been one of the problems of turning my back on nursing: what else could I possibly do? What else did I *want* to do? Now a new door was being opened and all I had to do was walk through it to more money, no more Sister Mandrakes, good prospects and what sounded like it could be an interesting and lucrative occupation. I would be a fool to turn it down.

The offered job became even more attractive a short while later. Wendy had come over for a dance and chat with me and Vale. I noticed this dish of a man talking to Charlie. I'd seen him at a distance a few times but had no idea who he was. 'Who's the tall, dark and handsome?' I asked Wendy.

'Oh that's my cousin Harry, he works for Uncle Jack.' I swallowed; my future boss was gorgeous. Perhaps we could share all that lovely money and the mansion.

We were into the last hour of the festivities. The new Mr and Mrs Charles Bree had departed to spend their first night at an expensive hotel on the outskirts of Manchester. It had seemed a bit extravagant to me and Vale; as she'd observed: 'It's a long time since they had their first encounter.' In the morning they were off on honeymoon somewhere in Wales.

Mother, who had belted out tune after tune, was beckoning from her piano stool. 'Get me another drink, love,' she said. 'I'm fair parched. I'll have a few more bits off the buffet if there's a sandwich left.' I bought her a gin and lime, her favourite tipple, and piled up a plate with left-over food. 'Have you enjoyed yourself?' she asked. 'It's been a good do.' I was just about to answer in the positive when a glass sailed over my head and hit the wall behind the piano. Mother ducked for cover and the two of us dived under the grand piano. 'Thought things were going too well,' she observed, unruffled. 'Most wedding receptions end up with a good punch-up.' She retrieved her drink and eats and we settled down in relative safety as battle raged. Over the years I'd been with Mother to a number of these events and become immune to the accompanying violence which often erupted. Sometimes it ended up with the police being called and us making a hasty retreat; usually it quickly calmed down as ruffled feathers were stroked. We were joined after a few minutes by Vale.

'What's made things kick off?' I asked.

'Oh, Chris heard one of the cousins saying there was more under his sister Wendy's wedding dress than her undies.'

'Bet Mr Broadbent isn't best pleased, him wanting to keep her condition quite.'

'Mrs B's in tears, and her side of the family are quite put out, blaming the other bunch and Charlie's pals.'

'Well, they can't blame them for Wendy's bump. She said before she left that if it's a girl she's going to call her Susan Vale,' I said.

'Poor kid, I always wanted to be called Chastity or Virginia,' said Vale, as we both fell about laughing.

Mother sipped her gin, obviously getting slowly sozzled. I was always amazed how she could still concentrate on

233

the music after a liquid indulgence. It was a good job that Mr Broadbent had laid on a taxi to take us all home. 'You know, you've been a good influence on our Sue,' Mum drawled, putting a motherly arm around Vale's shoulders. 'Real timid she was before she met you. I really worried for her but you've done her a power of good.'

Vale beamed. 'Glad to be of help, but she's all for splitting up this partnership and leaving. I don't think a mere six months influence will be enough. You tell her to stay at Benny's.'

'As long as she's happy, Vale, that's what counts. I don't care what she does as long as she's happy.' She patted my hand, hiccupping. I was on the point of announcing my new occupation when Jack Broadbent's head appeared under the piano.

'You okay down there, girls?' he asked. 'You can come out now, it's all calmed down. Quite a few have left, fights being beneath their dignity. Tom and his mate are nursing black eyes and whiskies, and I'm pouring fresh drinks and sympathy on the rest. Don't think your services will be required again tonight, Mrs Salt, but you've played beautifully.'

We struggled out from our refuge as Jack pressed an envelope into Mother's hand. We helped pack up her music into two battered cases and, wrapped in our coats, headed out to the taxi. It was only when we were settled in its warm depths, heading for home that I had chance to make my great announcement.

'I'm going to be an antique dealer.'

'What?' Vale looked at me bleary eyed. She'd had a few good measures of punch with the odd port in between and she must have thought I was in a similar state. Mother merely smiled. 'As long as it makes you happy,' she repeated between yawns.

I outlined Jack's proposal. 'It's a good offer, isn't it?'

'You don't want to spend your life poking round dusty old piddle-pots and stuffed birds,' Vale slurred.

'Well, it's better than spending all day scrubbing sinks with Gumption and being treated like rabbit droppings by Sister Mandrake.'

'Don't leave, Sue, your life will be so dull without me,' said Vale, an alcohol-fuelled tear lurking behind her mascara.

The street lights flashed by and a fresh flurry of snow hit the windscreen. The taxi hurried through the quiet streets of Thorpe, the silence broken only by a few late-night revellers turning out of the pubs. As the window wipers ticked back and forth, they seemed to be repeating: Stay? Go? Stay? Go? Stay? Go?

Chapter 14

Christmas

It was the 22nd and, like most Christmases, the last few days were a frantic rush. One minute it was weeks away, then just days. There were those last presents to hunt down and the great food stocking-up session. 'You'd think the shops were closing for a month, not just a couple of days,' said Mum, as she filled the cupboards and hoarded bread. She spent the afternoon baking, putting the finishing touches to the party food ready for that evening.

It was a tradition we'd kept for years: three days before Christmas Day we had the neighbours in for the evening. Mum provided mince pies, trifle and a selection of sandwiches. The Simpsons, Margaret and Bill, brought pork pies and bread sticks; Molly Price, the widow next door, made her special fancy cakes, and Sam and Alice from across always provided pickles, onions, crisps, crackers and cheese. The remainder each brought a bottle and by 7.30 the house was heaving.

I was in charge of hats and coats and expected to keep a good selection of music on the record player when mother wasn't at the piano, replenishing plates in between. It was very much an adult affair, each year a couple of mums taking it in turn to babysit the youngsters.

The party was at its height, food and drink flowing in equal measure, with lots of laughter and chat. Mum was heading to the kitchen to refill the egg and cress sandwich plate and I followed to top up the mince pies. 'It's going well. Hope yer dad doesn't drink too much this year,' she said, with a knowing nod.

Just then we heard a terrible screeching coming from the back yard. Mum dashed to the door, flung it open and rushed out. 'That damn stray cat,' I heard her shout, flapping a tea cloth, 'attacking our Tibs again! Go on you great beast, leave him alone, get out!' I was on her heels, just as concerned. Poor old Tibs, we'd had him for years, I couldn't remember the house without him. He was a dark tabby with the most loving nature and excellent habits, but he was growing old and no longer able to command his territory. This wretched stray, a big ginger rogue with ragged ears and a bent tail, had been hanging around since the autumn. A few years back Tibs would have rapidly seen the back of him but now, sensing weakness, the stranger was closing in, asserting his authority.

Never one to flinch from trouble, Mother wielded her cloth like a knight with a sword. Tibs screamed as the stray went for his throat, Mum plunged and made a grab for our wounded pet. In the half-light from the back window I saw a tumble of fur and heard the rising howls of a bitter battle. Desperate to help, I grabbed the yard-brush, bringing the bristles down into an arched ginger mass. With a final squeal of combined anger and fear, the rogue turned into the darkness and vanished over the wall.

Hugging a trembling bundle of old tabby fur with a blood-stained hand, Mum came back into the kitchen. At first I couldn't decide where the gore was coming from: was poor Tibs bleeding to death or was it human skin that had come off worse? It was a bit of both. Tibs' right ear was mangled and dripping profusely but, after pushing Mum's hand under a cold tap, I realised she'd been badly scratched and her ring finger sported a nasty rip.

Tibs shot off upstairs to mop up with his well-practised tongue. 'He'll drip blood all over everywhere,' said Mum, ready to speed up the stairs behind him.

'Never mind him, let's sort you out,' I said, realising from my limited nursing experience and past girl-guide first aid that my mother's lacerations were quite deep. 'You'll have to take your ring off,' I advised. The cut was still bleeding heavily and the finger was already becoming red and puffy.

'It's never been off since your father pushed it on nearly eighteen years ago. I don't think it'll come off,' said Mum, wincing as she tried to wriggle the ring up her finger. Dad came through from the party, all concerned, adding that 'she was a daft bat' thinking she could deal with two tom cats in combat. We tried soap and water but with the oozing blood, pain and increasing swelling it was impossible.

'You'll have to go to Cas and get it cut off,' I said, sounding quite professional. Dad nodded agreement, obviously impressed.

'Cut what off, the finger?' gasped mum.

'No, the ring. Your finger's going to carry on swelling. The ring's already cutting off the circulation.'

'I can't go to the hospital,' Mum exclaimed, busy wrapping a clean hanky round her hand. 'We're in the middle of a party, what will the guests think? I'll go in the morning if it's no better.'

'Your finger might be black by morning then you *will* have to have it cut off,' I warned. 'I really think you should go straight away.'

'That's settled it,' said Dad, taking my expert advice. 'Off you go to t'hospital lass, with our Sue. I'll keep party going and look after everyone.'

Typically for the sixties, no one on our street had a car; in fact I knew only two people who boasted this luxury, a distant uncle who was a mill manager and mother's eldest sister who'd married money. 'Do you think you could manage the bus?' I asked, hoping she wasn't feeling faint.

'I've only cut me finger,' she scoffed. 'But for the damn ring, I'd just put a bit of cream and a bandage on.'

So it was decided, as Mum struggled reluctantly into her coat, that I'd escort the wounded hero of the great cat conflict to Cas via the local bus, while dad held the fort. The guests flocked round with sympathy and advice as word spread. 'Our Barbara's friend did something similar,' consoled Molly. 'Her whole arm turned black. Gas gangrene,' she added solemnly.

It was getting on for 9.30 when we walked up the road to Cas. We'd caught a bus fairly quickly, it was a good service and quiet in the evening. The dark windows of orthopaedic yawned across the yard as we turned into the main entrance to the accident and emergency department. The waiting room, usually a bustling thoroughfare with every seat taken during the day, was almost deserted. Just a small scattering of patients waited to be called and a porter stood with a young chap who was sitting in a wheelchair, his leg plastered and propped. 'He'll have to return for plaster check on Monday,' I couldn't help thinking. 'But he'll have to come here, with orthopaedic being closed for the holidays.'

The reception desk wasn't used after 6pm. Nurses popped out of the department every few minutes to see if anyone new had turned up. We were soon noticed and a third-year student I didn't know came across to us. 'What's been happening to you?' she inquired kindly, unwrapping the bloodied handkerchief which enclosed Mum's hand.

'I got in the way of a cat fight.'

'Not to be recommended if you don't possess claws,' said

the nurse, examining the wound. 'Next time I'd throw a pan of cold water over them.' She turned the hand over and, even through her touch was gentle, Mum flinched, letting out an involuntary cry. 'I'm afraid that ring must come off then we'll clean it up, dress it, give you a tetanus shot and a course of antibiotics. I don't think you'll need stitches but we'll let Doctor have a look, see what he thinks.' She brought out a form and filled in all the particulars. After making sure Mum was able to walk and not feeling dizzy, she led her into the inner department, me in tow.

It was strange to be in the familiar surrounds, unencumbered by Gumption and without the terrorising presence of Tizzy. Though I was not the patient, it was different viewed from concerned relatives' perspective. It seemed somehow wrong when, as Mum was laid on a bed behind the cubicle curtains, I was offered a chair. 'Well, fancy seeing you here,' came a voice from behind me. It was Staff Nurse Fraser who I'd worked with during my Saturday morning stints; she was accompanied by a small Indian doctor. 'This is one of our nursing cadets,' she said. 'So we'll have to take extra special care of her mum.' I couldn't help feeling a thrill of pride at these words. As a mere first-year cadet, I'd been made to feel insignificant, an unimportant figure in yellow, only fit to wield a cleaning cloth. But those few unexpected words somehow elevated me to a member of the staff, part of the hospital.

They let me stay while Mum's gold band was expertly clipped off. 'Sorry,' said Fraser, dropping the offending tourniquet onto mum's palm. 'But I dare say you can have it repaired so you can wear it when your hand's better.' I noticed Mum's eyes were damp and understood that a combination of pain, shock and the emotion of having her precious wedding ring cut off had reduced my normally stoical parent to tears. 'I'll get you a cup of tea,' said Fraser, adding with a wink at me, 'we always spoil our own.'

She'd moved onto nights a month before and when night sister was off duty, she ran the department. 'After working with Tiz, nights are a doddle,' she confided. 'We can get really busy if a big RTA comes in, then I can always ask for extra help. I love never knowing what's going to come through the doors; it can be anything from a drunk with a head wound to an overdose. How are you getting on?' she asked.

'She's thinking of leaving,' said Mum, sipping tea and starting to look a bit brighter.

'That's a shame,' said Fraser. 'Why?'

'I've had a lousy time on orthopaedic and I don't think I can stand much more.'

'But you won't be going back to orthopaedic after Christmas, will you?'

I shook my head. 'But there's so many like Sister Mandrake. Sister Tissleton, for example.'

'Oh, don't let Tiz bother you, her bark is really worse than her bite. You have to learn to laugh at her. As for Monica Mandrake, she's just grown embittered over the years.' It was strange to hear Sister Mandrake called Monica. I'd worked in her department for six months and never seen beyond the sarcastic outer cast. Fraser cradled her teacup. 'She nursed the troops overseas during the war, won a medal but came home to find her parents had been killed in a bombing raid.'

I was astounded. I'd been so busy trying to cope with her cruelty and unfairness that I'd never thought of her as a person with a past. I'd only looked at the flint-like face, the unsmiling mouth, the hooded eyes. I'd seen her stiff shoulders, heard the swish of her crisp, starched apron and her highly-polished shoes beating down the scrubbed corridors, but I'd never glimpsed the woman hiding inside. Suddenly I felt guilty, a judgemental child, incapable of understanding this inscrutable matriarch. 'She was married,' Fraser went on. 'He was a doctor, that's how she came to move to Thorpe, but he was killed in a train crash over ten years ago. No children. I suppose she just grew hard as a way to cope but she is a good nurse.'

I had plenty on my mind as Mum and I walked back to the bus stop.

***

It was Christmas Eve and I was overwhelmed with advice. The resignation letter sat on the mantelpiece like an unwelcome Christmas visitor. 'Well, I think you should jump at it,' said Dad. He'd been set up since I told him about Jack Broadbent's offer. 'It's a grand opportunity. Good money, nice and handy, you can walk there in five minutes. A job with prospects is not to be sniffed at.'

'I know you've had your heart set on nursing since you were little but perhaps it's just not for you,' mused my worried mother. She nursed her bandaged hand but was insistent it was much better and determined to replace the dressing with a plaster. 'I want you to be content and enjoy what you're doing. That time on orthopaedic has made you look real peaky. If you worked for Jack, you could come home for your dinner each day. That'd be nice. Your granddad did well out of antiques sometimes, though he had his failings.'

'Failings?' I inquired, as an unexplained dark page in my family history made an appearance.

'Women,' whispered Mum.

'Gambling', said Dad as Mum gave him a scowl.

'My uncle was an antique dealer, made a mint,' advised the lady in the corner shop. 'My cousins were brought up in a big house with a garden and a greenhouse.' All the shop customers who were listening nodded, looking impressed. 'They should never have wanted for anything, if me uncle hadn't been taken sudden.'

'What happened dear? Was it his heart?' asked old Mrs Potts.

'Drink,' said the shop lady.

I was wrapping presents and admiring our tree, which looked very impressive with tinsel and delicate glass ornaments. So many of the trinkets had been around for ages and were brought out like elderly friends year by year. The star which adorned the crown of the tree had been made by my father when he was learning to be a brass moulder in the local foundry. The multicoloured paper chains had been licked, stuck and put up. Surrounding the central ceiling light there was an ornamental green paper decoration which threaded through a wire circle. This was always a focal point for our Christmas, being sited over the main table. I never knew its origins but it was very old and starting to look a bit weary. I was making a poor job of covering an oddly-shaped package with fancy paper when there was a knock on our front door. It was Vale.

'You any good with string?' I asked.

'Obviously better than you.' She attacked it with professional paper-folding skills and looped the string into a neat bow. 'Are you doing anything this evening?'

'Not really. Mum and Dad are going out for a drink then bringing friends back late on. I might stay up.'

'How about coming to the hospital with me?'

'Whatever for? You'll have to accept it Vale, I've left.'

'But you haven't posted the letter yet,' she said, nodding towards the mantelpiece.

'That's just a formality. In here,' I tapped my head, 'I'm moving on.'

'To dusty old antiques?'

'To a good wage and being treated like an adult. What are you going to the hospital for?'

'To see the carol singers.'

'I can go down Thorpe market for carol singers and the

Salvation Army band.'

'This is different. The off-duty nurses volunteer to go round the wards singing. That student nurse Beryl I got friendly with on Cas, she's on night duty in women's medical and she says we can pop in and listen.'

'I suppose there'll be bother if we're caught, another written-in-blood rule we'll be breaking.'

'What do you care, you've left anyway?'

'Well, I don't want you to get into trouble.'

'No one will see us. Beryl said if we go about nine thirty everyone will be busy and we can pop into the sluice. They put the lights out at ten and the carol singers come soon after.'

'You can go without me. It's cold and there's a good film on the telly.'

'Oh, come on, Sue. It won't be the same by myself. You're deserting me for a load of mucky old antiques, so the least you can do is come with me this one Christmas Eve. I'll most likely hardly see you again when you start your new job.'

'Don't be daft, we'll keep in touch. I'll see lots of you.' As I spoke, I knew it wasn't true. Circumstances and shared experience had pushed us together and we'd built a special friendship, but when we took separate paths we'd gradually drift apart. Vale had Brian and, if all went as planned, they'd be getting married in a few years. We lived a good bus ride apart and neither of us was on the phone. We'd make promises but we'd break them. It would be both and neither of us to blame.

'Okay,' I said relenting. 'What're you up to until then?'

'I've a bit of last-minute shopping and Mum's some friends coming about four and I promised to be back. How about if I meet you at the main gates about nine?

I agreed, and Vale left me to my parcels.

***

244

It was a dark, wintry night with a hint of frost as Vale and I met up. Benny's looked very different at night, the wards filled with golden light. Looking up at the lines of windows, we could see nurses and patients walking about, bed tops and curtains. Many of the windows glinted with Christmas decorations and they gave a feeling of comfort and safety. 'This is one of our nursing cadets so we'll have to take extra special care of her mum.' The words echoed in my mind and I felt sad knowing that I would never again be a part of that partnership of care.

We chatted as we made our way up to the top section of the hospital, treading the well-worn path that I had dashed up and down for the past six months. 'You'll never guess what Brian's bought me for Christmas,' said Vale.

'Lacy black knickers?' I suggested. Vale was into knickers. I never knew a girl that had so many pairs; she was a knickerholic.

'Salt, you are awful,' she laughed. 'You'd never have come out with that a few months ago.' She was right, I had changed during those months on orthopaedic. I'd grown up and learned how to rub along with all sorts of people. I could crack jokes I'd have never dreamed of before, I'd learned how to see the funny side of hospital life and, to the consternation of my parents, I'd even learnt how to swear!

'No, he bought me a fob watch. I'll show the Nightingale. She'll not be the only one who can flip a watch under her chin and look professional.'

'I think Mum's bought me one, she's been saving up. She was all mysterious a few weeks ago when I found a jeweller's receipt.'

'Pity you won't be using it.'

'I suppose I can wear it in the shop.'

'Perhaps she'll be able to swap it for a wristwatch.'

'Perhaps.'

We reached the main door of the upper hospital buildings. There was no need for security in those days and everywhere was deserted as we slipped in past the empty porters' station. The hospital smell hit us as the double swing doors closed behind us but we didn't smell it as much these days. In the first few weeks it had been overpowering and seemed to stick to everything we wore. Now it blended into the background, along with the tranquillity of Benny's at night.

Polished corridors stretched in both directions. I never remember seeing a dirty corridor, no matter what the weather; they always shone with a confident cleanliness. We turned right and hurried along, past the main theatre doors then down a passage to Ward 12, women's medical. Fairy lights with holly trimmings sparkled around the entrance door. Beryl had been watching out for us and waved us into the ward.

I'd been working in the hospital for six months and never set foot on a ward. Women's medical was a long thirty-bed ward of the traditional Nightingale design, with two acute single rooms and three side rooms. Forty beds altogether, which were looked after at night by a senior nurse and three juniors. With it being the night before Christmas, as many patients as possible had been discharged but there were still twenty-five ladies in residence and a very ill woman with meningitis in one of the acute beds.

'We're just finishing settling everyone, then we'll get the lights out. You can watch from the sluice door,' said Beryl, pointing to a door halfway down the ward which led to the main ward cleaning room. 'Merry Christmas,' she added, before rushing off.

'It's quite exciting really, isn't it?' I said to Vale. 'I've never spent Christmas Eve like this before.'

'I spent last Christmas Eve in bed with the mumps.'

'Well, anything's an improvement on that.' We waited,

peeping out of the door and watching the nurses who seemed to do so much in such a short space of time but never appeared to be rushing. 'I'd be a fool to turn down that job in the shop,' I said.

Vale nodded. 'Daft as a bat. I know I've been moaning at you but I'm just being selfish because I'll miss you. It's a great offer.'

The main lights popped out, leaving a small vision of fairyland. A tall Christmas tree nestled in one corner of the ward, clothed in layers of multicoloured lights which cast shadows across the antiseptic white of the walls. A silver star capped its peak and groups of tiny angels hung from the branches. The centre of the ward had been transformed into a miniature village. Streets of little houses, each about a foot high, with lights dancing from mock windows. At its heart stood a church with a pointed steeple and its own tiny Christmas tree standing outside, circled by matchstick-sized choristers.

The patients were propped on their pillows and a sense of expectation seemed to drift from bed to bed. It reminded me of being that eager child, lying in the dark on a Christmas Eve as Santa came creeping into my bedroom. I would tingle all over but never dream of opening my eyes in case he vanished and took the crackling paper parcels away.

The four ward nurses stood by the tree as we heard the distant sound of singing. The patients' eyes watched the ward doors which had been propped open, and I saw at least one reach for a handkerchief as the voices grew closer. A line of flickering lights approached as the nurses' choir, holding lanterns, streamed up the corridor and into the waiting ward.

There were twelve in the choir, all wearing their uniforms, with white caps and aprons, but with their navy-blue cloaks turned red side out, and the red straps fastened cross-wise. Holding the lanterns, they started to sing 'Silent Night' and, as they sang, they walked in a neat line around the ward, bed by bed, patient by patient.

A shiver ran down my back and I struggled to control my emotions. 'Silent Night' had never sounded so beautiful and I knew I would never forget those few gentle moments. I wanted to hold onto them forever. I glanced at Vale, not expecting the same reaction, but her eyes were dancing with tears which glistened in the reflection cast by the tiny lights.

I suppose I made my mind up during those few minutes we stood hidden in the doorway. I had to be a part of it. I knew these drifting angel-like nurses were the far end of the spectrum from Sister Mandrake. Two opposite ends of a long line. For every Mandrake there was a Wendy Broadbent; for every Leslie Nightingale there was a Thompson or Fran Hughes.

I wanted to be a nurse. I didn't know why I wanted to be a nurse, I'd never really known. It was something invisible, deep inside. I didn't know where it had come from, I didn't know where it would lead me, but I knew I would never be at rest unless I tried. Sister Mandrake, Gumption and all the stupid rules were just sideshows, as was Christmas Eve and the nurses' choir; the main show sat in those beds around the ward. The ordinary people who needed, depended, upon those four nurses who had their care this winter night.

It was both a terrible and wonderful thought, that some day I could be a nurse like that. Charged with the care and responsibility of a ward full of people who would look to me for help and comfort, whose lives I would hold in my two small hands. It was a scary challenge that if I turned away from now would always leave me wondering if I could have done it.

The choir had assembled around the tree as the last

chorus of the ancient carol drifted across the ward, and I knew Christmas would never be the same again.

Then they were gone, gliding like red boats out of the ward, their lanterns like guiding lights. They twinkled their way down the corridor and faded away off to the next ward, the soft sounds of 'Away in a Manger' floating in their wake.

***

The cold air crept under our coats, as we headed through the dark hospital grounds. Vale was catching the last bus to Moresbry and I was going to walk into Thorpe.

'Merry Christmas, Sue,' she said, pressing a small package into my palm. 'It's nothing much, I'm too hard up. Been quite a night, hasn't it?'

I passed across a bag I'd been keeping in my coat pocket. 'You beat me to it.' We laughed as we unwrapped our presents under a lamp post. I'd bought her some hankies, she'd got me a little cameo. 'I wonder where we'll be sent in the New Year change list.'

Vale paused, taking in what I'd said. 'You're coming back?'

'It's most likely the daftest decision I've ever made.'

'You're priceless, Salt,' she said, as we went our separate ways into the gathering snow.

About the Author

Jackie Huck was born in a typical Lancashire town of the,1950's/60's against the background of the fading cotton industry. Aged 16 she began working as a nursing cadet, at the local general hospital, leaving 14 years later having progressed to Ward Sister.

An only child: from an early age cats became her friends and companions and this was the basis for a life-long 'love affair' with a string of feline friends.

She moved to Cumbria in 1974 working as a District Nurse, before marrying a local farmer in 1976 and settling down to nurse cows and cats.

Jackie has written poetry from childhood, much of it reflecting the Industrial North, the beauty of her adopted Cumbria, and of course her cats. She often performs her poetry and short stories throughout Cumbria and the North West of England. This is her debut novel.

Lightning Source UK Ltd.
Milton Keynes UK
UKOW02f0610141114

241575UK00001B/24/P

9 781910 077238